All Last Summer

STEPHANIE J. SCOTT

Cover image © DepositPhotos – nejron

Cover Design © Designed with Grace

Edits by MK Edits

ISBN print 978-1-954952-01-0

Contents

❤

Author's Note

♥

Each book in the Love on Summer Break series can be read on its own.

Throughout the books, you'll find common characters and settings that take place place during different summers.

To keep up with book release news and discounts, join my author newsletter at www.stephaniejscott.com

Chapter One

♥

Experiences of Summer List

- Trip to Brazil Countdown: 1 day!
- Meet and bond with host family
- Meet and bond with Matt's host family
- Go on one student excursion trip per week
- Art museum with Matt
- Open air market
- Historical sites tour
- Reggae cafe (See TourScout rankings list)
- 1 pic Instagram a day/trip

There had to be a logical explanation. The very thing about to ruin my carefully orchestrated social life played out in front of me and I couldn't think of a single thing to stop it.

"It's not what you think." Matt, my boyfriend, sprung from his buddy's couch, his tanned hands moving in front of him and into his hair. The longish, messy brown hair I loved running my fingers through. His hands kept moving

—in front of him, around, everywhere. Everywhere except back on the body of the girl beside him.

"Lila." Matt stepped toward me as though approaching a frightened woodland creature. "You weren't supposed to be here tonight."

Of course, I wasn't supposed to be here. I was supposed to be packing. In less than twenty-four hours we were boarding a plane to Brazil for a summer student exchange trip. *Together.*

I'd been impulsive, which I should have known would only lead to trouble. Surprising my boyfriend by showing up to an impromptu house party went strictly against my planned-out agenda. My personality was Type A of the bolded, capital A variety. Packing for an eight-week summer abroad trip required multiple packing lists and down-to-the-last-minute run throughs.

Think, Lila. Think. There had to be a reason for Matt... *entwining* himself with this girl. Maybe he was mere moments from telling her he was committed in a solid eight-month relationship. After all, I'd done everything according to plan. We were Matt and Lila. *Freaking Matt and Lila.*

The girl on the couch, with honey blond hair and pale freckled skin, had the nerve to *yawn*. She didn't go to our school or I'd recognize her. Matt looked back at her, whispering.

The girl adjusted her gauzy blue top. "Matt, just tell her."

Just tell her. Tell her—me—a thing that apparently had already been decided? Memories of Matt flashed through my mind. Smiling at each other in Algebra 2. Holding hands after his swim meet. Registering for summer study abroad. The early Spring night after hearing the news my grandmother passed away, when he took me to his old elementary school playground and let me cry while my parents sorted out the details at home.

My vision grew crisp, like a photo sharpened to fine lines. I sucked in a breath, letting the rage flutter back. "Tell. Me." A statement, not a question.

A flash of silver came from his pocket. His swim team medal, hanging from a blue and gold ribbon. He swung it back and forth. The metal glinted from the glow of a nearby lit fireplace. Well, wasn't this just cozy.

"It's this thing I meant to talk to you about," he stammered. "So much was happening, you know, with the team and the trip. And you, losing your grandmother. I couldn't—I didn't want to bother you."

I'd wanted to escape my house. It was why I'd been looking forward to the trip for so long. A whole summer away from home. Out of the country, with the guy I loved. What could be better?

Matt twirled the swim medal in some sort of nervous tic. "It's just, the time was never right."

The girl stood and scoffed. "I'm Meghan. Matt and I, we're together." She completed the declaration by hooking her arm through Matt's, the space between them swallowed up like a black hole. "Since the trip planning meet-up."

The trip planning meet-up two months ago. Students from five area high schools joined together for a summer exchange program training. I'd missed it because of my grandmother's funeral. I'd had to attend a second make-up session without Matt.

My blood turned to lava and flooded my face with heat.

This couldn't be happening. I turned to the door for escape and horror struck again.

We had a crowd. Witnesses to my humiliation.

Everything I'd worked toward was disintegrating. My instincts screamed *run, cry, run, cry*, but I couldn't.

I'd devoted myself to Matt. *Devoted.*

"Meghan and I, we thought you wouldn't understand," Matt said finally.

Meghan and I. He said it so easily, as if used to the pairing. "This was supposed to be *our* trip. If you didn't want—" *To be with me* was too hard to say, I couldn't. "You should have talked to me."

Matt scowled. "You were the one pushing me away. If you were paying attention, you would have understood."

I—what?

He shrugged off my astonishment. "Look, the good thing is, we'll be in different parts of Salvador on the trip."

Salvador was the Brazilian city we'd be calling home in the next twenty-four hours. He said this all while hooked into Meghan's arm. With his free hand, he let the swim medal dangle from his fingers, swinging in a lazy figure eight.

Salvador. Summer. Matt. Matt and Meghan. Matt and Meghan and me, a squeaky, rejected third wheel. An uncharted future flashed in my mind. Matt and Meghan wearing matching Brazilian soccer shirts. Historic landmark tours and cultural events—all the activities Matt and I planned to do, and she would be there.

"Are you okay?" Meghan asked.

I snapped to the present. *Meghan* had asked. I stared at Matt waiting for him to tell me this was all a joke.

"Am I okay?" I laughed, though no part of this was funny. He had no idea how deep this betrayal went. Matt *was* my identity as Matt and Lila. A surge of rage hit me like a gale force wind. "How was it supposed to happen, Matt? On the plane? In Brazil, when we're thousands of miles from home?" They stood there, still joined at the arms like a united force against me. Like I was the problem here.

The silver of the medal caught my eye again, dangling from Matt's fingers. Stupid precious swim medal. For the last two months, I'd been his own personal cheerleader at his swim meets. He'd already been with Meghan by then.

The medal swung back and forth, back and forth. A deep and fierce *thing* inside reacted for me. I snatched the medal from his hands.

I didn't think. I aimed.

I chucked that medal right into the fire.

The room exploded in sound. Matt yelped. Meghan gasped. A chorus of "Whoa!" and "No way!" came from gawkers in the doorway.

"My medal, it's *burning*." Matt grabbed for a fireplace poker and attempted to hook the singed ribbon, only it had already burned through.

Nice shot, me.

Staring at him and his shocked expression, I let my rage have its way. "Have a *nice summer*."

I took the chaos as my cue to storm out of this house and out of his life. Forever.

I moved past the gawk-squad, some of whom were pushing forward into the room.

At the doorway, my gaze connected with Aidan Pemberton. Pale-skinned, lanky with pointy features, he gawked with the rest of them. Funny, Aidan had been the one who'd told me about this party. Aidan, one of Matt's dorky friends from childhood who constantly eye-rolled at me, who attempted to thwart my plans with Matt. Aidan, who never showed up to parties like this.

Aidan, who smirked at me.

I shoved past him, past everyone. Hot tears hit my cheeks. Ugly cries were coming and I refused to shed them here. I made it through the front door, out of the house and to the street. Then I ran.

Chapter Two

♥

Today's list:
  Goal: Nobody talk to me
  1. Sleep
  2. Wake up in an alternate timeline
  Someone pounded on my bedroom door.

"Lila? We need to talk."

Mom. I loved her, I really did, but at the moment, all I wanted from life was total darkness and a face full of hypoallergenic fluff. I crushed my face back into my pillow.

The door creaked open. "It's well past noon."

Something soft hit me and I rolled toward the wall. I ran my finger against the pale pink wallpaper that had been here when we moved in and was too hard to peel off so on it stayed. If I didn't get up, then none of last night happened.

"Downstairs in ten. That's an order."

Ten minutes later, I arrived downstairs. My response to the order was Pavlovian. Having military parents did that to a girl. Now retired from active duty, my mom and dad owned a construction company where they managed crews doing small-scale commercial jobs. Basically, they made an occupation out of telling people what to do. You'd think they'd be tired of it on their off hours, but not the case.

My older sister, Lenora, now out of the house in college, spent most of her teen years creatively bending their orders or outright defying them. Me? I was the kid who learned compliance made life easier. Just do the thing. Way less lecturing.

"We need to talk about whatever happened," Mom said as she gave the kitchen stove a thorough degreasing.

Dad closed the case over his phone's screen. "Sit."

Because I wasn't my sister, I did what he asked.

Mom stopped scrubbing. "Can you tell us what caused this sudden change? We let you call off the trip. Now it's time for answers."

I'd really gotten the drop on them when I came home from the party last night and declared I was canceling the trip to Brazil. Dad's work crew called him Sarge—there was no yelling at a former Sergeant—but I'd talked louder and louder until they heard me. When I'd called the sponsor teacher (at home, at night), and then the airline, and rejected every inbound call from Matt, even from the landline my parents insisted we keep for emergencies, finally they realized I was serious.

"I don't want to go anymore. Yes, Matt is part of it." All of it. "He's a jerk and I can't handle being in another country with him."

I left out the part about barbecuing his swim medal.

Dad picked at a coffee mug ring on the worn kitchen table. "I want to ask you a question. Did that boy hurt you?"

I snapped my head up. "*No.* I mean, not like, physically."

Dad's shoulders relaxed at my confirmation that Matt only hurt me emotionally. Which was a messed-up realization.

"There was a Meghan," I blurted.

"Oh, honey." Mom circled in and put her arms around me. "I'm so sorry."

Dad squinted. "I'm going to need a translator."

"Another girl, Eric. Matt and another girl."

Dad closed his eyes and slow-nodded. "I told you the girls shouldn't date until they're thirty."

"Lila." She ignored Dad. "You should have told us you were having problems with Matt. Maybe we could have prevented this."

"We *weren't* having problems." Even if we had been, the list of things I'd rather do than discuss my breakup with my parents included but was not limited to:

• Collecting random doggy dook from the park with those flimsy plastic bags

• dental surgery

• dental surgery without pain numbing

• trying on swimsuits at a Walmart (don't ask)

Dad stood and filled his Michigan State Spartans mug from the mostly-functional Keurig. "What I don't get is why you're the one sacrificing the trip. This punk gets to go to Brazil and you don't? He should stay."

My mouth dried out. "I couldn't get on that plane, Dad." Despite the packing lists and my fully indexed trip itinerary, after seeing Matt with another girl, it was as if every one of those plans self-deleted, lost forever on a crashed hard drive.

Dad muttered about responsibility and following through on commitments. "I should go over there and give that boy and his parents a piece of my mind. Ridiculous."

"Time will heal." Mom squeezed my shoulder and gave Dad a look I interpreted as, *Take it down a notch, Sarge.* "I know it doesn't feel that way yet, but it will."

Dad sat back down. "Speaking of time, let's talk about money."

Because time was money, he always said.

The biggest Oh Crap moment I'd had after all the canceling was the realization I was out the trip money. All of it. I canceled the day before the plane left, a full two weeks past any hope of even a partial refund. My pillow became my best friend, smooshed over my head, once Dad started yelling at the travel abroad program people over the phone this morning. No refunds. We'd all signed the papers agreeing to the terms.

Mom said something to Dad in a low tone. Dad grumbled, shaking his head. "Fine." He looked to me again. "I wish I understood why you were throwing this trip away."

I was equally as surprised. I never gave up on a plan. Except this plan, this trip to Brazil, had all been Matt's idea. A whole summer without Matt had seemed like an eternity, so I decided to go on the trip he'd signed onto. I took Spanish, a similar foundation to Portuguese, and with tutoring sessions twice a week, I'd brushed up enough to qualify for the trip.

The truth lay bare in front of me. I'd simply been tagging along.

That realization hurt almost more than the betrayal.

I stood in the middle of my bedroom, absorbing the enormity of what happened. I was Lila of the House of Vaughn, the Cast-Off, Goddess of Unusual Outbursts, Lenora's Forgettable Sister, the Dumped One, and That Girl Who Hangs Out With Natalie--You Know the Natalie with Cute Hair.

I sank to the floor by my abandoned pillow and reached for my notebook. I paged backward to my semester level goal lists. New year's resolutions were for suckers. I had life plans in stages—daily, semester, yearly, long term, epic long term. The answer to why my plans were failing had to be in here somewhere. The failure was in the execution. I'd missed *something*.

The original list. Where this all began. I slipped an old notebook from the shelf above my desk. From freshman year.

Social Life Boot Camp
Goal: to make lasting friends and connections
1. Find a best friend
2. Get invited to a sleepover
3. Be part of a known clique
4. Share clothes with bestie
5. First kiss
6. Boyfriend
7. Homecoming dance date
8. Prom

It all seemed so simple then. I would acclimate myself socially through rigorous planning and strategy.

My head hurt. I had no answers. I chucked the notebook and reached for my phone. Scrolling through celebrity pics on Instagram, my feed landed on an unexpected photo. The elevator cables severed and dropped me in full freefall to the bottom. Matt. *Matt and Meghan.* Standing by the airport gate. Flight times overhead, pointing and smiling.

Just like that, I was out of the picture. Replaced.

I clicked my phone off. In the space in front of me, Matt and Meghan materialized, wrapped around each other. I blinked and their outline lingered like scattered white spots from a flash bulb.

I texted Natalie.

Me: *Parents are super pissed.*

The little dots indicating she was typing back flickered on the screen.

Natalie: *How are you? I'm so sorry I wasn't there with you last night.*

Me: *I'm OK. Just...shocked, I guess.*

Natalie: *I can't believe he's with that other girl. Who else knew?*

Good question. Meghan was out there in the open with Matt at a party with our classmates. What did Matt think would happen when people saw them together?

Me: *I wonder if his old friends knew. They never liked me.*

Aidan Pemberton, smirking in the hall. His other buddies, Mason and Dan, used to join in, bagging on Matt for turning into a popular Bro. Matt always shrugged it off with a laugh. *It's not like that,* he'd say.

I spent the rest of the day feeling sorry for myself and falling asleep at a time when old folks usually ate dinner.

The next day, I woke feeling like I'd slept twenty minutes instead of nearly half a day. My parents were long gone to the construction company office by now. I settled in on the couch in our family room and booted up our streaming service on the big TV. One high point of not going to Brazil meant I finally had time to catch up on my favorite sci-fi shows. I'd been dying to finish *The Expanse*, but with finals and softball, I'd let the episodes sit unwatched in the queue. I had no one to talk to about the show anyway.

Okay, I deliberately didn't talk to my friends about sci-fi shows. Before moving to Ginsburg freshman year, I spent my free time reading my parents' Terry Pratchett novels and taking online courses on topics that interested me. For fun, not for grades. I lived for school clubs—junior robotics, quiz bowl, aviary club (that's bird watching). Making friends never came as easily to me as it had for my sister Lenora. She had charm and charisma. At each school, the inevitable would happen. I would try to make friends, but eventually get branded a dork and ignored. My very existence repelled sleepover invitations. I defaulted to loner status. Every time.

When my parents retired from the military to start their construction business in Ginsburg, Mom's hometown, my list making took a deliberate turn. Why not study what it took to be popular? Add those items to a list, make a plan, and have the life I wanted.

Aligning with Natalie turned me from an awkward, not-intentionally-anti-social-but-not-exactly-social   transfer student to the semi-popular incoming senior I was today.

None of which happened by accident.

I hit continue on the episode and willed myself to get lost in Captain Holden's stupidly adorable eyes and Naomi's fearless resolve. Only my mind kept drifting to the party. To Meghan in the gauzy blue top. To Matt's deer-in-headlights expression. Tossing his medal into the fire—that would cost me. I'd be branded a jealous ex. And I had no idea how to recover.

At seven that night, the familiar sound of tires crunching over gravel sounded outside, punctuated by the automatic garage door grinding open. A flurry of sounds traveled in from the kitchen until Mom peeked into the family room. She audibly sighed. It could have been my blanket hut with pillow support beams. Or how I'd drank her last LaCroix.

A voice squawked on speaker from Dad's battered work phone. "Yeah, I hear ya." He stopped in the doorway. "I have to go to the Raintree site. Jim's clocking overtime already."

Mom swiped the empty cans from the coffee table. "I told you that job was understaffed."

"He's the only guy I've got right now who can tile." Dad's voice rose as they talked shop.

I turned up the volume to hear the show better. The fate of the universe hung in the hands of a chosen few!

A newspaper landed on the coffee table in front of me. Dad hovered over it, blocking the TV. "Time to start with the Want Ads."

I paused the TV—I had to have misheard. "What?" An honest-to-goodness print newspaper. People looked for jobs in those? "I can take a look online at some jobs, I guess."

"There's no 'I guess' here, Lila. You owe us the trip money."

Mom sat in the chair across from the couch. "We decided it's only fair for you to pay back the money for the trip since you canceled so suddenly. It's a lot of money to waste."

Of course it was a lot of money. I hated to waste it too. I really did. "I'll use some of my savings—"

"That's for college," Mom cut in. "You will not touch a single cent in the savings account your family contributed to for your education. Absolutely not. This is money you need to earn and pay back."

I stared at them. "But you didn't ask me to pay for the trip. You offered to pay. You even encouraged me to go."

Dad headed for the coffee machine. "We offered to pay for an educational trip. Now the money is gone. Canceling because you broke up with that punk wasn't part of the deal."

"But—"

"We let you cancel the trip," Mom interrupted again. "You begged and cried and pleaded. We agreed since you were so distressed. That doesn't mean canceling comes free of consequences."

I'd been surprised my parents agreed to the trip to begin with given the hefty price tag, but they never once complained over the cost. This was a big opportunity, going to Brazil, but it had been Matt's opportunity. The whole thing was turning out to be an expensive...mistake.

I yanked myself free of the blankets. "I'm sorry. I'll...I don't know. I'll try." I stood from the couch, at once absorbing their focused judgment of my lazy day watching TV.

"You'll do more than try. Here." Mom reached into the bag on the floor beside her and held out papers.

I took them and scanned. I couldn't help my mouth from falling open. My parents had used their company financial software to run a bill for me. With a due date.

Mom's handwriting looped below the sobering figure. *By summer's end, we want half of this paid back.*

Half? It was *thousands* of dollars. Not at all a daunting task. Nope, not at all.

That wasn't all.

No team sports or prom next year if you don't.

No sports or prom? What was the point of all the work I'd done to fit in if I could cash in when it mattered? I bit down on my lip to shut down the quivering. "I'm going to my room."

Dad returned. He gestured with is coffee mug at the newspaper on the table. "Lila, we're serious. Find a job."

#

I retreated to my bedroom and whipped the door shut. I caught the knob just before it slammed. No need to trigger an additional lecture on obedience. Once Dad activated Sargent Mode, there was no canceling out.

It did *not* pay off to go off-list. Then again, if I hadn't gone to the party, I'd be halfway to Brazil with a cheating boyfriend. That had never been part of the plan.

I opened the newspaper to the jobs section. I needed a translator for these job term abbreviations. Not that I qualified for ninety percent of the positions. How did I gain job experience if I couldn't get a job in which to gain experience?

Natalie helped at her mother's veterinarian clinic. A small office with no need of a second teenager to sweep pet hair, or for sure she would offer.

There was always babysitting, but the full-time summer gigs would be taken by now. Maybe my softball teammates would have job leads.

I sent out a handful of texts.

Immediately, responses came in.

Did you really burn Matt's swim trophy?

It was a medal, not a trophy...

Someone said you cursed it. Did U say a spell B4 throwing in the fire?

Maybe I should have. It might make Dad feel better if I'd cursed Matt's trip. Heck, *I'd* feel better.

Who is the other girl? I always miss the good stuff!

My heartbreak was *good stuff*?

None of this helped. The texts kept coming in, so I pitched the phone into my laundry basket.

Dinner was on-your-own leftovers as Dad headed back to a job site and Mom packed food for Grandpa a few miles down the road. My grandparents were the reason we'd moved to Ginsburg. Grandma hadn't been well, and because life truly sucked, she'd lost her fight against cancer two months ago.

Downstairs, the garage door closing signaled my parents' exit. I wandered back to the kitchen and poured myself a bowl of cereal.

I cleared space on the table between the kitchen and family room and set my bowl beside scattered papers. I focused on the marshmallow pieces in my cereal.

Hold up—the table was messy. Not normal.

Mom's leather work bag lay spilled open with her laptop positioned in front of her usual seat and the papers and folders spread out from there. A sticky note with mom's handwriting topped the nearest pile. I slid it closer. It looked like a bill with the logo from a bank in the corner.

My throat went dry.

A business loan. The total owed matched the cost of my trip.

Chapter Three

❤

Daily list:

Goal: get a job!

- Outfit advice - Natalie
- Search for missing Vera Bradley purse
- Apply online for anything that fits
- Drive into town, apply in person
- Schedule lunch with Natalie
- Unfollow Matt from Instagram

I dragged myself out of bed for job hunting day two. All I had to show from yesterday were a few submitted applications from the food court in a dead-as-zombies mall. Still no bites on the online apps. Today, I'd hit the road to look for jobs the way, as Dad said, they did in pre-historic times. Before the internet.

Outside, I yanked open the door to the Heart of Gold, my adolescent-aged sedan. Dad and I named the car after the ship from *The Hitchhikers Guide to the Galaxy* because of the fictitious infinite improbability drive, which in the book was discovered by chance, much like the car, that had been left abandoned on a job site with the keys in the ignition. Turned out, the owner had left the car, and the state, with no intention of returning. Due to Dad's opportunistic sleuthing, he tracked down the owner (the brother of one of our construction crew), had him mail back the title, and bought the car for one dollar. Happy sixteenth birthday to me.

I kept the nickname to family ears only.

When I turned the key in the ignition, the car whined and choked, then petered out. I turned the key again. And again. *Wheeze, choke, cough, kaput.* I pounded a fist against the wheel. "Alright, not funny." I tried again. And again.

My no-excuses parents would add interest to my bill if they found me binging on TV and LaCroixs again.

I sighed and got out of the car, hitting the automatic garage door open. My gaze landed on a tarp in the corner. A tarp covering Lenora's old motor scooter.

I closed my eyes, letting the inevitable possibility sink in.

I grabbed the scooter key from the pegboard by the door to the kitchen and climbed onto the bike. I unearthed an equally dusty helmet. So much for good hair. At least it would hide my face in case anybody I knew drove by.

The scooter coasted down the drive, shuddering awake from semi-retirement. I turned onto our road and tried to come up with a job-hunting plan. Overhead, the sky clouded over and little flecks of rain dropped.

Please let it stay a sprinkle.

I pressed the gas pedal as far as it would go. The scooter ramped up to forty. The speed limit was forty-five, so traffic could either pass me or bite it. A horn blasted behind me. I waved an arm behind me, signaling the driver to go around.

The car moved into the opposite lane of the two-lane road and whooshed past, hitting a stray puddle. Cold mud-wash splattered against my legs and arms. "Hey!" I shook my fist at the driver. "Karma will find you!"

I glimpsed the top edge of the giant Teed Off! sign ahead. The driving range where Matt worked.

The stoplight blinked to red. Great, now I had to sit here staring at the giant, silver gleaming golf club sign, fighting memories. The golf range sat at the edge of town, one of the closest businesses to where I lived, making it super convenient to stop by at the end of Matt's shift. Sometimes we hung out in the parking lot. I couldn't believe that used to feel special.

The marquee strobed *Now Hiring* like a seedy invitation.

The rain showered harder. We were at pelting levels of rain here.

I swore under my breath, hit my turn signal, and eased over into the lot.

Parking by the dumpster and stowing the helmet beside it, I rushed across the lot, up the front walk and into the golf range. As the glass doors shut behind me, water pooled onto the tile floor and streaked down my bare arms. My hair stuck to my neck in sticky strings.

Now what? I couldn't ask for a job looking like a drenched cat.

I headed to the bathroom off the main lobby. A little creative bending beneath the automated hand dryer and a wad of paper towels later and I was good to go. Damp to go.

Back at the registration desk, I approached a woman with shoulder-length dark hair and excellently shaped eyebrows Natalie would comment on.

"Hi. Um, I see you're hiring. Are you still hiring?"

Her attention snapped up. "Yes, we are. I'm Jen. I'm actually the hiring manager." She stuck a hand out. "I'm covering registration for a break, but here." She dug beneath the counter and handed me a paper form. "We still have a few print applications floating around. How about you get started filling this out and we can meet in my office in five?"

I grabbed the job application, mustering more confidence than I felt. This was my ex's workplace after all. Former workplace. But if it meant a paycheck and a chance to save my social life for senior year, I'd suck it up.

Ten minutes later, I sat in Jen's office as she looked over my completed application. "This is a nice list of school clubs."

"Thanks. I've volunteered for military charity functions since I was eight. Everything from coat check and registration to set-up and tear-down. I can run electrical cords." I was rambling.

"And robotics club?"

I'd listed everything I could think of. "Yup. Middle school."

"This is impressive for your age. I believe you're exactly what we're looking for." Jen stood, and before I could blink twice, we headed back to the lobby. It was almost too easy.

I froze in my tracks. Mason Park, one point in Matt's cronie trifecta, stood behind the registration desk. Beside him, Dan Thomas, the second cronie. They looked up as if activated by the We Hate Lila Vaughn Alert System. In unison, they turned toward Jen. Then glared at me.

When Matt worked shifts with his buddies, they'd tumble out together into the parking lot where I waited. Usually, one of them would crack how the fun gestapo was here (that would be me—they thought I wasn't fun). Why Matt put up with them, I had no idea. When Matt and I were alone together, he acted sweet, attentive, funny. He'd been everything I'd ever wanted from a boyfriend.

Well, until he wasn't.

"Lila, this is Dan and Mason. They both work registration, though not usually at the same time unless we're busy." She gave them a pointed look given no customers waited in the lobby. Dan nodded and took off, but not before lasering a hate-glare my way.

I'd be rotating in with the cronies. *Beautiful.*

"As for you, Lila, I'll show you to the supply closet."

"Supply closet?"

"My apologies. It's been a stressful few days." Jen could easily have been the before picture in an Advil ad. "The job is for a porter. It involves cleaning and maintenance checks."

Oh. "So, not registration?" I guess she never named the position.

"Registration is full." That comment came from Mason along with a hard stare.

Heat crawled up my neck. I kept my voice light, directed to Jen. "So, I'll be making rounds and looking for mishaps?"

"Don't forget toilets," Mason said without breaking his gaze.

Jen looked apologetic. "The job does involve scrubbing toilets. I'm sorry I wasn't clear with what we had on offer. We've shifted staff around to cover a few recent vacancies." She held up a hand. "Are you still interested?"

Obviously, I needed the job. Toilet scrubbing or not. "Yes."

Jen led me on a brief tour, apologized again for any misleading thoughts about the job, and after signing a few papers, I was free to go.

As soon as the front doors closed behind me, I breathed again. No more rain and I had a job. A toilet scrubber, yes, but a toilet scrubber who'd be paid.

I'd keep my head down and ignore Mason and Dan. Try not to think how I'd be spending my summer with my ex-boyfriend's friends.

I reached the scooter. Now to get home and change out of these muddy clothes.

Wait a sec. Where was the helmet? I'd set it beside the rear wheel. It was gone.

Had it rolled off somewhere? The helmet matched the scooter—bright tomato red—so I couldn't imagine anyone stealing it. Who would take a tomato red scooter helmet and leave behind the matching scooter? I mean, at least get the set.

I knelt against the pavement, angling to see underneath the dumpster. My hand squished against something cool and wet. *Ugh. Wet garbage.*

Springing back, I lost balance and pitched sideways, falling onto my hip. All this and I still couldn't find—

"Looking for this?" a voice behind me asked.

I let my eyes close. I really, really did not want to look up at penetrating rays of an extremely haughty expression cataloging my humiliation.

Aidan Pemberton. The third element of the cronie trifecta. Holding the coordinating tomato red, lightning-bolted helmet, wearing his favorite expression, a smirk.

Besides the obvious pitiful circumstance of interviewing at my ex-boyfriend's place of employment, I was currently splattered with mud, desperate to get home, only to have my scooter helmet taken hostage by Matt's best friend.

I snatched for the helmet, but Aidan swung it out of my range. "Where did you find this? I left it right here."

Aidan, leaner and more angled than Matt, grinned. "What happened to your car?"

"She needs to get fixed."

"She?" The smirking intensified.

Shoot. "Never mind. Anyway, I need to get going. Helmet. Give."

Aidan made a point of letting his attention land on my mode of transportation. "That's quite a moped."

"There aren't pedals, so it's not a moped," I said before I could stop myself.

As if correcting him on the difference between a moped and scooter made this any less humiliating. Because, facing the cold pure facts, this was humiliating. Aidan had already seen me publicly dumped by his friend, and now here I stood groveling for a job and begging for my bike helmet.

Then again, no reason to worry he'd spread this shame-worthy gossip to everyone back at school. Aidan, to put it delicately, was a dork with no influence. Matt connected him to anything cool, and Matt wasn't here.

It didn't take much for Aidan's stern jaw to turn into a downright scowl. He thrust the helmet at me. "You'll be lucky if you last a week."

One thing I hated was anyone telling me I couldn't do something. "Is that some kind of challenge?"

"Whatever point you're trying to make, you've made it."

"The point is to get a paid job. Now I have to *do the job*."

He ran a hand through his brown hair. Flecks of copper glinted from the sun now peeking out from the clouds. His over-sized Teed Off! polo practically dragged his arm back to his side. "You could have still gone on the trip. I'm honestly shocked you aren't down there, pleading with him to take you back. Isn't that what perfect girlfriends do? Win their guys back?"

I involuntarily shuddered. He had me so pegged. Even if I wanted him to be wrong, the words stung.

I smoothed back my hair, frizzy from the humidity now hanging out with us from the earlier rain. "It's hard to say which is worse—being stuck in Brazil with a cheating ex or working with you. I guess I lose either way. That should make you happy."

Aidan looked me over, the smirk fading to a dull grimace. "I don't know what you're up to."

Not my problem. My problem concerned a bill with a number and several zeroes after it.

"Well, it's been real." I slipped on the bulky helmet. In one swift motion, I mounted the scooter and turned the key until the Electric Tomato awakened. I revved that bad boy up, hit the gas, and peeled out of the lot leaving Aidan in the dust.

Chapter Four

♥

Reasons to Loathe Aidan Pemberton:

- Smirks too much
- Rented personality
- Behaves like a child
- Co-dependent with crony friends
- Can't tell a moped from a scooter

Dinner was classic Dad at the wheel: strip steak with grilled vegetables from the charcoal grill on our back deck. He set the plate of meat in the center of the table as Mom and I sat. We chatted about my car not starting as I avoided the inevitable turn in conversation.

"Any job updates?" Mom got her question in a mere second after Dad stopped talking.

I took a healthy bite of meat and veggies. "Yes, actually. I got hired. Close by."

Her face lit up. "That's great."

Dad squinted. "Only thing up the road is the junkyard. You're working at Pete's?"

Mom let out an exasperated huff. "Lila isn't working at a *junkyard*. Honey, where?"

I braced myself. "It's at Teed Off!" I didn't say it as excitedly as the punctuation suggested, but tried to sound at least a little chipper.

She stopped chewing. "Matt's work?"

Ka-boom. "Not exactly my dream job." To say the least. "But they're hiring." Which was the literal least.

"Well, that's...good." She looked at Dad.

Dad had his eyes shut, probably imagining what real retirement looked like somewhere tropical.

Mom turned back to me. "Won't it be an issue, working where he does? He's coming back eventually."

"Well, yeah, it's an issue. She canceled her trip to get away from the guy and now she's going to spend eight hours a day where he works."

"Dad, I'm right here. It's a dead zone out there. The golf range hired me on the spot. Believe me, I'd rather work anywhere else." Like somewhere not run by Matt's buddies. "It's a paycheck."

Dad heaped another spoonful of grilled vegetables onto his plate. "I'll call up Pete. Maybe the junkyard needs a gopher."

What a summer this would be, cleaning toilets and working with people who couldn't stand me.

Stupidly, I still felt excited. This was my first paid job. Not babysitting, or volunteering, or odd jobs around the house for allowance money.

First, my car.

A knock sounded on the door from the garage. "Where's the boss?"

I tumbled into the kitchen as Grandpa walked in. He set his toolbox on the counter beside our recycling bins. He wore a short-sleeved checked shirt and a cap with my parents' construction business logo.

"There she is," he said. "Let's get your ride fixed up. That's what you kids call it—your ride?"

I shook my head. "No. Just…no."

He grinned. I was honestly glad to see him smiling. Only two months had passed since Grandma's funeral. For two years she'd been losing strength and pounds, the pink in her cheeks dulling to colors not found in my old crayon box. Until her cancer escalated and suddenly, it was all over.

I followed him to the driveway where the Heart of Gold hadn't budged since yesterday. Grandpa loved the mechanical workings of cars, especially older ones he grew up fixing. Newer cars with so many computer-driven components were a different beast, but there was still a lot he could do. My car was like a living robot, a mechanical wonder.

"I did some troubleshooting online to see if it's the starter. I already tried the jumper cables," I added, knowing Grandpa would suggest it first. Part of me had wanted to start taking apart the dash, but I'd need to get under the hood, disconnect the battery, and well, I needed Grandpa-level support.

He opened the driver's side door and tried the ignition himself, mumbling over the sounds. "Mmhm."

I assessed for other obvious signs of trouble. Kicked at the rear tire. What had I been thinking taking the scooter to the interview? Natalie would never pull out a dusty scooter to ask for a job scrubbing toilets. I couldn't imagine Natalie scrubbing a toilet.

Grandpa unlatched the hood. "You want to grab the radio?"

"On it." An essential component of car fixing involved listening to a baseball game or talk radio. NPR was a total snooze fest…at least that was what I used to tell Matt. In truth, I liked *This American Life* and interviews with Terry Gross. Nerdery I chose to conceal for the hope of a normal high school experience.

I grabbed blocks to place behind the rear tires. Grandpa moved the jack beneath the car and raised the front tires off the pavement.

I handed him a socket wrench, but he shook his head and nodded toward the battery. "You can do this. I've seen you do it."

I disconnected the positive and negative battery terminal cables. Then we'd need to remove the battery tray.

"Heard you're having trouble with the boy."

Was there no escaping this conversation? "More like the boy is having trouble with life."

"Boys that age don't have sense. You'll be fine without him."

Grandpa always seemed to like Matt. Though, Matt hadn't been over to my house much. Too risky bringing him to home base where my lack-of-actual coolness could be exposed.

Grandpa nodded to the Heart of Gold. "Glad to see you're still taking an interest."

"Yeah," I responded absently. I hadn't worked on a car with Grandpa in months. Friends and school had taken a priority. No—I'd made those things a priority. In return, I'd made Grandpa less of one. "I'm sorry."

"I don't think it's anything you did, kid." He looked at the car. "Sometimes a car quits working right. We'll fix it."

I didn't correct him. I knew we'd get the car fixed. It was everything else that had a question mark.

Chapter Five

♥

Daily List:
- Make grocery list (see sublist, next page)
- Pack lunch
- Arrange rides to/from work (rest up, Goldie)
- Moisturizing mask
- Cancel fall sessions of Portuguese tutoring

I walked into Teed Off! with my game face on. That would not be golf game, by the way, but the jack-of-all-trades porter game. With the Heart of Gold waiting on a part, Grandpa dropped me off. I didn't feel like riding in on the scooter to additional humiliation again.

Jen handed me a green Teed Off! polo. She gave me the run-down with the supply closet, explaining each section, and what I needed to track. "Out on the floor, you're looking for hazards, spills, messes, safety concerns."

I sat in Jen's office to watch mandatory safety videos and complete paperwork. This all should have bored me to tears, but I found myself reading over the pages of policy like I would study for a test. When Matt talked about working here, it was all about pranks he and the guys pulled on each other. Or he'd say it was boring, and wanted to talk about my day. He'd been a good listener. Hadn't he? It couldn't have been all bad. Eight months together—that wasn't nothing.

I shadowed Jen for the next two hours. The only cronie on the premises I spied was Mason, who seemed busy at registration with a busload of senior citizens.

"Nice work today," Jen told me as we finished checking the bathrooms by the golf bays. "You're free to go after a quick all-staff meeting before the evening switchover."

Using her commanding voice, Jen called out to the servers to report to the kitchen, leaving one staff at the front registration during the lull in customers.

"Hello, everyone. Quick few things." She waited as the employees gathered. "This is Lila Vaughn. New Porter. Welcome her to the team."

A chorus of hellos filled the room. I smiled and waved back. My smile faltered when it landed on Aidan. He must have slithered in while Jen was talking. Mason stood beside him, elbowing Aidan and snickering.

Nope. Those dudes were not ruining my first day. "Hi, thanks everyone."

"Next," Jen went on, "I finally have news on the summer incentive. For those of you who weren't around last year, we provide an opportunity to earn a bonus. The owner likes innovation. Improve a process, bring forward a great idea. Not only an idea, but a plan of how we can implement. The innovation bonus is open to everyone and the winner is up to owner discretion. The prize: fifteen hundred dollars—before taxes."

One-thousand, five hundred *additional* dollars? Added to my earnings, I could pay back my parents the full amount this summer. Starting senior year with a zero balance? Yes, please.

I could be innovative. Maybe newbie eyes on existing processes would be the insight the range needed. Maybe I was fated to end up here.

Across the room, Aidan caught my eye. Watching. Scowling.

Tough snacks, dude. I needed that money.

Jen dismissed us. I texted both my parents my shift had ended and walked out front. I took a seat on a concrete bench bordered by pots of summer flowers. I needed a good idea to earn the bonus. What had Matt told me about working here? *Ugh*, stupid Matt. I hated digging up Matt memories. Each time the party flashed in my mind, I became a loser all over again. My brain refused to take the hint and kept replaying the breakup scene. I needed a way to push the emotional junk to one side and logically piece apart what could help me get to that extra money.

"No scooter today?"

This was exactly why I hadn't driven it. "Don't you have work to do?"

"I'm on break." Aidan's angular frame shadowed me, hands slid into his khaki's pockets. Threads frayed from the pocket with a swath of grease visible across one knee. I wasn't a fashion snob or anything, but didn't he care how he looked at his job? "I saw you get excited over the bonus. Don't."

Okay, this time I sighed out loud. "Is this what it's going to be like every time we work a shift together?"

He laughed with a sharp edge. "You're the one who showed up here. Taking Matt's job after he dumped you."

As if Matt scrubbed toilets. "I didn't take his job, I took *a* job here. Besides, working here was a last resort."

"Well, for some of us, it's not our last resort. That bonus incentive means something."

He was provoking me, intentionally. The perfect girlfriend always played nice with Matt and his cronies. Where had it gotten me? I wasn't about to take this heat from Aidan without dishing it back.

"You were at the party." I stood. "You saw how Matt didn't have the guts to break things off himself. He got caught. And you know what's interesting? The reason I knew about the party was from you. I stopped by the driving range to see Matt and you just-so-happened to mention the party. Which makes sense we had that conversation because you and I *always* talk about parties."

I leveled a steely look at him, hoping the sarcasm came through thick and accusatory.

Aidan blinked, his dark eyes surprisingly soft at the edges despite the steel in his own voice. "Funny how Matt hadn't told you about the party himself."

Obviously, Matt hadn't if he'd planned to smuggle in a Meghan. But why *had* Aidan told me? "You knew about Meghan and wanted me to see for myself. You wanted us to break up."

"I didn't sabotage your relationship, if that's what you're suggesting."

"I guess your plan backfired. Now I'm here, at your workplace, all summer, making your life miserable."

Aidan laughed, hollow of humor. "You'll have to try harder. Don't expect open arms here. We have a tight crew."

Great. Exactly what I wanted—a summer impressing the staff with my mopping skills. "I don't have Matt's job, by the way. He worked registration. Also, do you think I'd be here if I had any other choice? I owe my parents the money for the trip and if you've been to the mall lately, it's an apocalypse. Just sayin'."

Aidan twisted his mouth into a faux-sympathetic sneer. "Forgive me if I don't feel sorry you wasted your parents' money."

The accusation came like a crisp slap across the face. He was right. I'd wasted my parents' money, and I would never not feel bad about it. I pretended to look for my ride. *Hurry up, somebody.* My eyes pricked hot and wet. I wasn't prone to crying on demand, but these were not normal operating procedures.

All of this was my fault. Not only for letting things get bad with Matt, but for thinking I deserved any of this to work out. For thinking I could be the girl who had it all— friends, a boyfriend, a real social life. All based on *lists.* I was a fraud and I knew it. Now everyone else did too.

For some reason, Aidan still stood in front of me, all awkward and not saying anything.

Well, he'd seen me on hands and knees behind a dumpster looking for a 1990s scooter helmet, so witnessing sad-girl tears might be an improvement. "I'm sure it would have been great in Brazil." I bit the words off, the tears close. "Me, Matt, and Meghan. You must love knowing I've been replaced after I took away your friend. I was the girlfriend who got in the way of your little bro-gang. You win."

For a fleeting moment, I could have sworn sympathy flashed in his eyes, but it was probably pity.

Thankfully, Dad pulled into the lot, nearly taking out a curbside bush. He adjusted his cap and lasered his eyes at Aidan. If there was anyone who could scare the smarm off the face of a self-important teenager, it was my dad.

Aidan, bowing his head, scattered like a bucket of wayward golf balls.

"Happy first day on the job." Natalie sat across from me at an order-up-front Greek place. The type of place where "salad" was more in quotes. Sure, there was lettuce, but a heavy pile of seasoned meat and feta cheese topped the greens.

She pulled out a baklava dessert with a mini bow stuck on the top of the plastic container and slid it toward me. "So, tell me all about it."

This was where I needed to come clean. I couldn't lie to my best friend all summer about where I worked. "The job...it's at Teed Off!"

We went through the inevitable reactions—yes, the same Teed Off! where Matt worked, and where his friends worked, and wasn't there anything else I could find—all leading to Natalie's pout face, her classic *I feel so bad for you* expression which should have elicited major eye rolls, but she was so freaking genuine with her sympathy I usually wanted to hug her.

"There has to be something else," Natalie was saying. "I'll see if you can come to the vet's office. Maybe clean cages."

Cleaning up after animals didn't sound much better than cleaning up after humans.

"The woman who hired me, Jen, seems like a decent person. I don't want to ditch on her." Like I'd ditched my trip.

She leaned in. "You're working Matt's old job. *With his friends.* That has to be rough." The way Natalie spoke had a dramatic feel as she stressed certain words. She reached across the table. "I'm *so sorry* I wasn't there. I owe you an ice cream and Netflix night. Pick a date and I'm there."

"I'll get my full schedule tomorrow."

"I'm sorry this happened. I can't believe it. I thought you two would go *all the way* through senior year. Maybe into college."

A dull longing pulled at me. Sadness for what could have been. "I don't know. It's a lot of pressure to think so far ahead."

Of course, I'd thought that far ahead. Strategic planning ran through my veins. Matt assumed his college plans would fall into place after filling out a handful of applications.

"I just feel so bad," Natalie went on, spearing an olive so intensely her fork clinked the bottom of the bowl. "I mean, what's *wrong* with him? You were nothing but awesome to him and he *throws* this other girl in your *face*. Hooking up with her at the party in front of you? And our friends? Who does that? I'm...I'm *furious*."

"Hey, hey, it's okay. I'm sure I did something to annoy him." I laughed in one hot burst.

"Lila, no." Natalie set her fork down for emphasis. "This isn't your fault. Not even a little. If anything, I feel responsible. I pushed you two together."

"What? No. The only thing you're responsible for is any social life I have at all."

She folded her arms. "That's not true."

"It's totally true. When you met me I was the biggest dork." Even with my lists and a plan, it took time to adjust and win over Natalie.

"I mean, you watch those old movies, but that's not so strange. The one you showed me with the British guys dressed like knights and hitting coconuts together to make horse sounds? It was kind of funny."

Monty Python was always funny, but Natalie only watched *The Holy Grail* with me to be nice. She didn't laugh nearly as much as me and Dad.

"All I'm saying," I continued, "is I owe a lot to you. I'd never blame you for encouraging me to like Matt. We didn't know he'd turn out to be a jerk."

Natalie sighed. "Anyway, I truly believe it will be *emotionally damaging* if you continue working there. I never understood how Matt hung out with those guys."

One thing we could agree on. "You should have seen the dirty looks Aidan gave me." I decided to skip the saga with the scooter because then I'd have to admit to having actually ridden the tomato nightmare, and my ego was already limping. "Oh, get this. There's bonus money we can earn if we come up with an inventive business idea or process improvement. Aidan had the nerve to tell me not to bother. He even told me I wouldn't last working there more than a week."

Natalie's jaw dropped in predictable dramatic fashion. "That sounds *awful*, Li. You know, there's a panini shop in the new plaza by the vet. I can ask if they're hiring."

I filled her in on Grandpa fixing up my car. "The range is close to home. I'm going to stick with this job. If I'm lucky, maybe I can pay my parents back by the end of the summer. Then I can quit the golf range for good."

Natalie pursed her lips, attacking her salad. "You seem... *determined*."

"My parents threatened banning me from softball. And prom." Not that my skills contributed as super valuable to our softball team, but I liked playing and being part of the group. Prom was a destination I'd devoted an entire notebook to. I'd have to rethink now that Matt was torn from the plan.

"I'm probably freaking out," I added. I'd been burned. I'd lost money. I was the broken off half of a known couple at school. Naturally I was freaking out.

"Maybe don't put so much *pressure* on yourself to figure it out?"

Easy for her to say. This all came easily for Natalie. She could end a relationship and easily find someone else. I'd watched it happen for three years. For me, I had to plan. Figure things out or the figuring out never happened.

I'd worked too hard to let this riff with Matt ruin my life. Or my summer.

Chapter Six

♥

Weekly List:

- New idea for golf range
- Win bonus money and rub it in Aidan's face

Jen found me in the staff room after I swiped my badge for my next shift. "Lila. I need you to sweep the second-tier golf bays. Ketchup catastrophe."

"On it."

I kind of liked having a mission, ketchup catastrophe or not. Once I arrived at level two, no question which golf bay Jen meant. She wasn't kidding about the ketchup.

"Hey, new girl," one of the waitstaff called over. She stopped at a server's station and tapped at a touch pad screen. "I'm Nala." She looked college age and wore her black hair in tiny, long braids. Her brown skin had a rosy glow from the June afternoon heat coming from the open golf bays.

"I'm Lila. Was there a workshop here about exploring creativity with condiments?" Yeesh.

"That party was nuts." She gestured toward the tables decorated with smears of ketchup, mustard and a flourish of fry bits. "The parents complained the whole time our kids' menu wasn't *extensive*. Heaven forbid."

"Do many kids come here?" It seemed a pretty boring deal for kids. There were smaller sized golf clubs, but they'd be more fun in colors.

Nala picked up the stack of trays from the counter at the server station. "Yeah, they do and they're always getting yelled at. Hitting siblings with clubs, hitting the chairs with clubs. Everything gets hit with a golf club."

I returned to wiping, soaking, spraying. A final wipe with a clean towel and then I dried off the table and the chair backs. My cleaning rags were disgusting and I needed to rinse off these rubber gloves. I returned to the supply closet, dumped the gross rags in the dirty bin, and continued my checklist and rounds. Lila on patrol.

Nala passed by me in the hall leading to the elevator the staff used to bring food to the higher tiers. "Hey, girl, not trying to micromanage, but that ketchup mess needs to be fixed."

"I did it already."

She raised a skeptical brow. "I just came from there. Ketchup all over the table."

There was no way. I dashed back to the public part of the tier with the tables overlooking the driving range. I raced toward the table and stopped, my jaw dropping. The same bay I'd moments ago cleaned was covered in ketchup streaks. Almost decorative. Hmm. Not random splatters. No mustard. No fries.

My heartbeat picked up. I looked around, my focus landing on the customers the next bay over, who hadn't ordered food yet. The other side, two gray-haired men chatted wearing clean button-down shirts. No kids with ketchup-smeary hands in sight.

"Get to work, Porter."

I whipped around to find Aidan. Behind him stood Dan, six feet tall and all elbows and freckles with reddish blond hair, snickering into his hands.

I marched toward them. "Are you kidding me right now? I already cleaned this whole bay."

Aidan peered over my shoulder. "Doesn't look like it."

"Those kids must have come back." Dan spoke with a lisp and his teeth looked weirdly glossy, like he wore those invisible plastic molded braces.

I narrowed my eyes. "You have something on your sleeve."

Dan lifted his arm, searching. "No, I don't."

Ha. Made you look. Yes, I was that juvenile.

I blew out a breath and stomped off for more supplies. I imagined the two of them minutes before, dousing my newly-cleaned table with a fresh coat of fry dipping sauce. They'd better be gone by the time I got back. Or...or, I didn't know.

Back at the mess, on hands and knees beneath the table wiping up what had to be an entire unloaded bottle of Heinz, Jen's voice sounded behind me.

"This was a doozy, huh? I thought you'd be done by now."

I backed out from the table and stood, holding my ketchup-gloved hands a safe distance from my body. "Yeah, I was. Apparently, the kids came back."

Jen's brow furrowed. "That party checked out before you clocked in. I watched them leave."

Beyond Jen, Aidan filled a plastic tub with dirty plates to return to the kitchen. "You know Aidan—I think that's his name? He and the tall guy told me the kids were here again. Maybe you could ask him about it."

Jen turned to where I looked. "Aidan," she barked.

Aidan looked at Jen, then to me. His shoulders went rigid and he walked over. "Yeah?"

"You see some kids mess this table up with ketchup? After it was clean?"

Aidan's eyes flicked toward me. "I don't know what you're talking about. Those kids left probably twenty minutes ago."

Jen looked between us with a nonplussed expression. There were no plusses to be had. "Ditch the funny business. Both of you. Back to work."

She left us to face off with each other. Aidan's Teed Off! polo had a more fitted look today. Weirdly, his arms appeared...muscular. It had to be the lighting in here—half indoor bulbs layered in with natural light from the open golf bays. He wasn't exactly a pumping iron kind of guy. The most sporty these dudes got was watching Matt's swim meets and occasionally playing Frisbee on the quad during lunch at school.

Slowly, Aidan slid into view a plastic bottle, red with a white cap, from the pocket of his apron.

"You." I pointed at him and the offending ketchup bottle. "Are a jerk. You could get me *fired*."

He sneered. "That's the idea."

My jaw clenched. "*Not. Okay.*"

"It's not okay you're working here."

"It's not up to you whether you think it's okay."

He visibly flinched, but started coughing, as if that somehow covered up his reaction. I needed to play this cool. If I made it too obvious how much I needed this job, the cronie crew would try even harder to get me booted. Except they had to know how much I needed the job by virtue of me even standing here cleaning up their orchestrated condiment catastrophe.

Behind Aidan, Dan approached. "You're right, dude. I don't think she's going to make it. Phase one ketchup hazing and she already went tattling to Jen."

I glared at them. "*Tattling*? I'm not a child. Grow up."

Aidan's attention flicked to me. Not exactly apologetic, but maybe a flash of guilt if I got creative with my interpretation. "Come on," he said to Dan. "Let's get back to it."

The two turned and walked off, leaving me to deal with phase one ketchup. Phase *one*? As in, multiple, numbered phases? I returned to a crouch and wiped red droplets from the floor.

I went about my day, learning how to become invisible to customers. I made their messes disappear. Scrubbed and scoured and flushed them away. If only strict adherence to OSHA regulations worked for social lives.

Blending in had been a solid part of my everyday existence before moving to Ginsburg. I didn't have a posse like Matt had going back to kindergarten days. A posse so loyal they committed condiment crimes against their friends' jilted exes. *Jilted*. Was anyone other than an ex labeled *jilted*? I may as well put the word on my work polo stitched in scarlet.

Later, on break, I scarfed a sandwich and Pringles in the storage room. I'd never been more grateful for a thirty-minute slot of time that didn't involve rubber gloves or weapons-grade cleaning solution.

"Lila." I looked up to see Aidan walking toward me. A clipboard attached to one hand and a blue tooth device at his ear. His features were set to neutral, as if he'd convinced himself we were merely coworkers with no other history. "It's cage time."

These words were English, but they held no meaning. "Uh..."

"The ball retrieval machine." He nodded toward the massive green beyond the golf bays. Parked in the corner sat the orange metal monster that collected stray golf balls on the range.

"Do you mean Brutus?" That's what Matt had called it.

Aidan blinked, a moment of recognition hinting at our existence beyond working together. "The old one was Brutus, but he's retired. This one is the Cage."

"Ooh, *so* creative. How did you go from Brutus to cage? Is it because, let me guess, it's a wheeled cage?"

His eyes widened before he narrowed them. "It's actually Nicolas Cage."

I snorted. I wished I'd snorted out of sarcasm. He'd actually made me laugh.

Aidan's mouth evened out but seemed to be straining at the corners. Fighting off a smile? "You can call it whatever you want."

A golfer in the rowdy group near us cracked a golf ball into the green, sending the ball directly into the caged vehicle. Into Nic Cage itself. "So, when is the break for vacuuming the course?" I figured it was like hockey where players cleared the ice for the Zamboni.

Aidan's steely look finally gave way to a grin. "We don't hold up customers to clear the green." He held up keys dangling from a Teed Off! branded key chain.

"You want *me* to go out there?" I sensed something afoot. Definitely a foot involved. "Where's Jen? Why are you giving me work?"

He tapped the clipboard. "When Jen is off for the day, I assign tasks as needed. Here. Take these." He shook the keys at me.

I glared at him. He was one key-shake away from saying, *"Here girl! Come on, come get the keys!"* One scant key-shake from me chucking those keys out the golf bay.

"You don't want me to report you for insubordination your first week, do you?"

Insub—I...I would kill him. Take the clipboard, the keys, leave no survivors. "You don't have to be an ass about it." I snatched the worn brass keys.

Aidan turned a precise ninety degrees and started walking. "Follow me."

Such a weirdo. He wasn't my boss. Situational Floor Lead, maybe. No, Situational Floor Assistant. *Junior level.*

Crummy title or not, I didn't trust him not to report me to Jen. I couldn't risk losing this job.

I followed him to an employee-only stair corridor, taking us to ground level. A fenced-in walkway led into the golf range and the expanse of green turf. The caged monster, mere steps away. Outside the walkway.

He held open the door. Less a polite gesture and more the equivalent of a welcome mat placed on a cliff's edge.

"It's like a sturdier golf cart with a metal cage around it." Aidan thumped the gate with his knuckles. "Nothing to be scared of."

Did cage driving require a driver's license? Cage certification? Were there speed limits?

Jen had been thorough on my job duties, and driving the cage was not part of my training nor woodenly-acted out in any of the mandatory safety videos. I was a mopper, a stocker, an occasional glop-sopper. Not a cage driver.

I saw Aidan's look. A challenge. Aidan didn't think I could do this. He expected me to try to get out of it.

There's an age-old debate whether pride is a virtue or a vice.

I lifted my chin and sauntered past him to the green.

He followed me and cracked open the driver's side door to Nic Cage. A golf ball streaked overhead. I steeled myself, I could take it. I angled past him to the pleather seat, which welcomed me with a crackle when I sat. I pulled shut the cage door.

The functions seemed pretty basic. I buckled in, turned the key, and the engine started up. Attached to the front of the cart were wheeled baskets that rolled over and collected the stray golf balls. Kind of like herding grocery baskets.

Aidan closed the fenced door. And smirked.

That was enough to fuel me.

I hit the gas. Nic Cage puttered forward with less pick-up than the scooter. All this extra metal weighed the cart down. I pressed the pedal harder and the cart lurched forward. Sweat tickled my hairline, but a current of excitement ran across my skin. This was kind of cool.

I eased the cart right into a sweeping turn and straightened out to ribbon back across the green. "*Yeah.*" I pumped a fist in the air. "First try. Eat that, Aidan."

I didn't suck at this. Bonus: vacuuming the course didn't involve ketchup.

I looked ahead to my next turn, this time sweeping left and around, and adjusting to head back, now a modest distance from the golf bays. No twenty-point-back-up-and-scoot-forward turning for this gal. Me and Nic were going to be good friends.

A sharp, tinny *clink* sent me flinching. The first ball to hit. Good thing the Cage protected me.

Another *clink* chipped against the metal side. Then a *clunk*, like the ball struck more of the solid surface.

I squinted toward the bays. For one frozen moment, it seemed I'd launched into hyperspace as an array of white stars traveled infinitely fast toward my craft.

Then the pelting began.

An assault of golf balls poured down, like metal bolts dumped from the clouds. If I'd ever wondered what golf ball-sized hail would sound like if it were actual golf balls driving into the sides of a metal cage on wheels, well, now I knew. That sound would solar-power my nightmares.

It was almost like someone had done this on purpose.

I swung the Cage to drive back across the green, savoring the blissful silence now from a sky clear of golf balls.

"And...go!" a voice carried over from far off.

A second attack. I hit the gas pedal to the floor, but old Cage was maxed out. Balls battered the sides. The sound was like a string of metal cans kicked by more metal cans. I smelled fear and sweat. *My* fear and sweat. I zagged the Cage one way, then zigged the other.

And now my clean field was full of golf balls again.

Chapter Seven

♥

Additional Reasons to Loathe Aidan Pemberton:

- Pranks involving ketchup

- Coordinated, targeted, hazing

- Sent me to a death cage

- Should consider getting a life outside of work

Waitstaff and kitchen crew stood by the open food service doors clapping as I emerged from the golf green. I aimed for the dark solitude of the supply cabinet.

"For a first timer driving the cage, you did awesome." Nala patted me on the back. "It's tradition, you know." She took off toward her tables.

By tradition, she meant how every non-customer golf bay had been occupied by an employee, each sending their fiercest drives into Nic Cage. That had been *fabulous*.

A short, lean guy with olive skin and a cap sauntered over. He held his fist out. "You drove it like a champ. I'm Joe. I run the kitchen."

I bumped his fist. "It's almost like this was all planned."

He shrugged, a guilty grin on his face. "You did better than those teenagers over there. That guy couldn't even finish. Just shut down the cage and waited it out."

I looked where Joe had gestured, landing on Aidan's frame. Aidan's body appeared to be locked down from any abrupt reaction. "Really?"

He laughed, nodding. Ha. I'd done better than Aidan. Pride: dust off, and Lady Up.

"Don't get cocky," Dan said, breezing by.

Ugh. Not my problem if Dan felt irked. I returned to the supply room and shut the door.

I'd done a kick-butt job driving Nic Cage. Sure, I'd had to circle back, but I'd finished collecting golf balls on the whole course, despite the ball battering by the staff.

Not only would I last more than a week, I would last this whole summer.

I gathered supplies for my last round of sweeps before the range shut down. I opened the closet to find Aidan on the other side, his hand reaching out as if to turn the handle.

He stepped back. "Sorry, I didn't know you were in there."

He'd dropped the hardened boss act. "Let me guess. You don't actually have a promotion to be an after-hours Jen. You only sent me off to get me in front of an adoring audience with pent-up energy."

He held up a clipboard. "The promotion is real. So is the other part. The part about your adoring audience." He searched my face. "People seem to like you."

I wheeled the mop bucket around him. What was with his scrutinizing looks? "Everyone except you and the cronies. No surprise there." I headed toward the golf bays, feeling weariness seep in.

Aidan moved in front of me. "Why do you call us that?"

"You're in my way."

He didn't move. "You always did that. You called us cronies."

"You acted like his—Matt's—protectors. You were like henchmen."

"We're his *friends*." He muttered something I couldn't hear. "You're with your one friend a lot. The blonde. Are you her henchlady?"

Stupidly, I nearly laughed at *henchlady*. I couldn't give him the satisfaction.

I wanted to believe Natalie and I were equal as friends, but the truth was, I still worried I was tagging along. Though I'd never admit it to Aidan. "You were like little trolls. Any time Matt and I were out, you guys couldn't stop texting him."

"Again. Friends do this. Texting is considered normal behavior among those who befriend one another."

His lecturing tone made my hair catch fire. Or feel like it at least. "But all the time? Constantly needing to know where he was and when he'd be back? You guys treated him like your king. Your almighty ruler. How are you functioning with him out of the country? It's a miracle you're diffusing oxygen without his assistance."

Aidan took a menacing step toward me. "Maybe we wouldn't have cared so much if you hadn't been so obsessed with him. Hanging off of him like an accessory."

The accusation stung, but I wasn't about to stop. "You were jealous."

"We were *annoyed*."

"People grow out of pranks. People get girlfriends. And boyfriends. And non-gender-specific special companions. It happens."

"I realize we were never cool enough for you."

The fact we were debating my coolness while I held a dirty mop and wore a golf polo dappled half in sweat, half in liquid potent enough to strip paint off an oil tanker put my current reality in perspective. "Well, all I'm saying is, you could have been more understanding that Matt had a girlfriend."

Aidan moved in a step. "He *still* does."

His remark stared me in the face, leaving no escape. "You know what? Never mind. I don't care."

His expression didn't need interpretation. He knew I cared. I hated how he knew I cared. Why did I still care?

"You talk about Matt being our king. That's laughable. What about you?"

"I was his girlfriend. I treated him the way any girlfriend would." My response sounded scripted. I'd rehearsed it enough times, practiced, and lived it out.

Pathetic. The word went unsaid, but I heard it in the walls. I saw it on Aidan's face. He leveled his gaze at me. Fire crackled in his eyes along with something more. Something menacing. "I don't think you believe that."

My blush game came on so strong my mom probably sensed it at work two zip codes away. "I see. Apparently, you know everything, Aidan. The answer to life, the universe, and everything surely must be in the words you're saying right now."

"Did you just—"

I couldn't take this anymore. "Shut up, Aidan."

I had no idea why he bothered with this unnecessary conversation. He clearly didn't like me. I clearly didn't like him. Since we had no reason to continue talking, I turned and walked away.

I completed a week. A whole week of working at the golf range. *Eat that, Aidan.*

Even better, I'd driven to and from the range today on my own. As much as I loved my family, parental pick-ups only further gave me the sense I'd lost any shred of coolness.

"It feels so good to be driving again," I said across the dinner table to Grandpa. I'd worked a day shift today, making it home a little after six, and immediately sat to wolf down Mom's chicken enchiladas. Her cooking was admittedly not the greatest, but after my paltry lunch of a PB&J and going-stale Triscuits, I didn't bother to douse the enchiladas with salsa. "Thank you so much, Grandpa."

Mom smiled, looking between us with a wistful expression. "You know, we can add the cost of parts and labor to Lila's bill."

I guess I'd misinterpreted her look. "This whole *Lila's bill* business is getting out of hand. I helped Grandpa with the repair. I'm cleaning gutters for him on my day off."

"She's got those skinny arms," Grandpa said. "Good for scooping."

Dad shrugged this off. "Gutters aren't equivalent to car maintenance."

"These days we push kids too hard," Grandpa said. "Back in my day, we ran the streets until dark. My folks called us in for dinner. They'd shoo us out if we came home early."

I nodded at Grandpa's sage wisdom. Never mind that last part about running the streets—he had a point about this all work and no play business.

Dad settled his elbows on the table. "Lila is well taken care of and in no danger of overworking. We aren't an ATM of endless expensive coffee drinks and car parts."

"I only get coffee with Natalie. Half the time she pays so she can get points on her gold card."

Dad's grunted response didn't appear to help my case.

"We want to teach Lila responsibility," Mom said. "The trip to Brazil cost a lot of money. In this family, we don't throw money away."

Oh, for the ability to evaporate and mist out of a room. I chewed silently, and willed myself to turn camouflage.

"She should be off with her girlfriends, having sleepovers," Grandpa was saying, while Dad muttered about Matt being a punk kid more deserving of military school than a vacation in South America.

"Stop coddling her, Dad," Mom said to Grandpa. "We're the parents here."

"I didn't even want to go," I blurted.

Dad stopped chewing, one cheek stuffed with food like a chipmunk on pause. Mom and Grandpa watched me.

"What." Dad's *what* dropped like a lead ball. No question mark.

Crap. "Nothing. I don't know." I stuffed the rest of what remained on my plate into my mouth. *Chew chew chew* and pretend all of this is someone else's life.

Taking my plate to the sink, I scraped it clean and loaded it in the dishwasher.

All I'd wanted was to have what would make me happy—friends, a boyfriend, a social life. Now, no matter what I tried, I seemed to wreck everything.

I crawled into bed, tucking blankets around me into a fluffy cocoon. I didn't want to think about Matt. Thinking about him meant replaying the breakup, and replaying all the things I'd done wrong leading up to it.

Aidan had laughed at me when I brought up how he and the cronies gave me a hard time. I'd always felt like the outsider with them around. They were into geeky stuff I stayed away from once I'd started at West Ginsburg. Matt wasn't as into geekery as much as Aidan, Dan, and Mason, but they were all best friends from elementary school, and everything seemed to center on those old memories. I kept expecting Matt would break off from them, having outgrown their immature jokes and pranks.

I'd manufactured my personality to get Matt's attention. Writing out my lists and plans as if making friends and dating was a test I could ace.

I curled tighter in my blanket nest. I scrolled through Instagram, but the celebrity pics only made me feel worse.

I landed on one of Matt's photos in the Instagram feed. Obviously, I should have unfollowed him, but...I hadn't. The photo was of Shell Gas Station with palm trees and a sign in Portuguese behind it. Caption: *Shell gas. Just like home.*

Besides the airport pic I'd already seen, he'd posted another photo of himself standing in front of a house, his nearly six-foot height and white skin glaring among a shorter, brown-skinned group of five varying in age from teen to elderly. Caption: *My host fam. They are awesome and made us a HUGE dinner!*

The first comment posted on the photo was from @MeghanM233 *So good. Obrigada!*

Meghan. Saying thank you. The *us* was Matt and Meghan. Of course.

I wasn't sure what I'd expected. Obviously, life for Matt and Meghan continued despite my choice to stay here and not witness it.

In another universe, I might be there taking similar photos. Rubbing my skin with SPF 70 on the daily, working on my conversational Portuguese. Instead, I was huddled in a blanket hovel longing after someone else's life.

I sat up. No. I was not this pathetic. These lists. I needed to stop letting them dictate my life.

I pulled a notebook off my desk shelf. Then another. There were dozens of them. Some spiral bound, others bound journals. I grabbed a shoe box from my closet and jammed the notebooks inside. I wasn't done making lists forever or anything, but the ones with meticulous notes about popularity had to go. I had honest-to-goodness charts of the lunchroom at West Ginsburg. So embarrassing.

I took the box to the garage and lifted the lid on the recycle bin. No. Someone could find these. Snatch them off the recycling sorter and read my popularity plans on their lunch break.

Instead, I detoured to my car. I pitched the box into my trunk. I'd drop these off to the dump myself. Personally.

Chapter Eight

♥

Weekly Goal:

- Make friends at work
- Lay off on making so many goals

After dipping seriously low the previous night feeling sorry for myself, I had nowhere to go but up. A whole summer lay ahead. It was up to me to not settle for feeling miserable, and I was determined.

I bounded over to Nala's workstation, smiling bright and strong. "So, Nala, what's the scoop around here?"

She held up a hand. "Did you just ask, what's the *scoop*?"

"Yes, but it was meant to be funny. Like, intentionally dorky." Because you knew you were scoring with humor when you had to explain it.

"I'm trying to hit my sales goals. I'm pushing these." She pointed to the soft pretzel appetizer in a metal wire basket with attached cup holders for three different dipping sauces.

I needed an idea to get going on the bonus money. Pushing pretzel dippers wouldn't get me anywhere since my job involved blending in with the woodwork. Or polishing the woodwork.

"You know who's cute?" Nala turned to me with a grin ready to give up some gossip. "Aidan."

My eyebrows shot up. Aidan with the ratty khakis? Aidan with a permanent scowl? "Oh?" I played it cool. "He's in high school. I mean, not that you're...old, but since you serve drinks, I assumed you were at least—"

Nala swatted me. "Not for me. For you."

"Me?" I shook my head, my laugh sharp. "No. Not after he sent me to drive the cage with everyone waiting to blast me with golf balls."

"They do that to everyone. I could tell he felt bad, though. He tried to stop it all from happening, but Joe and the kitchen staff wouldn't let him off the hook. You have to find your fun where you can, you know?"

I nodded like any of what she said made sense. Aidan wouldn't stop my humiliation, he'd instigated it.

"You don't have a boyfriend, do you?" Nala asked, now eyeing a group of women walking to an empty table in her section.

"Nope. No worries there."

"Girlfriend?"

"What? No. Sorry, I guess the way I answered was confusing. I had a boyfriend, but we...ended things right before I started working here." I debated telling her it was Matt. She obviously would know him—all the staff knew each other. I wanted Nala to know me for me. To know me apart from my old attachment.

She gathered four menus. "I'm sorry. If you're looking for a rebound" —she made a clicking sound through her teeth— "I'm telling you, I think Aidan has his eye on ya."

A summer storm rolled in. The overhangs in the golf bays sheltered customers from the bulk of the rain, but a fine mist covered surfaces with a thin wet sheen.

Jen found me toweling off a table. "Lila. We need supplies from the basement. Grab the cart and I'll show you how to operate the service elevator."

I followed Jen in with an empty cart. She put a key into a slot by the elevator's floor numbers and turned it. The elevator shifted lower until it reached the bottom and the doors stuttered open. Dank and dark, but once the lights flickered on, it appeared less like a horror movie.

"We store extra paper products here, and oh, it looks like we'll have to order more liquid soap." Jen did her assessment, circling items on her clipboard and making notes. "Alright, here's a list of what we need upstairs. This key gets you back up—you have it on your keyring." She checked her watch. "Let me know if you need anything."

"You're leaving me?" Darkness from the far corners of the basement sent a trill of panic through me.

"Sorry, I know it's kind of creepy down here. If you can't find everything on the list, ask Aidan for help. I've got to run."

Mission clear: find everything. Avoid Aidan.

If I stood where the lights shone down, the basement wasn't so bad. I loaded the cart with items from Jen's list.

One last thing I couldn't find—batteries for kitchen smoke detectors. I searched the shelves again, but nothing. I rolled the cart around the corner, realizing the basement had a second section partially walled off. The next section was coated in darkness. There had to be another switch somewhere. I blinked and the outline of a horror movie clown appeared. No. Just my eyes playing tricks.

I stepped to the next section and trailed my fingers along the cool cement wall. My finger made contact with a switch. I flipped it and lights blinked on after a few takes. I laughed.

"Of course." Boxes of golf balls stacked up nearly to the ceiling, taking up one corner of the room. I wasn't sure what I'd expected, honestly.

Beyond me stood another opening with no door attached. *Curiosity, curiosity.* I'd made it this far, hadn't I? I reached the entryway and felt for a switch, but the walls were smooth. My eyes adjusted. I could make out bulky shapes. I stretched my hand farther along the wall and bumped against a switch not flush with the wall. It probably wasn't safe to flip random switches, so I took out my phone and clicked the flashlight app.

And screamed.

Motionless eyeballs stared back. Were there *actually* horror movie clowns down here?

I flicked my flashlight app toward the wall, fully prepared for blood-trails on the cinderblocks. Instead, I found a switch. I flipped the switch and dim light grew stronger overhead.

Sculptures filled the room. No, not sculptures. Statues? A windmill, a boy and girl with peach skin and brown button eyes, like you'd see in a retro kids' picture book. Was that a dinosaur head?

Maneuvering around a stack of boxes, I peered into the junk mass. A long wooden sign was propped up against a pile of boxes. I angled to see better, sliding aside a box of rainbow-colored golf balls to read the sign.

Uncle Albert's Mini Golf

Beside me on top of a box stack, a framed photo with cracked glass rested. The photo featured a white family posing in front of the same Uncle Albert's Mini Golf sign stashed in this room. The kids held mini putters and behind them, the dinosaur head on top of a dino statue body, and those boy and girl statues. Or similar ones. The statues in the photo were posed differently.

Wait a sec. I circled back to the statue children. I crouched to their eye-level, wiping off dust from the face. The arms, the body—this wasn't all one solid piece. I grabbed the head and looked behind it. A panel. A port for a plug. This girl statue was alive. Alive by wires.

I grabbed the little notebook I kept in my back pocket for spur-of-the-moment note taking. I had an idea.

Chapter Nine

♥

Business Plan:

  (for the Teed Off! Bonus money incentive)

1. Write a business plan

2. ???

3. Profit

"This is a terrible idea," I said to my mom the next morning as she crouched in front of a garden bed pulling weeds in our front yard. "I need your help with it."

Mom chucked a wad of weeds into a bucket. "You're starting a school project now?"

I watched her trim back a plant I didn't know the name of. Grandma Rose used to tell me about every plant and flower in their garden. She would spend hours pruning and tending to her flowers. "It's not for school. I have a chance to win a bonus at work. They're looking for an innovative idea to improve the driving range. And I have one."

"I thought the idea was terrible?"

Terrible for the Lila I'd carefully constructed to win over friends and Matt. Not so terrible if I wanted a chance at the money. "I need a business plan. I figured you'd have some suggestions since you and Dad developed the construction company."

Mom stood, her shoulder length hair tied in a knot at the base of her neck. "I don't think you need to add more challenges this summer."

"You handed me a bill, Mom. It's going to take me through college to pay you back unless I do something else."

She wiped her garden gloves against her worn jeans. "Tell me about this plan of yours."

"The basement at the range has a bunch of old stuff from a miniature golf course. Old robotics that I guess were set up around the little golf greens according to the pictures I found. Nala, one of the servers, told me how kids get bored at the driving range. What if they brought back mini golf? Teed Off! says it's an entertainment venue on the sign. They're missing a key...what do you call it? Like, a whole customer group. I mean, there's already families coming there, but this could mean more for them to do."

Mom opened her mouth but didn't speak. Finally, "What are you thinking you'll do with this idea?"

"Part of the bonus incentive is to present a plan for how the idea is implemented. That's what I need to know how to do. How to draft up a plan to make it all work. The idea would be to bring back the old mini golf. The driving range is modern, but the mini-golf is like a wink to a past era."

"It's certainly ambitious." Mom reached for her small garden shovel-thingy.

I pictured Aidan and his smirk. I needed to be ambitious to win.

Inside, Mom and I outlined what would be needed to bring back a miniature golf feature at Teed Off! Most of the list, I'd discovered, started with my own investigation. Did the golf range own the land in the empty lot beside it? Did they own the mini golf equipment, or were they housing it for someone else? Would there be enough interest in the mini-golf idea, enough to merit the range investing in the project?

By this time, Dad had joined us, setting down a mug of decaf coffee beside his own. "Anyone can have an idea. A solid plan, that takes work."

Oh man, Dad was loving this.

"You could take a look at those robotics for them," he went on.

I took a breath. Never mind how the robotics drew me into this idea in the first place. The problem was, this project required stepping back into Old Lila territory. I'd already been shoved halfway there thanks to the breakup, but this next part was intentional. Deliberate.

Though I'd never made a grand announcement to my parents about leaving behind my old interests—reading paperback sci-fi novels, star charting, taking apart old radios —they got the hint once I'd started hanging out with Natalie. For my after-school interests, I joined the softball team since Natalie played.

Then I kept going. I signed up for yearbook (bonus: influence over the high school memory narrative) and the Spanish and Portuguese Student Coalition. I started going to parties not supervised by parents. They knew I'd changed.

"I always thought it was a shame you didn't carry on with robotics," Mom said, giving voice to my thoughts. "There are a lot of opportunities for women now in STEM fields."

"Mom, I *know.*" My words came out pinched and harsh. I knew what I'd given up, distancing myself from what I enjoyed, what I was good it. Tinkering with electronics got me sorted as a Class A Geek at my old schools. It for sure hadn't won me many friends.

As much as I tried to talk myself out of being excited, I was excited. I had a new idea I could make work. If I was willing to allow myself.

My next shift, I covertly began gathering data. With my basement key, I could easily get back downstairs for recon whenever I needed. Preferably when Jen was off duty.

"What's going on with you?" Nala asked, setting her tray on a recently vacated table. "You're acting like you're up to something."

So much for stealth mode. "I have a plan." I pressed a finger to my lips. "For the bonus money."

"If it's larger bathrooms, I'm all for it. I hear that complaint from customers a lot."

"No way." Larger bathroom equaled more toilets to clean. Speaking of. "Time to get back to work."

Down the corridor, I stopped short. Aidan, Dan, and Mason stood grouped tightly together. A toxic glob of cronies blocking my path to the supply room. *None shall pass!*

If I was going to beat them to the bonus money, I needed to be able to *walk by* the three of them. Facing them was only the beginning to total Teed Off! domination.

Aidan straightened and tapped Dan on the shoulder. Dan and Mason headed the other direction.

Scatter! Scatter like the underlings you are!

I pushed forward toward the supply room. I channeled Beyonce. If only I had a wind machine.

Aidan caught up to me, clipboard in hand. "Are you closing tonight?"

I channeled indifference with an air of confidence. "Yeah. On Jen duty, huh? Lining up another firing squad?"

Aidan flinched, but otherwise remained neutral in expression. He was better at the indifference thing than I was. "Everyone gets hazed in the Cage."

"Even Nala?"

"Nala was a friend referral so she had a heads up about it." He shrugged.

Funny how Matt never mentioned the hazing. Could have used *that* heads-up.

"I only asked about closing because I have to cut someone for the night," Aidan said. "We're slow. I thought if you had something better to do." He waved a hand toward the open air and the green.

"I don't have other plans." I swallowed, aware of how lame this sounded. Then again, may as well lean in at this point. "You probably heard, I ditched a trip to Brazil to scrub toilets at a golf range for minimum wage."

He burst out a laugh. "I heard something about that." He held up his clipboard. "I'll keep you on then." He nodded and took off.

Well. That interaction was...more friendly than expected. *Skeptical Lila was skeptical.*

When I stopped by the kitchen to drop off antibacterial soap, Joe the line cook beckoned me over. "Hey, Lila. When's your break?"

I checked the clock above the sinks. "In an hour. What's up? Do you need something?"

"A few of us eat together in the break room. I haven't seen you in there."

Mainly because I hid in the supply room for break and ate sandwiches from home. "I only go there to clock in and out."

"You're welcome to join. A few of us are up in an hour. See you there?"

Hadn't I wanted to make work friends?

When break time rolled around, I made my way to the staff room. A long table bisected the room where four staff sat setting food along the vinyl checkered table covering.

"Lila," Joe called and waved me over. He was way older, like probably married or had kids. He wore a thin gold chain at his neck and had a close-clipped beard. "Join the feast."

"Oh, I've got food." I held up my lunch bag and took out my sandwich and a string cheese.

A woman I recognized as a server tapped a plastic bowl in the middle of the table. "I'm Kara. I brought chili. I made extra." Kara was already spooning chili into a paper bowl. "I will be personally offended if you don't at least taste my chili. My kids say it's the best and they're picky. They don't flatter me often."

"Well, with an endorsement like that." I accepted the bowl and took a bite. A hot burst of jalapenos hit my taste buds first, followed by the rich chili sauce. I let out a breath. "My parents make our chili hot too."

"And with beans? I'm not a fan of that Texas no bean mess."

"We lived in Texas for a year. My dad hates no bean chili."

Kara grinned. "That's my girl."

I couldn't imagine any of us had much in common other than we all worked here, but we talked easily. Kara worked part-time while she raised her kids. Joe had been here five years and knew everybody's business. The other two at the table were college students, one on break for the summer, the other a grad student who commuted to classes.

Kara was complaining how many school fees her kids racked up the past year when a guy named Chet brought up the bonus incentive and how it should involve the kitchen.

"As long as you don't take my idea." Joe snapped his fingers. "I'm serious though. Stay out of my way."

Neither shared details. Saving money in the kitchen sounded promising. Unlike my idea of spending who-knew-how-much on expanding the golf range with a decades-old miniature putting course. Crap. My idea *was* terrible.

"You thinking of entering?" Joe asked.

Everyone's attention landed on me. Subtle. Stealth. "I'm... exploring options."

Joe busted out laughing. "See, I knew she was up to something."

"Am I that obvious?" Maybe this was Joe's entire reason for asking me to have lunch.

"I didn't mean any offense," Joe explained. "Usually the high school kids they hire here do the minimum and goof off. You take the job more seriously."

"I'm a military kid," I offered as explanation. "I've been hard-wired to be punctual and to keep things clean and tidy."

"Nothing wrong with that." Joe bit into a biscuit, also supplied by Kara. "You're setting the example."

"Their leader is gone this summer, so they don't know what to do," Kara mumbled. "Sorry, did I say that out loud?" Kara and the others laughed.

Joe gestured toward me. "They're talking about a guy who worked here. Another high schooler. He left for the summer to a foreign country with his girlfriend."

I coughed, a chili bean lodged halfway between my mouth and esophagus. Did they know Matt's girlfriend as me, or as Meghan? Had Meghan been here? OMG. Had they met Meghan? Had they met Meghan before I met Meghan?

Kara smacked her hand against the table. "Come on, Joe. She probably knows him. It's a small community out there."

Playing dumb was likely best. "Oh, I don't know. There are a few high schools around. Private schools."

"This guy, he was good looking and knew it," Kara said. "Thinking he was top dog all the time. Had trouble running his mouth."

"Jen couldn't stand him." Chet laughed. "Remember that time she threatened to call his parents?"

Joe gestured with his chili spoon in the air. "Come to think of it, it was Matt who couldn't hack driving old

Brutus, not Aidan. He's the one who parked it in the middle of the range and just sat there."

Laughter chorused around the table again. This was surreal. All the time I'd spent wanting to be known as Matt's girlfriend? Now I didn't want to be known as his ex.

Kara noticed my strained expression. "We're venting. We won't talk about you when we leave. It was rude of us to let loose like that."

"We?" Joe placed a hand at his chest with a dramatic flair. "I believe all petty talk began with you, Ms. Kara."

The two bickered back and forth as I ate the rest of my chili. Matt never let on he wasn't liked here. Maybe he never bothered to notice anyone beyond the cronies. Joe confusing Matt for Aidan said enough for me.

Chapter Ten

♥

Experiences of Summer List (amended):

- Make $$$
- Hang out with Natalie (when not working)
- Go to a party (with Natalie)
- Beach day
- ???

My crummy summer job was taking over my life. Natalie and I managed to work opposite schedules so we kept missing out on meeting up. I hadn't seen a beach, not even one on TV. I had managed to clean gutters at Grandpa's house. Truly, I led a glamorous life.

Today was my day off. A day I refused to squander.

I headed to the vet clinic to see Natalie. Inside, a caramel and black terrier jumped and barked excitedly at my entrance.

"Hey, *little pupper.*" My voice switched to the voice every animal lover instinctively knows. "Who's a cute pupper-dupper?"

Beside the dog sat a cat carrier with kitty eyes peering out. I knelt to the floor. "Is there a bitty kitty in there?"

Natalie appeared and scooped her arm through mine. "Let's get out of here before we have an abduction."

We rounded the corner to a smoothie shop. The girl running the register gave Natalie her drink for free since she was a regular.

"Are you getting anything?" Natalie asked me.

I couldn't exactly afford to. "I'm good. I'll just hang out with you."

Natalie turned back to the smoothie slinger. "Can you get hers too?"

The gesture only reminded me of my state of brokeness. "Thanks. Um, I'll take a lemonade."

We sat by the window where a steady stream of cars passed. "So, what have you been *doing* lately? It seems like all you do is work."

Yeah. That was about right. "I'm working on this idea for the bonus money. It's kind of a long shot."

"What is it?"

I hesitated. Natalie knew I'd done robotics in middle school. We'd known each other since freshman year and she knew the most about who I used be. No biggie and she never asked about it again.

"I found these animatronics from the old mini-golf in the basement of the range. They're sitting there collecting dust. I thought it would be cool to fix them up. Then, I thought maybe it'd be even cooler to bring back the whole miniature golf course as a way to bring in more families to the business."

Natalie blinked. "Wow. That sounds like a lot of work. I thought you weren't into the robot stuff anymore?"

"I'm not," I said quickly. "Well, I mean, I'm out of practice. At first I thought the robots were statues, but when I realized they had a back panel and switches, I kind of got an itch to maybe do something."

"Sounds cool." She sipped her bright yellow citrus smoothie. "Olivia and I are taking a summer theater class. There's one at the civic center. It starts in a week."

"Oh?" I hadn't realized Natalie was interested in acting.

"It's a beginner's thing. You know Olivia. She'll try anything once."

I did not know. Olivia didn't exactly talk to me directly.

Natalie gasped. "Maybe you could join us. Wouldn't that be *so* fun?"

"It's free?"

Her shoulders slumped. "No. Sorry, I keep forgetting about the money thing. But you're making money at your job. You could probably swing the class, right? Maybe we could see if it transfers as actual class credit."

"That's sweet, but my schedule is tight." I hadn't even been paid yet by the golf range. I wasn't about to spend money on an acting class I didn't want to take. Besides, I'd been acting around her long enough.

During my shift the next day, I sped through my usual rounds. I needed to return to the basement.

The mini-golf remains looked pretty old. And basic.

That stuff didn't matter right now. The animatronics were what interested me. The boy and girl robots had movable joints at the shoulders and elbows. Their heads appeared to move side to side. A back plate was held together by screws. I'd need tools to get a good look at them. The dinosaur had a seam at the neck where the head likely turned. I also found a giraffe in two heavy pieces, a panda, and a chicken.

I returned to the staff elevator and rode up to the lobby level. The doors opened to a green Teed Off! polo on a skinny dude. Dan Thomas.

He looked me over. "Basement level. No cart. What are you up to?"

"Be my guest if you want to go down there. That place gives me the creeps." I walked past him, shuddering for effect.

For whatever reason, Dan followed me. "You did a decent job driving the Cage."

Do not take the bait. I'd find something to busy myself with soon enough.

"I mean, I thought you'd suck," he went on. "You came to work on a busted red scooter, and I don't know. Seeing you here, it's like, blowing my mind."

I stopped and faced him, causing him to nearly collide with me. "You weren't here the day I had my interview."

"Aidan told me. He said you were covered in mud and riding some 1980s scooter."

"A 1990s scooter. *Late* 1990s." This was not helping. "How exactly am I blowing your mind?"

"You without Matt." He gave me an incredulous look, as if I should have instantly known what he meant. "You're different."

I held my hands up, marveling at my palms. "You're right. I'm...*human.*"

He clapped once and pointed at me. "That. Right there. That's what I'm talking about. You never talked like that before."

"I didn't?"

He shook his head. "You always waited for Matt to speak. You were like his shadow. Just, like, *existing* next to him."

This was the most Dan had ever spoken to me. Triple the amount of words spoken to me at one time.

Honestly, I couldn't argue with him. I *had* been Matt's shadow. The part who thought for herself, I tended not to show around Matt or his friends.

"Aidan was right. When you let your guard down, you're a totally different person. Everyone here loves you."

I rubbed at my arms, unsure how to respond. "I have friends, you know. What do you mean, Aidan was right? What has he been saying?"

Dan looked beyond me. I turned to follow his gaze, landing on Aidan talking with a customer, pointing toward the bathrooms.

"He said not to give you such a hard time. I guess he feels bad about what went down with Matt and that other girl." He shrugged. "I don't know. Anyway." He directed a pointy elbow into my side. "Smell you later."

Smell me later? Any progress Dan made up the maturity ladder instantly slid to the lower rungs.

"Everything okay?" Aidan stood beside me now, close enough I could sense heat from his body. "Are you looking for something to do? We need a sweep of the range with the Cage."

"Sure. Just call me the Ghost Rider."

Aidan's mouth parted.

"I meant like the Nicolas Cage movie."

"No, I got it. That movie is terrible. I've seen it seven times."

"Seven. Times."

"Six wasn't enough."

Because I was not in control, I laughed. I was not supposed to laugh with Aidan. I disliked Aidan and he disliked me.

Aidan had a different air today. An easiness replaced the usual tightness around his mouth. Softened edges. His hair looked more styled and he wore a more fitted polo.

Clearly, I only noticed this now because Aidan was acting nicer toward me, and telling Dan to lay off the criticism. That had to be it. Only, he wasn't off the hook. He'd warned me off this job and the bonus. He'd planted the seed about the party knowing Matt would be there with Meghan.

Even if we were cordial at work, I couldn't forget. Aidan was not my friend.

"Lila?"

I blinked. "Sorry. Tired is all." I yawned for effect.

"I cut two staff for the night already. You'll have to stay until close." He didn't say it in a mean tone, more as a fact.

"I'm good. Ready to get back to work."

"Good." Aidan watched me.

"Great." I watched Aidan.

A beat passed. Another.

I made a point to look beyond him, anything to break the claustrophobia of standing so close and refusing to move. "Don't you have people to manage?"

A quiet laugh came through. "Yeah, I guess I do."

His grin. Oh my goodness, his grin was...not terrible. I tore myself away from staring at his lips. And his white and very much imperfect teeth that were possibly endearing in their slight crookedness.

The Cage. Yes, the Cage was where I needed to be right now. A nice cramped space all by myself.

Chapter Eleven

❤

Notes in the margin:
Aidan - enemy or friend?
Is "frenemy" still a thing?

Payday. Oh, sweet payday. I ripped open my printed deposit statement and skimmed to the dollar amount and... There had to be something wrong here.

I drove home, stewing. Came into the house, slammed the door.

"They take *this much* out for taxes?" I shook the paper statement stub I'd so carefully torn along the perforated edges. I was ready to chuck the offending sum into the garbage disposal.

Dad slung an arm around me. "This is why happy hour exists."

"Happy hour is what I clean up after." I shirked away. Okay, it wasn't his fault minimum wage was so...minimum. Or that taxes were so non-minimum. "Maybe I'll be a political science major and run for office. This is ridiculous."

"Our daughter, the enlightened fiscal conservative," Mom quipped to Dad.

Har har.

Paying off the trip debt would take *forever*. I desperately needed the bonus money. Except my idea, it was too big. I needed to scale my plans down or make them more practical.

Back to work the next day, I entered the Cage. Row after row of clearing the course helped clear my head. The bright turf laid out in front of me like a green canvas, refreshed and re-set.

I steered Nic Cage back to its parking spot, checked the sky for soaring golf balls, and made a mad dash back inside.

At the top of the stairs by the golf bays, Mason stood beside Dan.

Dan held up his fist for a bump. "*Kick-ass* job, Lila."

Tentatively, I met his fist with my own. "Um, thanks."

Mason held up a hand for a high five. "You really *left behind* the mess on the course."

"You're a real *national treasure.*"

It was like seeing someone open their mouths to speak but hearing tuba sounds instead of English words. "Oh, I get it. Those are Nicolas Cage movies."

Mason spun his phone in his hand. "We're going on break. Want to join us?"

I searched their faces, looked at their hands, their stance. Why? What was the trick?

Dan noticed my lack of response. "It's not a set-up. Aidan's not here today and we're bored."

Perhaps a slight disappointment trickled through at hearing Aidan wasn't working today. No, not disappointment. Further skepticism? Why was it okay for them to talk to me when Aidan wasn't here? "Sure. I have my lunch in the fridge in the break room."

We fell in step, the three of us, walking toward the staff area. "Joe acted all cryptic about his kitchen improvement idea today," Dan said. "Did he say anything to you?"

"Chet is the one with the kitchen improvement project," I answered. "He hasn't said anything to me, since you're drilling me for details."

"Come on, Lila. I'm trying to make conversation here. I swear, this isn't some scheme."

"Dan's not even going for the bonus," Mason said. "He's too into writing sci-fi stories to think about work any more than he has to."

"Trying to be the next Terry Pratchett?" I asked.

Dan raised a brow. "You read Terry Pratchett?"

"I didn't say that." Or, inadvertently, I had.

His shoulders slumped. "Well, regardless, no one can replace Sir Pratchett. He is an enigma and a genius."

I nodded. "Totally."

I followed Mason and Dan into the empty break room. I decided to give them the benefit of the doubt. "I know we haven't always gotten along. To be clear, I know some of the stress between us was me. Maybe all of it was me."

Dan looked at Mason, his pale skin turning blotchy at his collar. "We wouldn't have asked you to have lunch with us if we hated you."

That made sense. Now it left me to believe it. To re-set the course, so to speak.

I grabbed my lunch from the fridge. Napkins were scattered at one end of the table beside an open cardboard box holding one lone half donut. I tapped at the pastry remnant with a plastic knife. "Ugh, peanut."

Mason peered over my shoulder. "Why do they always get donuts without us?"

"I'm telling you," Dan said. "You have to open to get the treats. Jen brings in the good stuff for the openers. Never for the closers."

Mason took out his own lunch, a hoagie large enough to feed three full-grown men. My own PB&J and yogurt seemed pretty chintzy, but I depended on my parents and their grocery buying. With the money I owed them, no way would I ask them to buy me better lunch options.

Dan and Mason talked about a rude customer and progressed to a glitch in the registration system they kept reporting to their outsourced IT help desk, but nothing was ever done about it. I ate my sandwich, listening.

Mason pulled his phone out with a puzzle game briefly lighting up.

I caught sight of the familiar screen. "Are you playing Word Storm?"

"What? No."

Dan elbowed him. "Yes, you are. You're obsessed with it."

"What's your highest combo?" I asked.

"You play?" Mason flicked the screen back to the game, tapping to pull up the stats. "I got a triple blast sentence chain and an ultra-bomb combo."

"Nice. I'm working on those sentence chains. I want to unlock the Clause Beast."

"For a free game, Word Storm is pretty cool," Mason went on. "I'm sort of a mobile game geek. I'm working on developing my own."

"Really?" I took out my own phone and scrolled through my games. "That's cool."

"I didn't figure you for a Word Stormer," Dan said to me. "No offense."

"We don't exactly know each other," I shot back.

He flinched. Not a full flinch, but a notable flick.

"Sorry." I turned to Mason. "What else do you play?"

He pulled up a game with a name in another language. "I play a lot of Korean games. My cousins and I play this." He showed me an 8-bit fantasy image, like old-school Nintendo. "Classic side-scroller. Fun if you're into those."

I wasn't, but his knowledge of gaming apps was impressive. I'd been so insistent to shun Matt's friends, afraid I'd regress to Nerd Lila, I'd never bothered to find out their interests.

The room fell quiet. Dan picked at the foil edges of his bag of chips. "Have you...talked to Matt?"

Hello, Elephant. Meet room.

Instagram didn't count, though you could say I'd checked on his whereabouts. "No."

"Me neither."

I looked from Dan to Mason. "Neither of you?"

Mason sat back, arms folded. "We don't like Meghan."

"To be fair, you didn't like me either. Maybe you don't like that Matt has girlfriends."

"I don't like how Matt *acts* when he has a girlfriend," Dan answered in a clipped tone. "It seriously has nothing to do with you. It's about him."

Huh. Dan sort of implied this the other day, but I hadn't fully understood. "What's different about Meghan that you don't like her?" I could hardly believe we were talking about this after so much of never talking about anything. Let alone talking about Matt and our connections to him and to each other.

"He shouldn't have started anything with her before ending things with you." Mason shifted in his seat. "We tried to tell him. If he didn't want to be with you anymore, he should have told you. He would complain to us and not do anything about it. No offense—it's just, we saw the other side."

Heat crept up my neck. I'd seen what I wanted to. I'd given Matt a pass on a lot of things because I didn't like confrontation.

Why had I agreed to lunch again? I stuffed the nearly empty yogurt into my sandwich bag.

Mason tapped at his phone. "We were basically done with Matt by the party, but the party was the final betrayal."

"Betrayal?" That was a loaded word. "Did something else happen?"

"We've been friends with Matt going back to kindergarten. It was like we weren't good enough for him anymore. To him, we're like a last resort. If no one else cooler is around."

Even though his friends were into geeky stuff, Matt always played down the geekery in front of me or at school. Matt had been trying to change his image, same as me. An unsettled feeling washed over me. If Matt betrayed his friends in favor of cooler friends, of popularity, of acceptance, who had I betrayed?

"I'm sorry."

Mason looked genuinely confused. "Why? Matt's the one who acted like a jerk to you. We didn't get it until that night."

"Anyway," Dan said, "Aidan said we should talk to Matt about how he was acting before he left for Brazil. Then Matt brought Meghan, and then we saw you." He shook his head. "Messed up."

Aidan had smirked at me after I caught Matt with Meghan. He'd *gloated*. None of this fit together. With Dan and Mason, seeing the looks of disappointment on their faces as they discussed Matt, I could believe they were being honest about cutting Matt off. But Aidan?

None of it made sense.

Or maybe it did. Aidan was mad at me for ruining his friendship with Matt. I belonged to the crowd he'd gotten ditched for. Even if Dan and Mason seemed okay with me, Aidan wasn't. Any change in attitude he'd shown me had more to do with his shift position. He *had* to be civil.

Mason turned off his phone, looking at me without distraction. "I didn't mean to get you upset. Sorry."

"It's okay, really." I swept up my crumbs, leaving my spot at the table at least a little cleaner than I'd found it. I had a lot more cleaning house to do.

The following night, I raced through my closing duties, leaving the Cage for last. I had my sweeping method down to the point my mind could wander. Aidan's smile strobed in my thoughts. His slightly imperfect teeth. What? No. *Bad, Aidan smile.*

Enemy, frenemy—whatever. Thinking about Aidan in any other way could not be good.

We closed the golf range by 11:07 p.m., which had to be a record. Nobody wanted to stay here a second longer on such a beautiful summer night.

I fired off a text to both Mom and Dad that I planned to stop by Natalie's before coming home. I hadn't gone anywhere but work since the infamous party and I wasn't about to let this summer night go to waste.

I headed to my car. A blue truck beside me made the auto-unlock sound.

"Hey." Aidan. He stopped by the truck.

I did a double take. "That's yours?" I couldn't for the life of me remember seeing him drive a truck. Or see Matt riding in it.

"Uh, yeah. I bought it off my cousin. Or at least my parents did. I owe them in installments." He nodded toward my car. "You heading out?"

"Yeah." A decal on his side window caught my attention. A sword and a dragon over the image of a red crest with little scroll designs. "What's the sticker?"

Aidan checked where I looked. "It's from a Renaissance Faire. I'm part of the Firebreather faction."

"There are factions at the Renaissance Faire?"

"Yeah, if you're a LARPer." He watched for my reaction. "That's live re-enactments with a game element."

I knew what it stood for. "I didn't realize you were into that stuff."

"*That stuff* is pretty fun. It's not for everyone, I get it."

"I wasn't making fun of it. I didn't know you did LARPing. Matt never—" I stopped. "I didn't always know much about what you guys did, apart from school and whatever." Matt for sure would never have dressed up for a Renaissance Faire.

Aidan leaned against his truck. The doors auto-locked again. "I guess we both have lives outside of the person who connected us."

"There's a Ren Faire near here?" I'd been to several faires in different states as a kid. I had fun watching the live joust with knights and horses.

"Yeah. About a forty-minute drive."

"Oh, wow." I tried to sound both interested and not overly interested. I was still sort of amazed we were having a discussion outside of a task list or toilet paper stocking. Or threats to my job.

He jangled his keys. "Anyway, I wanted to make sure you were on your way home since we're the last ones out."

"Yeah, I was about to go."

"Cool. Me too."

Neither of us moved.

He swung his keys around in a loop over a finger. "Are you going out somewhere?"

I swiped my phone awake to check the new text. My parents gave me the all clear to stay out until one a.m. at the latest. I grinned. Being the typically responsible daughter paid off from time to time.

A second text from Natalie told me she was out at a movie with Olivia.

Shoot. "I was supposed to, but Natalie's out."

"Oh. Okay." He craned his neck, looking up at the sky. "Nice night."

"Yeah. It is." The stars danced overhead like an invitation. *Stay out. Play.*

Aidan had just opened his truck door when it hit. That feeling from when I'd nestled under the blankets, wondering whether I'd ruined everything, if I'd been destined to never be the girl with the social life and a yearbook filled with happy memories. The less I had to do to fill my time, the more I was forced to confront silent pestering.

I was not at all in the mood to confront my pestering conscience.

Aidan clicked unlock again and opened the door to his truck.

"Hey," I said before I could stop myself. About those instincts? The ones telling me to do the opposite of what my gut implied, and the reason I'd made friends and scored a boyfriend? That drive surged through me fierce and strong. I blamed it on those pesky, inviting stars. "This is probably crazy, but do you want to go somewhere?"

Chapter Twelve

♥

Mental note:

Danger! Danger! Frenemy warning!

Not ten seconds later, I sat in the passenger side of Aidan's truck with the engine humming. I must have teleported. With numbed fingers, I reached for the seatbelt and clicked it into place. The click, a final confirmation this was happening.

"This is weird, isn't it?" I blurted at the same time Aidan said, "We should acknowledge this is weird."

"Did you say this is weird?" I asked.

"I thought you said weird. I heard you say weird."

"I did. And it is."

Neither of us spoke.

"We don't have to do this," Aidan said finally. He traced the seam of his seat with a finger. "If you don't want."

"I don't feel like going home. So, I figured we could go somewhere."

"Because I was the only one left in the parking lot."

"Well, yes."

"And your other friend is busy, but your parents aren't expecting you home yet."

"Something like that." Precisely like that.

Aidan tapped at the steering wheel in an oddly familiar beat. "Summerfest is happening."

"Oh, yeah." I'd forgotten all about it. The downtown Ginsburg festival site had carnival rides and live music.

"Let's go check it out." He pulled forward and out of the lot. "What music do you listen to?"

My answer depended on which Lila I wanted to be. I was so over trying to gauge what other people would think about me, so I said the first thing I thought of. "There's this Australian singer named Utra. She writes music out of her bedroom, but she's getting a lot of attention online. She sounds like Lorde and Ellie Goulding, but moodier."

"Utra? I'll have to check her out. I like Lorde."

"What I like about her is she does concept albums. You have to listen to each one with the tracks in the listed order to get the full experience. The one I like is all about galaxies and planets. She has lyrics about quantum physics that sound like poetry."

We slowed to a stop as a traffic light switched over to red. Silence blared.

"Not simply physics, but quantum physics, huh?"

He was making fun of me, I just knew it. Only when I looked over at Aidan, he wasn't smirking. Instead, he wore a curious expression.

"Um, yeah. She's great." I gestured toward the digital interface on his dashboard. More advanced than Goldie. "We can listen to anything."

The light turned green and Aidan tapped the gas. "Satellite radio. Here's an electro pop station. Does that work?"

We reached downtown having had a thorough discussion about whether remakes of old songs into acoustic versions with barely-there vocals were cool or annoying. Aidan turned into a three-story parking structure across from the street fair.

"I think the music at the fest goes until midnight. If you're interested, we could check out the last band. They're all local."

"You're into music." Captain Obvious over here, though it hadn't been obvious to me until we'd ridden in his truck together and had this conversation.

"Yeah. I dress for my dragon faction and wield a pretend sword. I'm layered."

"All while coordinating employee tasks at a golf range. Layers indeed."

Aidan parked and unhooked his seatbelt. "You ready?"

As I ever would be. Which was not, really, but I had limited time to cram in fair food and a ride or two. Oh, and check out the band. It was already the last week of June and I'd done nothing fun since canceling my trip. Working second shift had a way of stealing summer.

We fell in step together. Guitar music from the distant event stage echoed toward us, partly swallowed up by children's squeals and adult laughter. Lights from the carnival lit up the city block like an alien wonderland daring us to join in.

Immediately, I recognized one of our teachers—Mrs. Halloway who taught Biology and Earth Sciences. If I recognized a teacher, easily someone from school could recognize me. Or Aidan. Or us, *together*.

"Did you see Mrs. Halloway?" Aidan asked me.

"Yeah." I pushed the paranoid thoughts aside. "It's always off-putting to see a teacher outside of class. When I was little, it totally confused me. I thought teachers lived at the school."

Aidan laughed. "I never assumed that. Both my parents are teachers."

"Where do they teach?"

"Mom's a professor at Pine Valley College. My dad is an assistant principal the next county over. He never wanted to teach in the same district where me and my brother went. Turned out great for me. I wouldn't be the super stud I am if my parents were watching me every day in the halls."

I shook my head, smiling. Stud was a terrible word to describe anything other than a breeding horse, but he certainly wasn't...repulsive. He'd likely had girlfriends. I wasn't sure why he didn't have one now. Unless he did and I didn't know.

We reached the ticket gate and Aidan handed over cash.

"Hey, wait." I dug in my pocket for the twenty from my extremely limited stash of allowance and chore earnings.

"No, I've got it."

The word DATE flashed in my mind, spelled out in the bright bulbs of the midway. "Okay, but only if I can buy your food tickets." I handed over my twenty to the ticket lady. Everything purchased at the fest required us to pay with tickets.

We walked beneath the Summerfest archway decorated in smiling suns wearing sunglasses. Light-up palm trees anchored the sign as posts. In Michigan, a digital palm tree sign was as close as we'd get to tropical. Once we cleared the entrance, I handed him a string of connected paper tickets.

"You didn't have to do that."

"I don't want you thinking I owe you."

He stopped walking. "That's not the way I think."

Why had I thought coming here with Aidan was a good idea? "I'm sorry. Let's get some food and we can go."

"Hey." Aidan stepped closer, making room for a family passing by to the popcorn vendor a few steps away. The stinging salt in the air made my mouth water, but Aidan was so near now, I couldn't be torn away. "I should tell you I'm sorry. I'm sorry about the party and how things played out. I'm sorry about a lot, but mostly how I've been...unfair to you. I took sides with Matt when I didn't have to. I didn't want to."

There was so much so fast my brain couldn't keep up. Aidan was *apologizing* to me. I didn't want to talk about this. Yet here I stood with Aidan during my off-work hours and didn't make a move to leave.

I had to say something. "Thanks. For the apology."

His shoulders eased.

Carefree voices swirled around us. The festival was like an artificial backdrop for a scene we were expected to act out. Only I had no idea how to act this part.

"This is probably too weird, you and I being here," he said.

I let out a breath. "Yeah. It's weird."

He nodded toward the entrance we'd just walked through. "We can go."

I held out the tickets. "I won't be able to come back before the fest ends." I refused to waste more money.

Also, Aidan's apology seemed genuine. He wouldn't have driven me here on his own time if he truly hated me.

"You know, I never wanted to be mad at you and the guys. You just seemed so irritated by me and I guess the mutual disliking built from there."

Aidan jammed his hands into his khaki pants pockets. He shifted weight to the other foot. "We did gang up on you sometimes. Matt would turn into a different person around you. He'd pretend to be so, I don't know, fake, I guess."

My throat tightened. "I liked how Matt acted around me. It was how he acted around you guys I couldn't stand."

Aidan's gaze fell to the pavement. I found myself staring down too, connecting dots of flattened popcorn pieces and discarded hot dog wrappers.

"I guess we saw different Matts," he said finally. "You shouldn't feel bad for liking how he acted with you. For us, he acted different, like a stranger." He shook his head. "Seeing you away from him, you're not at all like what I expected. You're a whole person. You're Lila, not Matt and Lila."

My breath caught. A sense of relief flooded over. I was a whole person—just me on my own. With Matt, I'd intended for people to see us as a couple. Hearing Aidan say this now, the intention came off shallow and misguided. I was ashamed of it.

I swallowed past my dry throat. "Did you actually see me that way? Less than whole?"

As I waited for his answer, the sounds around us deadened, hollow, like hearing it all below the water's surface.

"I think I did. I didn't know you then. I still don't."

But you want to? The question slinked into my thoughts like a casual invader. *I'll just show up and settle in.*

"Maybe..." My voice came out quiet. What did I want? I wanted Aidan to want to know me, and I wanted to know him back. I wanted to get over old hang-ups. I wanted to move on. Holding onto an image of Aidan as a henchman kept me angry and hurt. He wasn't those things. I channeled Natalie's confidence. My sister Lenora's brash attitude. "Maybe we could start over. Tonight, square one. We start clean." I still had questions, but we had to start somewhere.

A breath seemed to catch on his lips. "Yeah. I'm good with that."

"Okay."

"Good." Aidan grinned. "Now that we've settled our grievances, we could stare awkwardly at each other some more, or we could get curly fries and slushies and go see that terrible sounding band."

"Yes, but replace curly fries with a soft pretzel and slushies with cotton candy."

"You're replacing a liquid with a solid?"

"Hmm. Cotton candy is more of a wisp that melts in your mouth. You could make an argument for a liquid."

"You could make the argument and you'd be wrong. It leaves your mouth sticky, so you want a drink. It's the opposite of liquid. It teases you with the melting and then makes you thirsty."

I mean, he wasn't wrong. I wouldn't let him know that. "Up for debate."

We departed separate ways to order food from different vendors, giving me a short time to calm my internal freak out. What was I doing here with Matt's bestie? Okay, former bestie. More importantly, why did I *like* it?

I picked up my pretzel and pop from the order window and met back with Aidan as he balanced a fry basket and slushie in one hand, and a blue and pink swirled poof of cotton candy in the other.

"Here." He handed over the cotton candy. "Since you have a drink, now you can deal with your sugar thirst."

Something about the bright, pillowy cotton candy made me happy at the basest level. And he'd spent fair tickets on me. "Thanks." It came out more serious than I'd intended, like he'd paid my parking ticket.

A memory flashed in my mind. Matt and I at a school fundraising carnival in March, sharing cotton candy. His birthday had been that week, and I'd won him a little stuffed football from a ball toss game. He'd won me a plush cat.

But we'd gotten in a fight over going to the carnival at all. Matt had canceled plans with Aidan, Dan, and Mason to go with me. I'd recently been sick and was still feeling pretty crummy. I was off my game, and being social in large groups didn't come easily for me. I'd tried to back out, to stay home sick, but Matt said if we didn't go the day would have been wasted. After all, he'd canceled plans with friends for me, wasn't I grateful? He'd apologized later. The whole fight felt stupid looking back.

Aidan and I found an open spot at the back of the crowd by the event stage. The band, a mix of guys with graying hair who wore faded rock T-shirts with logos of bands my parents liked, were decent if you liked wailing guitars and lyrics ending in, "yeah."

I bit into my pretzel. "They're not so bad."

"The drummer is great." Aidan watched for a few beats. "I used to play."

"Why did you stop?"

"I wasn't very good." He laughed. "I used to be in band and orchestra in middle school, but I didn't bother trying out in high school. Too much pressure, you know?"

Our high school's band was not for the casual musician. They marched in statewide holiday parades and had flown to a big-time college bowl a few years ago. "I'm also instrumentally challenged," I admitted.

"I'm not great at sports either. Not for lack of trying. Soccer, Little League, pee wee football, gymnastics. I tried it all. I'm bad at all of it. This left me a lot of time after school to explore geekery."

"Is that where LARPing comes in?"

He took a long draw of slushie and winced. "Brain freeze." He blinked and waited before sipping again. "LARPing happened because of going to the Ren Faire enough years."

On stage, guitars wailed into a frenzy until finally the song ended, followed by medium-strength applause.

"Well, that was something." His eyes widened.

"What?" Then I saw it. A sea of faces turned toward us. Everyone at the concert headed to the exit at once. We stood right in their path.

Aidan raised brows in silent communication. *Bolt now?* I telegraphed back, *Yes.*

We dashed back to the midway, zigzagging through clusters of people. I stopped short, blocked by a wall of plaid. No, a man. A refrigerator-sized man in plaid.

"There." Aidan pointed. He led us to an open space by portable metal gates separating the carnival rides from the food trucks. He guided me with a light touch to my back, steering me toward the gate and putting himself nearer to the crowd. I found myself leaning into his hand at my back. I imagined him encircling his arms around me. Protecting me...

Snap out of it.

Now safely tucked in our alcove, we watched the concert horde shuffle by.

"Upon closer inspection, they're walking pretty leisurely." Aidan slow-nodded. "Yup. We nearly escaped a woman on a scooter."

The mention of a scooter had me immediately defensive, but what Aidan spied was a mobility device, the four-wheeled type rather than a totally radical, tomato red dream machine.

Aidan held up a hand. "Not that kind of scooter. I didn't mean—"

"I know. I wasn't thinking you meant any other type."

"Because I wouldn't bring that up."

"I wouldn't expect you to."

"For the record, you rode off on it like a boss. Honestly, I found it impressive."

Score. My pride at peeling out of the Teed Off! lot hadn't been solely in my head. "Except you said you didn't mean that kind of scooter."

"I hadn't. Then when I said it, I thought of your scooter."

"My sister's," I corrected. Oh, what was the use? Moving on. "Do we have time for a ride?"

Aidan chucked his empty fry container and napkins in the trash. "Sure. Which one?"

"Ooh, how about Gravity Insanity?"

Aidan squinted past me. "You mean the tilty-spinny?"

I nearly choked on my cotton candy. "The what?"

"I don't know what it's called, but every carnival has it. You stand against the wall in the round thing and it gets tilty as it spins and your feet lift off the floor."

I bit my lip, smiling. "Centrifugal force. The force is equivalent to three times the force of gravity, thus lifting the feet."

"I see." Aidan nodded. "As I said. Tilty-spinny."

I ditched my own trash and grabbed his hand, leading Aidan to the ride where teenagers and kids allowed out this late scrambled into the metal contraption for a final ride. It wasn't until we were inside, leaning against our wall panels, I realized his fingers were entwined in mine. I quickly moved to retract my hand, but Aidan squeezed back.

I dared to look at him, my heartbeat ramping up the same as the ride prepping to spin us off the ground. Aidan watched me. Something was different now. I felt it in my bones. His hand in mine connected us and all of our memories. Thoughts of him swirled in my head—how he looked at me, how I'd thought he'd looked at me that maybe wasn't as critical as I'd always thought. He inched closer and my breath caught.

The ride operator appeared in front of us barking instructions for our safety. I didn't hear a single word.

Aidan squeezed my hand again. And the spinning began.

We tumbled out of the gravity ride drunk on physics. As tonight's Summerfest wound down, we made our way back to Aidan's truck. My head felt deliciously light.

On the drive back to the golf range, the radio filled the silence. I rolled my window down. Against my skin, the night air tickled like a lightning bug's light touch and go. These were the moments of summer to grab and hold onto. Like digging toes into fresh cut grass and slow-roasted pavement cooled by a summer shower. A sense of peace, of certainty, settled over me. I was right where I needed to be.

Which was weird because I was a passenger in Aidan's truck.

Then again, so long as the entirety of my summer wasn't mopping floors, who cared who the time was spent with? Right?

When we reached my car in the driving range lot, Aidan got out too.

"Thanks for coming tonight." Nerves suddenly took over even though we'd been sitting together in his truck moments ago. "And for whatever tonight was."

Aidan's smile wavered. "Yeah."

"Oh, no. Do you feel sick? Gravity Insanity is no joke."

He turned, rubbing his chin. "No, I'm good. I just wonder what Matt would think. Of us hanging out together."

Despite being thousands of miles away on another continent, we couldn't escape Matt.

I folded my arms against the growing chill. "Matt has nothing to do with this."

"I know, but you and Matt have history. Me and Matt have history."

"Despite our *history*, Matt hadn't bothered telling me about Meghan."

In a flash, the night and everything we'd built up cracked open. Every time I seemed to put the breakup behind me, I somehow managed to dig up the roots.

I held up my hand. "My point is, I don't want my future decisions or plans run through some sort of Matt filter. He made his choice and now he's gone."

Aidan scuffed his shoe against the ground, grinding stones beneath the sole. "Besides, we only hung out because I was the only option, right?"

This was the part where I was supposed to laugh like everything was fine. It didn't feel fine, but I wasn't great at navigating awkward discussions. I didn't like disappointing anyone or confronting issues. I preferred to apologize for any wrongness and move on.

I smiled, pretending none of those thoughts mattered. "Look. I had fun tonight. We don't have to hate each other. I call that a win."

"I never hated you." His words came out quiet but firm. "I'll see you tomorrow."

This conversation felt like it needed...more. I wasn't ready to see him go, regardless of my pending curfew. "Oh, I'm off tomorrow." I watched his face, waiting for a note of disappointment. Never mind—it didn't matter. The important part was Aidan and I weren't enemies. Now I could breathe easier during working hours. "I'm back the day after—midday shift. So, see you then."

He looked back one last time before getting into his truck. "Good night, Lila."

He was right. It had been a good night.

Chapter Thirteen

♥

Reasons to Loathe Aidan Pemberton cont'd:

- Maybe loathe is too strong a word

Natalie called the next day, saying her plans moved to the following weekend, so she was free after all. She invited me to her house and asked if I wanted to go to Summerfest.

On the way over to her house, I debated what to tell her. If I told her I'd gone already, then I'd have to tell her who I went with.

And as much as I'd said Matt had nothing to do with Aidan and me hanging out, explaining I'd spent the evening with Matt's best friend felt like a loaded conversation.

Wait, this was stupid. Natalie had been my trusted sounding board for the past three years. Why was I worried to tell her? I absolutely needed to tell her.

She waited on the bench swing on her front porch when I arrived, phone in hand.

"I ended up going to the festival last night, after my shift." I kept my voice light. "With...Aidan." There. Like a Band-Aid, ripped it right off.

She squinted at me. "Aidan who?"

"Pemberton. Aidan Pemberton. From work."

Her hand flew to her mouth. "Aidan *Pemberton*? You went to Summerfest *with Matt's friend, Aidan Pemberton*?"

"It sort of worked out that way," I said in a rush. "I think maybe we're friends?"

Natalie pursed her lips. "Come inside. I need to hear everything."

I followed her into the house and up to her room. Natalie's bedroom could have been pulled from a Pottery Barn catalog, decorated in grays and muted purples with white ruffled curtains and a white faux fur stool and rug. The room smelled like lavender and pricey hair products, both a comfort and a reminder of how much I relied on Natalie for anything fashion-related or trendy.

Anderson, their aging sheepdog, lumbered into her room before she closed the door. He attempted to camouflage on the fur rug.

"So, let me get this straight. You're hanging out with Matt's *best friend*? On *purpose*?"

"We hung out once. We work together." I was starting to question whether I should tell her about the holding hands part. It had only been for a second. Okay, more than a second. "The best friend title is more of a former title."

"Did you guys talk about Matt?"

"A little. Aidan apologized for what happened. He was at the party. He saw the break up go down."

"Oh." Natalie paced from her bed to the door.

"Matt was acting like a jerk to him. And to Mason and Dan. They didn't like the person Matt was turning into and tried to talk to him about it. They tried to talk to him about Meghan and—"

Natalie covered her ears. "I cannot *stand* hearing that girl's name. I can't *believe* what an idiot Matt is."

She crouched in front of me and reached her hands to mine. She looked at me like I was the timid woodland creature. "Are you sure you're okay?"

My muscles tensed. Normally, I would eat up this level of attention from Natalie. She was one hundred percent into my issues—a best friend who cared. But hadn't I managed okay these past few weeks? "Why do you keep asking me if I'm okay?"

A hurt look crossed her face. "What do you mean?"

"I know you're being nice, but it makes me think you see me as this, like, fragile person." A squirrel ready to scamper beneath a blanket nest. I was out here, trying to move on. Doing pretty well, if I said so myself.

"I wouldn't say fragile, but I'm just saying you don't have to pretend not to be sad about losing Matt. You two were so *into* each other. I can't imagine it's easy to separate from that."

It also hadn't been easy to keep up the role of perfect girlfriend. Playing Matt's girlfriend took work. Clocking in at the golf range gave me a place to be myself without the act. Honestly, it was almost a relief to not have to be Matt's girlfriend anymore.

Holy crap. I felt...relieved.

This was a good thing, right? I attempted to reframe. "Think about it. Senior year has so many more options now that I'm single."

Natalie stared at me, her face not landing on a specific expression. She seemed to work her way through confusion, disbelief, and questioning.

I wasn't sure Natalie would understand. I wasn't sure I understood myself. "I know you're concerned, but I'm fine. I think I'm in a good place."

She sat on the carpet beside me, petting Anderson. "All of this seems sort of rushed. Like you're showing everyone you're fine but maybe you're not."

"I've had plenty of sad moments. I don't need to drown myself in ice cream pints to get over the guy who cheated on me."

My remark hung in the air, the sting reverberating. "I'm sorry," I said quickly, remembering Natalie's offer to stay in to watch movies and eat ice cream. "I didn't mean your idea was bad."

Natalie smoothed back her effortless waves. They floated back to frame her face. "I know. I guess I was thinking back to when things ended with Darren. I didn't want to do anything."

I'd been around for her breakup with Darren. All pre-Matt, where my social devotion had been solely aimed on Natalie. "I remember. I did that for a couple days, but I had to get a job. Remember that bill my parents wrote up for me?" I didn't necessarily want to press the money subject too much. Natalie worked too, but the car her parents bought her on her sixteenth birthday wasn't found abandoned in a construction lot. She owned the latest iPhone, where my phone had belonged first to my sister.

"Anyway, Aidan and I cleared the air, which works much better for me since we have to see each other all summer.

We ate fair food and rode one ride, to give you the full summary. That's pretty much it." Except for the hand holding. I wasn't ready to share that yet. I liked that it was my secret to keep.

Natalie looked away, staring through the gauzy curtains to the watercolor-like green leaves out the window. "Let's do something. You know what? We're going to make this summer *amazing*. Forget Matt and the girl whose name I will never say. Let's take back your summer, Lila. It's time to get out there. How does that sound?"

This I could agree with. I needed to do something else with my summer besides work. "Okay. I'm ready for fun. What should we do?"

Natalie pulled out her phone and tapped the screen. "Let's see what Olivia's up to. I'm sure there's a party somewhere."

If I could count on Natalie for anything, it was to give my social life the kick-start it needed.

Flames danced in an orange burst ahead of us as we entered the backyard bonfire. The house belonged to the Hayes sisters. Grace Hayes, a fellow incoming senior at West Ginsburg, had a big-time party reputation. Not someone I regularly hung out with, but like Natalie said, it was time to get back out there. My summer bucket list was light on check marks: Teed Off! and visits with Grandpa didn't count. Well, and Summerfest with Aidan.

Aidan who was very much not at this party and that was a good thing.

"Look who's here." Olivia came toward us. Olivia, a Latina with dark hair swept up in a bun, was almost as exuberant as Natalie with her declarations.

"Hey, Liv!" Natalie flung her arms out and the two embraced.

I waved. "Hi, Olivia." I didn't have Liv nickname privileges.

Natalie and Olivia both had dressed in halter tops and distressed denim. Natalie in a jean mini-skirt, and Olivia in shorts frayed at the ends. My own outfit looked like the dorkier version of theirs—longer cotton skirt and a top that wouldn't give anyone a peek at my midriff. I'd felt fine about my clothes at home, but now...

Ugh. I hated comparing myself to other girls. I needed to ditch that like I was ditching my old bad habits.

Evening shadows reached across the lawn to tempt us forward. We made our way toward the fire, stopping first by an open cooler full of sodas. Parents were home, so no alcohol. No complaints here. I wasn't a partier on that level if I could help it. Too much at stake to get caught drinking and kicked off the softball team.

Okay, honestly, I avoided drinking because my parents would go nuclear. I'd witnessed their combustion with my older sister and I preferred to avoid regular groundings and threats of being sent to a nunnery. We weren't even Catholic.

Olivia chose a diet soda, wiping the can free of ice droplets. "What have you been up to, Lila?"

"Working. I'm at the golf range off Route 50."

"Where Matt works?"

I internally winced. "Work*ed*, past tense. He's gone for the summer."

"Oh, okay. I didn't realize you both worked together."

"I was supposed to be gone this summer too, but now I'm not, so I got the job after the...breakup."

Her nose scrunched. "Sorry to hear about that. Bummer."

"Yeah."

Olivia smiled politely and migrated toward the fire where Natalie and Grace Hayes were surrounded by more of our classmates.

Why had I clammed up? I did fine at the range making friends. Sure, they were old and liked potlucks, but that counted as social. Right?

"Hey," a voice said from behind me. "It's Lila, right?"

I turned to see a white guy with tanned skin wearing a sports jersey. The heavy scent of a body spray took over. "Hi. Yes, I'm Lila. Brandon?"

He nodded, grinning. "What's up?"

My tongue tasted like the Sahara. I usually relied on Natalie...or Matt to take the lead when we socialized at parties.

Now the lead fell to me.

"Oh, you know." I cringed at my own non-response.

Brandon appeared unfazed. "So, what happened with that Matt guy? Somebody said you burned his swim gear."

"What? No, it was an award medal. I mean, I doubt it *burned*—it's made of metal. Probably just the strap got singed."

I waited for Brandon to scowl, or turn away, or say only unstable hot messes threw their ex-boyfriend's prized possession into a fire, but he only nodded and drained the rest of his energy drink. He belched but had the decency to look a little embarrassed. "'Scuze me. Anyway, that was low, him breaking up with you like that."

"I broke up with him." Important clarification.

"But he was with that other girl already, right? So, he ended it first."

"If he'd ended it with me, he should have had the guts to actually end it with me."

He laughed and held his fist up for a bump. "Feisty. I like it. I'd never do a girl wrong like that. Not my style, you know what I'm saying?" Brandon moved in closer, the spice scent of his body spray mingling with the syrupy sugared energy drink. "You seem like a cool girl."

I laughed to cover my nerves. I was *so* bad at this.

An arm hooked into mine. "He-ey." Natalie's voice came through like a song. "I wondered where you'd gone off to."

"Right here." I blinked at her with my BFF SOS.

She gave me a reassuring smile. "You're fine."

"My family has a boat." Brandon mimed a fake lay-up and jogged in place. "We dock it at Bishop Lake. I can take you ladies out on the lake some weekend."

Natalie beamed at me. "That sounds *so* fun. We should see if Olivia wants to go."

"I have to check my work schedule," I reminded her.

Natalie smiled at Brandon. "We're *totally* in." She turned to me. "Hey, I need to go to the house. Want to join?"

Apparently, her question was not a question, and I was swept away. I followed her through the sliding back door into the Hayes' kitchen. We reached the bathroom and she closed us both inside the small space. My back pressed against a towel bar as she ran the faucet and washed her hands.

"Isn't Brandon nice? He'd be a good rebound. A perfect summer boyfriend, don't you think?"

Girls like Natalie had options like seasonal boyfriends. "Or he's moving in quick because he thinks I'm an easy hookup."

Natalie turned off the faucet. "I've known Brandon since first grade. He talks himself up like he's a player, but believe me, he's a good guy. He's *so* cute."

I wasn't sold on the *so*, but he was cute if you were into hair gel and miming sports moves. Which, I realized that instant, I wasn't. "Earlier, you said you thought I was rushing things. Now you want me to find a rebound guy?"

She sighed and opened the door. "I want you to be happy, Lila."

And finding another guy would make me happy? "Maybe this summer can be about us. Hanging out together." That's what I thought she'd meant about taking back the summer.

She moved into the hall. "I still think we should go out on Brandon's boat. We'll get a bunch of us—it will be fun. I swear I won't bug you about dating him."

I took my turn washing my hands since I was here. For some reason, hand washing seemed to legitimize both of us going into a hall bathroom together.

I contemplated following Natalie back to the fire, but detoured to the patio first. I was an independent young woman who could handle socializing on her own. I had lists of tips from online articles and magazines. I could do this.

I grabbed a hot dog and a layered s'mores parfait in a clear plastic cup. I looked up to see Grace's younger sister

Holli hovering by the patio table near all the food.

"These are so cool," I told Holli, holding up the s'mores parfait.

Her eyes lit up. "Thanks. I found the recipe on Pinterest. Tala and I spent all afternoon making them."

She and her friend Tala hadn't joined the rest of the party, from what I'd seen. Kind of like how I'd treat a party if I'd never intentionally gone against my wallflower instincts. Holli, who'd just finished freshman year with straight-As, was a general bookworm type who also ran cross-country. The kind of friend I would gravitate toward if not for my grand social plans.

"You should join us," I told her, nodding toward the fire. Maybe she needed coaxing, like I had with Natalie.

Holli looked toward the partiers. "My sister's already annoyed with me."

I could relate. "I have an older sister too. She tested my parents' limits. It's made it both harder and easier for me. One, I know what I can and can't get away with. But on the other hand, my parents know what I can and can't get away with. But mainly, I know I don't have to be her. I can be my own person."

I thought I saw an eyeroll from Holli's friend. What was I doing lecturing them on hanging out?

"Anyway." I needed to move on or I'd find myself glued to the wall. Or patio. "It was nice seeing you."

To my surprise, Holli and Tala followed me to a circle of kids on the grass set back from the fire. We sat to join them mid-conversation about a concert at one of the big venues in Detroit.

A girl next to me looked me over. "What ever happened after that party where your boyfriend showed up with some other girl?"

Okay this was ridiculous. All anybody knew about me was my ties to Matt and that stupid party.

Today was a new day. I could take my summer back. "I dumped him. Then I took his job."

Her mouth dropped open. "Oh my gosh. Are you serious?" She tapped the girl beside her. "Did you hear what she said? Tell her what you said." She looked at me, waiting.

On my other side, Holli watched me with interest. The group quieted to wait on me.

This didn't have to be humiliating. Not anymore.

A spike of adrenaline surged. "So, he was cheating on me with this girl from the summer abroad program. They started seeing each other the weekend of my grandmother's *funeral*." I could hardly believe these words were coming out of my mouth. Words that should have been humiliating, but I was done feeling sorry for myself. "She was totally impatient with him, telling him he had to tell me or she would. Like, I almost was broken up with by the girl he cheated on me with. He could barely face me. So pathetic." I laughed, cold power running beneath my skin. I liked the feel of it. "Anyway, I told him bye and took his job at the golf range."

So maybe I hadn't taken Matt's actual position, but my version sounded better.

Yes, my version. I knew how to do this just fine. All I needed was to craft a new persona—one without Matt.

Chapter Fourteen

♥

The Real Me:

- Plays on the softball team
- Part of Yearbook staff
- Has a best friend
- Fully intends to pay my parents back
- Enjoys hanging out with Grandpa
- Reads...but mostly for school
- Secretly watches Sci-fi shows
- Recently digs reading about old robotics
- Is actually glad I'm not in Brazil

Working at Teed Off! was swiftly turning me against all condiments in squeezable plastic containers. As fun and strangely empowering as the bonfire party had been, my daily reality kicked back into gear when I clocked in to work.

Once again, on hands and knees, I mopped up a nasty spill of the red stuff.

"It wasn't me, I swear," I heard behind me.

Dan stood a few feet back. Took a hesitant step, then crouched beside me holding a wadded paper towel.

"Here." I handed him a damp rag soaked and wrung-out with cleaning solution. I wouldn't turn down free help.

He grinned, the sheen of his invisible braces glistening from the late afternoon sun. He wiped the splotches nearest him and closed his free hand around the top of the busted ketchup container. He chucked it into a nearby waste bin.

"Everything okay here?"

Aidan joined us holding his clipboard. This was the first I'd seen him since our night at Summerfest. His brow furrowed. Not a small amount of annoyance was directed at Dan.

Dan held up a hand. "It was Nala. She knocked over the ketchup. Not me. Lila saw it."

"You're such a child." I gave Dan a good-natured shove. "*It wasn't me.*"

Dan shot back an exaggerated sneer. "Well, it wasn't."

"Did you need me to do something?" I asked Aidan.

Aidan watched us. "Uh. Yeah, I was, I mean I came over to ask..."

Dan slapped Aidan on the shoulder. "Dude, I'm clocking out early. Jen said as much. I have a meet-up to go to."

I dropped my dirty rags into an empty bucket on my cleaning cart. "Is it your sci-fi writers' group?"

"Yeah. We're doing critiques. I'm reading." He looked back at Aidan. "I re-wrote that whole chapter after the article you sent me. I'm going to see what the group says."

"Oh, great," Aidan responded, his tone absent of emotion. Definitely absent anything resembling *great*.

Dan took off, leaving me standing with Aidan, whose mouth formed a thin line.

"What's up?"

He scanned his checklist. "I guess you two are buddies now?"

"We talked in the break room the other day—he and Mason and me." I watched Aidan's reaction. Definite movement detected on the strange-dar. "Kind of like how you and I cleared the air, we did the same. I guess we're all starting over."

"Uh-huh." He didn't look up.

"I'm ready with whatever you need."

His cheeks reddened. "Just...do what you were doing."

"The floor is clean. I'm caught up."

"Are you asking to be cut?"

"No." I definitely needed the money. "All I'm saying is I'm here. I'm available." Wait. That sounded... *Lila, you are a moron.* "I can be assigned tasks, is what I mean."

I did not know how to talk to guys. Not to Brandon, who'd clearly been flirting at the bonfire, and not to Aidan who clearly—well, it wasn't exactly clear how he was acting right now. He was trying to assign me work as my supervisor. Then why was he blushing?

"Maybe check basement storage for our hand soap inventory."

The request was petty and we both knew it, but if business had slowed enough for cuts, I'd take the assignment.

I rode the staff elevator to the basement and breezed by the liquid soap, noting the same number of hazy transparent jugs as last time. I headed straight for the back storage.

I'd been debating whether I should ask Jen for permission to snoop further, but every time I thought through that conversation, I'd get to the part about rebuilding animatronics to open a mini-golf, and all I could envision were eye rolls and utter confusion. This idea was big. Only, I couldn't stop thinking about it. If I could show them the potential and show them what I could do, this could *work*. I only needed to dazzle them with a cool presentation.

Yes, I wanted to *dazzle* my coworkers. I needed help.

I lined boxes flush against the wall to clear space. The robotics I grouped together, resting them on their sides. I took out the folded paper of my inventory notes along with a pencil.

I knelt to examine the robot nearest me. I squinted to look closer at the back panel and how the body parts connected. I needed a workbench and tools. More space and light. What I needed was to take one of these robots home.

I would have to ask Jen after all, but she was always so busy. Plus, this was a real job, not a school project. To be taken seriously, I needed to figure this out on my own. Besides, it would be stupid to bother her with the details of my idea if I couldn't get the robot working in the first place. And I couldn't get it working here in the dark during my shift.

"What are you doing?"

My heart slammed against my chest. I bolted upright. *Crap*. Aidan.

"Oh. Hello. I'm..." In an area I'm not supposed to be. "Just cleaning up a bit."

He took in the room. "I've never even been back here. I followed the light when I couldn't find you."

"You sent me down here, remember?"

He let out an exasperated breath. "I know." He took a second look at the surroundings. The dinosaur head gawked at him to his right. He squinted at the giant dino eye. "What is this stuff?"

"It's from an old miniature golf course before the driving range existed. I don't think anybody has touched this stuff in a long time."

He tapped a finger against the clipboard edge. *Tap tap tap tap.* "Well, you shouldn't be this far back. If one of these boxes fell on you, Teed Off! would be liable. Jen would ream me out."

Even more reason to take a robot home to work on. I grabbed my pocket planning notebook with sketches and inventory and made a move to walk past him. Only Aidan blocked the way.

"What's that?" He pointed to the papers.

"The...inventory. For the soap."

Aidan's face turned stern, like an older sibling showing disappointment. "Let me see."

"No. Why?" I knew I sounded defensive.

"Let me see." He reached for the notebook.

I stepped back and swung my arm behind me. I couldn't believe we'd held hands only a few days ago. "Okay, I lied. It's a journal. I'm sad and I came here to write my feelings on paper."

Aidan's hand froze mid-reach. "Really?"

His expression softened, and instantly, he became the Aidan from Summerfest. Not my curmudgeony, sometimes-supervisor.

I swallowed. "No, but I can't show you."

"Why?"

"It's a secret?"

"Lila, come on. What are you doing down here?"

I sighed. "It has to do with my proposal."

He blinked. "For the bonus."

I nodded.

"I can't say we're hurting for storage space. Cleaning this up won't make a difference."

Cool, he didn't suspect anything. "Sure. Of course."

He let out a breath. "You're not telling me everything."

I pressed my tongue against a sharp incisor to keep me from spilling. "Look, you're going for the bonus too, so discussing our ideas would be a conflict. Besides, you told me not to bother, remember?"

He looked away, kicking his heel against the floor. "I'm sorry I said that. About not bothering."

"But you're still entering. It's a lot of money."

He searched the room, avoiding a direct look at me. "Of course I am. It's just, I can't..." He paced by the doorway. "I can't figure you out, Lila."

We weren't having the same conversation here. "I promise, I'm not trying to be difficult." I folded the papers and shoved them into my back pocket. "These are about my proposal. I was using the downtime to plan it. That's all."

Aidan half-shrugged, seeming to accept my response, but appeared no less agitated. "How is it that you and the guys are all chummy?"

"Dan and Mason?"

He nodded.

"They reached out to me. It's like starting over, remember? I didn't know Dan wrote science fiction until the other day. Or how Mason plays Word Storm and is working on his own mobile game. Same as how I didn't know you were in a faction at the Ren Faire until we talked the other night."

"But we don't know about *you*." He leaned against the open-ended cinder block door frame. "That's always the mystery. It's like you're one person for show and another outside of school."

Little pinpricks formed along my arms. I'd tried so hard to make the transition seamless. The point was to be the same person regardless. I wasn't trying to act different only at school, or only with Matt or around Natalie. That was who I'd wanted to be. "I don't know what you're talking about. That's an incredibly rude accusation to throw at someone."

He pushed off from the door. "Since we're starting from scratch, I guess I figured you might be honest."

"Did you ever think maybe I'm trying? Why do you care so much?"

He laughed without humor. "You're upset with me because I care? About you?"

He cared. About me. *Aidan cared about me.* I tried to process this as quickly as possible without letting my emotions rat me out. Because I guess I cared that he cared. No, not a guess. I *did* care.

Not everything made sense yet. "You knew about Meghan and never told me."

Aidan's gaze went to the rolls of green turf slumped against the wall. "Yeah. I tried to stay out of it. I guess I could have done more. I could have told you he was with someone else. I could have dropped being friends with him."

He could have, but why would he? He didn't owe me anything. Obviously, I already knew this, but standing in front of Aidan now, it made clearer sense how he'd tried to work with Matt. "He was your friend. Of course you kept trying." I didn't know what it was like to have a friend you knew most of your life and to see them change in a way that hurt so personally.

Aidan kicked at the rolled-up putting green. "Who wouldn't have a problem with their friend constantly ditching them? Then ditching on the girlfriend they'd been ditched for? It kept happening until he wasn't the guy we used to know."

For so long, I'd blamed Matt's friends. Turned out, they were trying to gain back some of the old Matt they grew up knowing. I hadn't wanted any part of their shenanigans because it took away the version of Matt I knew and loved. The one I'd crafted into a perfect, unrealistic version of him.

"You know what you said before about Matt being my king?"

"Can we forget I said that? I could have said it better. Or not at all."

"I won't argue that." I nodded. "So, I spent my life moving every year or two as a kid. When my parents left military service, we settled in Ginsburg for good. I wanted permanent friends and a boyfriend but didn't really know how. I thought being a good girlfriend meant acting as close to perfect as possible. Because we were putting down roots, if I messed it all up, there wouldn't be anywhere to run."

He thought this over. "But everybody fails. It sucks, but it's life. Failing is honest. Failing hard is brutal honesty."

"I think you just called me brutal."

"You can be." He grinned.

His grin reminded me of one nagging detail. "You smirked."

"What?"

"At the party. You had this smug look on your face during the most humiliating experience of my life. You set me up to go that party and get dumped. And then when it happened, you smirked."

Aidan's mouth hung open for a second. "You mean watching what happened? I don't know what you mean about a smirk."

"In the hallway. You looked right at me and your face—it was a smirk." How could he not remember? I twisted my own mouth as close as I could get as a demonstration. "You know, like a smarmy, know-it-all grin—"

"I know *what* a smirk is." He shook his head, attempting to put the pieces together. He snapped his fingers. "Yes, I looked at you. Maybe I was making a face, but not because of Matt. Because of what you said to him."

"Huh?"

"That was the first time I'd ever seen you not let Matt walk all over you. You called him out. You demanded he say sorry. You told him to have a *nice summer*."

"That made you *smirk*?"

He cycled through a few words before fully speaking. "It was like seeing you become someone else. Like you were waking up."

I had no idea he'd been paying attention. For so long. "No offense, but smirking at my breakup was a confusing signal to me at the time."

"I'm sorry. I guess I was caught between smiling at you taking him down and not wanting to look like I was laughing about it. I wasn't laughing. I was...proud."

That actually made sense now that I had this crisp twenty-twenty hindsight. "Thanks. I guess you were rooting for me, only I didn't know it. I couldn't see it."

"Yeah. Maybe I was." He grinned faintly. He shook his head and blew out a huff of frustration. "Friggin' Matt."

I nodded in solidarity. "Friggin' Matt."

"I only told you about the party because we'd given Matt an ultimatum. Tell you about Meghan or we would. We didn't know he'd *bring* Meghan."

Another piece of the puzzle in place. "If I hadn't gone to the party, I'd be in a subtropical city on another continent and actively hating my cheating boyfriend. Maybe it's happening in a parallel universe. In the multiverse, me in Brazil could be one timeline over—" I stopped myself at the look on his face.

"Multiverse?"

"Or whatever." Shoot. Which Lila did I go with here? Popular-seeking Lila with no Matt attachments? Or just me, making sci-fi references to someone who would probably appreciate them for once?

If only I could clone myself. Yes, cloning would solve everything.

"Lila?" Aidan watched me with intensity. "What are you actually planning down here?"

I scanned the boxes and piles of old equipment. My idea was ludicrous. "World domination through mini-golf?" I sighed. The bonus money felt even further off than ever. "I thought I had an idea, but I'm back to square one." I shrugged. "We should probably get above ground again or people will think we clocked out."

Aidan shook his head as he looked over the room. He followed me to the elevator. "I have so many questions."

You and me both. Aidan and I may have been starting over, but I needed time to adjust to starting over too.

Chapter Fifteen

♥

List Organization:

- Mini-golf inventory
- Sketches of proposed new mini-golf (incomplete)
- Business proposal outline
- Power Point presentation?
- Schematics for robots (search online)

At closing that night, I prepared for the perfect moment to return to the basement. The mini-golf idea was my best and only shot at the bonus money for now. Getting one of those robots home would at least let me know if my idea had legs. Ideally, operational mechanical legs.

I readied an empty cart and waited for Aidan to disappear. As he ran his closing rounds, I'd roll out the robot to the parking lot. I planned to wrap it in empty garbage bags. I'd parked by the dumpster, so not a stretch if someone saw me taking out trash.

In the basement, I tipped the girl animatronic upright and carefully nudged her onto the bottom shelf of the cart. Only one robot would fit.

I stared at the robot. Did I for sure want to do this? Putting geekery behind me to pursue long-term, acceptable popularity had been crucial. Now, here I was pursuing exactly what I'd avoided for three years.

I needed the money. I had an idea and a skill, and maybe a long shot, but I could do something with this robot that could work. I wrapped the empty trash bags around the robot to disguise her and headed out.

The elevator doors opened revealing an empty hall. *Score.* I looked both ways before pushing the cart down the hall and around to the front lobby. A server whizzed by paying me no attention. The registration desk sat empty since closing mainly involved the kitchen and locking up the golf bays. I was free and clear.

My heart struck harder at each footfall. *Don't look back. Just head to the dumpster, look like this is totally normal.*

I slid my keys from my pocket and popped my trunk open from the key fob. The trunk unlatched, but did not open fully. Good cover since I headed to the dumpster first where I'd then check surroundings again.

Stopping at the dumpster, I turned. One of the servers walked out the front door, waving to someone behind him. I slinked back into the shadows. Another person came out —kitchen crew.

I couldn't put the robot in my trunk yet with witnesses around. Maybe this would be a two-part process. I could put the wrapped robot in the bin and come back for her. Yes, that would work.

I hefted the robot from the cart. Darn it. I had to open the dumpster lid first. I set the robot back down, flipped the lid on the large bin, then carried the robot up and gently let her down on top of piled trash bags. Hot garbage fumes stung my nose. Before closing the lid, I knotted the garbage bag tie an extra two times along the end so I could recognize the bag when I came back.

The server made it to his car and gave me a chin nod before entering. I gave him a salute back. My eyes fell shut. *Why, Lila? Why a salute?*

I headed back inside at a light jog, pushing the much lighter cart in front of me. I wheeled it past registration and back to the supply closet. *Whew.*

Grabbing my stuff from the break room, I clocked out. I opened the door to the lobby and stood face to face with Aidan.

"Oh!" I smiled brightly. "Hey. Are you done?"

"Yup. Everyone's out."

"Cool, let's get out of here," I said.

We walked out together. I waited as Aidan locked up, my gaze focused on the dumpster.

"What are you up to tonight?" Aidan asked as we approached his truck.

I yawned for effect. "I'm beat. Going to bed." After I got my hands on that robot.

"I hear ya. I'll be up late, though. I'm—" He stopped.

"What?" My heart raced as his attention drifted toward the dumpster. No, he was looking at my car. Shoot—I'd left the trunk popped slightly open. Could he see that through the dark?

"Oh, nothing. It's about the bonus project. I'm working on something, but it's probably weird to talk about since we're competing. Or are we? Didn't you say you're back to coming up with ideas?"

I gained back the breath I'd been holding. "Something like that. I haven't worked here long so it's hard to know what I can improve."

"Maybe you're onto something with that storage space in the basement. You went down again tonight, right?"

I froze. *Think quick. Deny or accept?* "Uh, yeah, I needed some trash bags."

I couldn't tell whether Aidan suspected anything. If he knew I'd smuggled out a robot—and thrown it in the trash —he would absolutely tell Jen. I was sure of it. Our truce was related to our common bond of hating on Matt. I didn't trust that his newly-established friendliness extended to being cool with me removing property from the range.

He nodded. "Huh. Well, have a good night." He squinted past me. "Is your trunk open?"

At least the dark masked the panic in my face. I jingled my keys. "Oops. Hit the wrong button. See you later, Aidan."

I dashed to my car and slid inside. I waited a good thirty seconds, but Aidan hadn't left yet. He had his truck running but made no move to drive. What was he doing back there, texting? His headlights illuminated the dumpster beside my parked car. I imagined heat rays melting the metal to expose the stashed robot.

Of course. Aidan would want me to leave first. He'd follow me out for safety or something irritatingly noble.

I turned the ignition on Goldie and backed out of my space. At the exit, I turned left. Behind me, Aidan turned right. As his taillights faded into the distance, I angled into the lot of a landscaping company, then circled back for my stash.

Operation Robot Smuggle turned out successful. And it also turned out, I hadn't lied about everything to Aidan. I'd actually been so tired by the time I returned home and carried the robot to our basement, I really did go to bed early. Early considering I'd worked until midnight.

I slept in late the next morning. After going through the list of chores my parents left for me, I was due back at Teed Off! for my mid-afternoon to closing shift before I had a chance to work on the robot. I would need to put together a solid plan and a schedule to get anything off the ground. Things I was good at but found tedious to consider right now for some reason.

Aidan was on again in his new role while Jen took time off for the Fourth of July holiday. At the close of our shifts, we did our lockdown routine and ended up in the break room at the same time.

I swiped my badge on the time clock mounted to the wall.

Aidan did the same and we walked out to the lobby. "All done. It's just us now."

Just us. I craned my neck toward the empty hall. Kind of cool to have the entirety of the driving range to ourselves. Not that I wanted to be alone with Aidan or anything.

"You don't seem as in a hurry tonight," he said.

The tips of my ears grew hot, thankfully sheltered by my hair. "I'd like to say I have plans, but I don't."

Instead of responding, Aidan laid both hands on the registration desk, shifting his weight forward, almost like doing a standing push-up. His arm muscles grew taut. He was surprisingly muscular, which was especially noticeable now that he wore more fitted polos. He pushed back from the desk. "You know what? Come on. I want to show you something."

He headed toward the golf bays. It was eleven thirty on a summer night. On a holiday week with Fourth of July this week. Which, of course, we were both working and expecting non-stop customer traffic. Tonight, there were parties to go to. Probably. Bonfires and midnight movie dates. Here I debated following this frustrating boy back through the workplace I'd clocked out of.

He turned the corner, passing by the staff kitchen door on the long hall to the supply room.

I caught up. "Where are we going?"

He pivoted to walk backward and held up the master key ring.

"Is it a super-secret supply closet?"

"No, though I wish it was. You'd like organizing it." He grinned and gestured toward the door leading to the driving range.

I followed him, a sense of déjà vu crackling around me, recalling the first time I'd followed him to the Cage. We walked outside, through the fenced hall and out the door. He kept walking right into the middle of the green.

He stopped and spread his arms wide. "Not often we get to do this—safely, I mean." He crouched and lowered himself to lay flat on his back.

"Okay, weirdo." I laughed and remained standing. Alright, he had me. This was cool being out here with no one else.

I joined him lying on the grass. The turf pressed cool and a little damp into my back. Above us, the navy sky brightened at the edges like a halo as the floodlights encircled us—huge lampposts illuminating the fenced-in green. Red sparks shot into the sky. "Hey, look. Fireworks." The sparks crackled and fizzled away. "More like firework, singular."

A burst of silver followed, not overhead, but high enough above the tree line to see.

"This must be somebody's early Independence Day personal show," Aidan said from beside me.

We waited for more, but the silver had apparently been their finale.

"Mason dared Dan to lay out here during business hours."

I turned my head toward Aidan, viewing him sideways with little tufts of green sprouting around his limbs. "Did he do it?"

"He waited until closing and laid by the Cage. Technically, he fulfilled the dare."

"I'd go with a technical interpretation on that one. Assuming you guys also planned to get the staff in on a coordinated ball launch."

"Hey, it's one thing to do firing squad at the newbie in the Cage. But with no protection?"

I laughed, feeling it down to my belly. "What a weird thing—a driving range. There's a ton of open land on the other side of this fence. Real grass never looks like this. It's too green. Too perfect."

"Teed Off!, where you'll find optimal golf conditions you'd never find anywhere else."

"Teed Off! Where every time you say the name, you have to be excited."

"Did you know, for the first four months we worked here, Dan insisted on shouting the name Teed Off! because of the punctuation? Then he switched to not shouting it, but saying it enthusiastically."

"*Teed Off!*" I inflected the words with as much spirit as I could muster, causing Aidan to laugh. I decided I liked his laugh. It was a gentle rumble and didn't emerge easily. I refocused on the sky. "I'd like to see a driving range with real obstacles. Like a wind machine with hurricane-force gusts."

He propped himself up on one elbow. "Or like a giant windmill with slowly turning blades. Like a mini-golf, but sized up."

Mini-golf. I waited for him to say more, to mention the basement or the robots, but he didn't.

"Have you ever played?" He looked like part of a movie set, sitting half upright on the too-bright green with the sharp overhead light brightening his face and clothes.

I sat all the way up. "Not real golf. Only miniature golf."

"You work at a driving range and you've never swung a real golf club?"

"I wipe up ketchup and stock napkins. They never play-tested me with the golf equipment."

Aidan stood and held out his hand. "We're fixing that right now."

I took his hand, a warm grasp when I expected cool, and got to my feet. "We'd have to open one of the bay gates." I pointed above us to the metal gates closing off the open-walled tiers.

"Then that's what we'll do." He spun the master key ring in a lazy loop.

I stifled a laugh. "If you had any idea how ridiculous you look right now showing off your key set."

He patted his chest. "That's right. Impressing the ladies with my master keys since last Memorial Day."

Never mind I *actually* was a little impressed.

We left the green and hiked up the stairs. I called ahead to Aidan: "Top tier, right?"

"Absolutely."

He led the way, and I split off to the clubs stationed at a middle bay as Aidan powered open the mechanical gate. The night sky opened up to us again. Aidan set down a bucket of golf balls.

"We should have put empty buckets on the green as targets."

Aidan shook his head. "Mason and Dan tried once. Way too hard to hit."

"So, you've done this before? Played after closing?"

He chose a club for himself. "More like after customers left but we were still open. When we were supposed to be shutting down for the night."

"Figures. You guys are always messing around."

"I've participated in nary a mess-around for weeks."

True, he'd been acting notably responsible. I didn't care about that right now. I considered more how we had this small amount of power, to keep a golf range open past public hours. We could do anything we wanted, and here we were, *golfing*.

"So, what you're saying is," I said. "This is your first time playing here after hours. With no one else in the building."

"Yes. Technically."

That realization satisfied me. I don't know why, but it did. "Are you going to tell me the difference between all these clubs?" I recalled hearing about a nine iron at some point. Probably from Grandpa, who was not above watching golf on TV. "Which one is the nine iron?"

He handed me a club. "My advice? Get a feel for it first. We'll try a couple different clubs."

I plucked a golf ball from the bucket and placed it on the square swatch of green in front of me. "Clear!"

Aidan stepped a good few feet aside. I set the putter part beside the ball. Adjusted my stance like the golfers did in the ten minutes of TV golf I'd watched. Pulling back with the club, I let 'er rip.

Momentum kept me twisting and the club whipped around, sending hot pain prickles in my shoulder.

"Whiff!" Aidan called out.

"What?" The ball sat in front of me, unmoved. I'd hit air. Nothing but air.

"My first shot I missed, too. It happens to the best of us."

I rubbed at my shoulder. I focused on my stance again, shifting forward and back, straightening and relaxing my knees. I should have been embarrassed, but an excited thrill ran through me. The two of us together on a summer night, sending golf balls into a green abyss. Or not, as the case was for me.

"Hang on. Is it...are you okay if I...?" He mimed moving closer. "I can show you a good stance."

"Oh, sure." My voice hitched as Aidan stepped behind me. The energy from his body connected with mine as he closed the gap between us.

His arms lightly circled my back to the club I held in front of me. "Is this okay?" he asked, barely above a whisper.

I shivered from feeling his breath on my neck beneath my ponytail. "Yes." Any awkwardness evaporated into a comfortable thrill.

A warning flashed in my head. *Danger!* I silenced it. Why danger? Because Aidan was friends with Matt? Or because he was a temporary superior to me at work? His warm presence hovered around me, more a forcefield than actual contact. I found I wanted him closer.

He stepped back and suggested I try again. Using the stance he'd assisted me with, I swung again. The club connected with the ball and it shot forward like a bullet.

A soft clap followed. "Solid swing."

I tried a few more times while adjusting to Aidan's advice. When I hit the ball so hard it soared toward the lights, I whipped around to Aidan and squealed. "I did it!"

He beamed. "Nice work. Credit to your coach."

I swatted him lightly on the arm, liking the feel of his shirt against my skin a little too much.

I took in the sight of him again and blinked. Suddenly, I saw Matt beside him, scowling. A memory of Matt, obviously, but it felt so real. So much so I rubbed at my eye. I blinked again. Matt was gone.

"We should go," I said.

"You tired?" Aidan asked. "It's getting late."

I nodded and hung my club back on the rack.

Aidan closed the bay doors. "Maybe we can do an after-hours thing again for the Fourth. You're working, right?"

I grabbed the ball bucket and jammed it beneath a table. "We probably shouldn't press our luck doing this again." Borrowing the robot unasked and now staying past closing for our own amusement tested my rule-following limits.

"Did I do something wrong?" Aidan asked. "I mean, in the last ten minutes. I screw up a lot, so I'm talking about a specific timeframe here."

"I don't know what you mean."

He bit at his lip. "It felt like things might be changing between us and I liked it. I like seeing you here. You're... different."

I liked seeing him in a different way too, but I couldn't bring myself to say it out loud. A heavy sensation weighed down. Suddenly, nothing felt easy.

"It's about him, isn't it?" Aidan sighed. "Thousands of miles away in another country and you still care what Matt thinks."

"No, I don't." Did I have to remind him he'd played a similar part being Matt's friend when he'd had problems with him for months? "I don't care what he thinks."

"You deserve better than him."

My heart pounded, thrumming from my chest and up through my ears. "Matt was your friend. Until recently, he was a good guy. I was the one who didn't see the signs. He was bored with me. My plans to be a great girlfriend—they didn't work."

Aidan shook his head. "Can you even hear what you're saying? You're blaming yourself? Matt cheated on you, and you still think it's your fault. This is why you aren't ready to move on, to be...whoever you are."

The pounding in my chest bottomed out to my gut. "You have some nerve saying I'm not ready to move on. You don't have any idea what I'm ready for."

Aidan stepped back. "I...you're right. I don't. But, Lila." Aidan moved closer again. His breath carried over, crisp like peppermint and salty like fries, because it was hard to avoid smelling like a fry basket working here. "You deserve better. I wish you could see it."

"I know." The words came out bratty and insistent. He obviously felt sorry for me. Pitied me. He was probably readying a self-esteem lecture which would send me diving out the golf bay. My whole idea for creating the Lila I wanted to be was to have some control. Now? I didn't know my next move. I'd lost control.

"Hey." Aidan moved into my sight lines. "Hey."

This time I looked at him, his voice a calming buoy in a rowdy sea. "I don't know what else to say right now. I feel sort of lost." I closed my eyes, not willing to witness his reaction to the words I let tumble out.

"You don't have to say anything."

I opened my eyes. He hadn't moved. A magnet force surrounded us, inviting comfort. One step, and I shifted into his body's heat. Saying nothing, Aidan slid his arms around me. I pressed in, my arms still at my sides, a statue with no life-giving wires to bring it animation. Without another word, he hugged me.

It was everything I needed. One person who understood. The swirling shame and hurt and awkwardness settled and sank. Not gone, but no longer rising to the top.

Chapter Sixteen

♥

Things I Will Never Do Starting Freshman Year:
  (social boot camp NEVER List)
- *Talk about science fiction books, movies, TV, unless my new friends do and then it's OK.*

- *Cosplay (can talk about it but not actually do it - too dorky)*

- *Robotics*

- *Watch learning modules outside of what's assigned for school*

- *Make my friends feel like they aren't as smart as me*

- *Wear ugly shoes (bye bye utilitarian sport sandals)*

I replayed the previous night over in my mind. Aidan's arms around me, assisting my golf swing. Lying next to him on the green. Closing up a second time, just the two of us. Him holding me when I'd admitted I'd lost control.

These were things friends did together, right? Friends and coworkers. It could have been any of the golf range staff with the master keys who decided to stay open a little later for some fun.

If not, I faced the real possibility I was crushing on my ex-boyfriend's best friend. Crushing *hard*.

Ex-best friend. That part was important.

Downstairs, boxes piled in the front living room with stacks of stuff on the floor and separated along each couch cushion.

"What's all this?" I asked Mom as she zipped past to the kitchen and back.

"Oh, just cleaning. Some of this will be donated and we can sell. Ginsburg's trading group on Facebook has promising sales."

I took in the array of stuff more closely. Our bread making machine and a panini press sat in one box. "Isn't that the bread maker from Grandma?"

Mom kneeled on the floor and stacked two pots in a box. "We never use it. Might as well sell."

A sharpness hit my chest. The machine hadn't been a gift from Grandma. It had *belonged* to Grandma. And now Mom wanted to sell it for quick cash?

I plucked the machine from the box. "You can't sell this. I'm keeping it."

She glanced up. "Have you ever made bread?"

I hugged the bulky machine to my chest. "I can learn. We just need flour. And yeast. And...other things I can look up. What about the panini press? Dad uses that."

"These are just things. We need to de-clutter."

As far as I could tell, we had plenty of living space for a few extra appliances and pots. This was about money.

But I couldn't let her sell off precious things just to make a buck. This was a part of Grandma Rose, and all we had left were her things. We couldn't cast them off in some online garage sale like they meant nothing.

"Just let me keep this, okay?"

Mom rocked back on her heels. "She loved that bread maker, didn't she?"

I thought of last Christmas when Grandma made a gingerbread loaf. My eyes grew hot and wet.

"Lila." Mom stood. "I miss her too." She hugged me—and the bread maker by default since I refused to set it down. "This is a good time to clean house. Now scram or I'll end up keeping too much."

Having moved often, we'd always been fairly lean with the stuff we'd kept. I was used to regularly sorting through my clothes and toys so we could move with a lighter load. Since coming to Ginsburg, we didn't have to worry about keeping our belongings to essentials. Our stuff had accumulated, but it had never been a problem.

My parents needed money. They had that loan to pay back and nothing to show for it since I cancelled my trip.

I couldn't let them sell off what was precious to us, which meant I needed to get back to work making more money.

After returning the bread maker to a lower cabinet in the kitchen, I headed to the basement. Ours was a half-finished walkout emptying into the backyard through a set of sliding doors. A crumbling brick patio with a forgotten lawn chair sat outside the door. Inside, the main part of our downstairs was home base for what my parents envisioned as a rec room. "The room has great bones," Mom liked to say. Then she'd stack another box in the corner on the old, industrial carpet nearby a plaid couch my grandparents had transported from their neglected basement to ours.

The girl robot still lay wrapped in plastic bags in our workroom area.

I peeled back the layers of plastic. "Ew." The garbage bags smelled like, well, *garbage*, given the robot's stint laying low in trash. I wadded the bags and shoved them into the trash bin beside our workbench.

I rolled the robot so her back faced up. Grabbing a 4.55 mm screwdriver, I removed the back panel. I held my breath. I hadn't done this sort of work in a while. Never on a robot as old as this.

The back panel lifted off. I expected a circuit board. There wasn't one. "Wowee, okay. Hmmm." Making these sounds helped cover my shock. This robot was ancient as far as robots went. It was analog.

I figured as much, but still. I angled a mini flashlight into the robot. There were motors, timing wheels, relays. Mechanical stuff.

A manufacturer name was embedded into the back panel. I grabbed my phone and pulled up the internet browser. I typed in the name to search for schematics. Maybe someone scanned a similar version at some point.

I made notes and bookmarked websites to return to. An excited energy ran through me. These robots were cool! If I could get the girl robot working, next step would be to try another one. I'd focus my live presentation on the robots, and then show the plans for a mini golf using a mix of old and new tech.

Grandpa would be a good resource. Next step: I'd schedule us a date with a robot.

I arrived back to work that afternoon feeling energized.

Mason swung by the supply closet as I prepped for closing. I'd hoped he had donuts for me, but he arrived empty-handed. He was right, the donuts were never for closers. "Hey, Lila. I'm meeting the guys after work. Want to come?"

An actual invitation with the guys? Outside of work? "Um —"

"If you're busy, I get it." He waved a dismissive hand. "We're going to the diner over by the highway."

My parents would hopefully be cool with me staying out another hour after closing. I'd stayed out a few nights now —two of those with Aidan. "Okay."

"For real? I thought you'd say no."

I shrugged, trying to play casual. Natalie hadn't texted in a few days. I'd been trying not to overanalyze, but this was me. Analyzing was my DNA. Not part of it, but my *actual* DNA. Maybe I'd blown it at the bonfire. Maybe she didn't think I could handle rejoining our social circles. Now Aidan, Dan, and Mason, guys I'd avoided, shunned even, were the more appealing option. When had that happened?

"I'll text the guys."

As I closed with the remaining staff on shift, I couldn't help but smile at my after-work plans. I'd show up in my Teed Off! shirt and none of them would care. Low stress. Plus, I was *starving*.

Aidan and the guys weren't hard to find at the diner. Mason said that Aidan and Dan would be coming directly after a Ren Faire faction meeting. Dan wore a brown cap with a long feather reaching out from the side like a yesteryear antenna. His guffaw carried over to the front.

Mason, who'd arrived ahead of me, threw a napkin wad at him.

When I came into view of Aidan, my breath caught. He wore a weathered gray vest with black leather clasps over a faded white peasant shirt. It was...well, it was pretty hot. If you were into dudes wearing vests from historical eras.

Which I discovered I was. I smoothed my clammy hands against my work khakis.

"Hey, guys." I slid into the booth beside Mason, directly across from Aidan. Closer up, their outfits were even cooler seeing the details. "Great costumes. I'm glad you kept them on so I could see them." Kept them on? I cringed. *Why, Lila? Why?*

"Anything goes around here." Dan gestured to a nearby table where a group dressed in all black held up a puppet who appeared to be ordering. "You could show up in nothing and you'd be fine."

Aidan's cheeks flamed red.

Mason smacked Dan's arm from across the table. "Dude. Be respectful."

"Oh. I wasn't saying you *should*. I was saying no one would notice." He held a finger in the air. "I now see where I've gone wrong." He tipped his head at me. "Apologies, M'Lady."

I focused on Dan, not daring to look Aidan's way or I'd disintegrate into a pile of charred crumbs. "Apology noted and accepted," I returned in an English accent.

"Not bad." Aidan slid a menu toward me. His own plate held remnants of an omelet.

I leaned my elbows on the table. "So, tell me about the LARPing group."

"Tonight was more of a LARPing subgroup," Dan said. "Right now, everyone is prepping for opening day."

I looked around the table. "Opening day of what?"

"Of Ren Faire," Aidan clarified.

"Ah." Of course.

"Tell her about the queen," Dan told Aidan.

"The queen? Sure. She's in a local guild. She came by our group tonight to share costuming tips."

"The new queen is the best I've seen," Dan cut in. "She was part of the regular cast at a Detroit theater company. She used to do off-Broadway. Lots of Shakespeare."

Mason grinned. "Dan's into her. From what Aidan said, she has to be like, close to thirty."

"I can be into her talents," Dan fired back. "She's bringing new life to the role."

Aidan and Mason teased Dan about his devotion to the new queen. Aidan went on to describe the highlights of the Ren Faire. As he spoke, my attention drifted to his fingers as he traced the edge of his plate. Then to his hands. I immediately called up the texture of his skin against mine. The sure grip, the thrill of spinning in the gravity ride and stumbling out together. The dizziness that couldn't have all been from the ride. His body close to mine helping me practice my putting stance. How did Aidan make golf sexy? Was *Aidan* sexy?

The server came by and I fired off an order for a bagel, side of scrambled eggs, and a decaf coffee. The guys resumed talking over one another, feeding me stories of faire folk and the fantasy faction game Aidan played as live action role playing. The LARPers held events at a nearby park where they enacted fantasy battles or played more casual games while dressed in costume.

"There are indoor events too," Aidan explained. "Some are low-combat. Not everyone can run around for hours in heavy costumes holding weapons, you know?"

"Like Allison," Dan said.

The server arrived with food for me and Mason, setting the plates in front of us and topping off the coffees. "Who's Allison?" I asked.

"A LARPer," said Dan. "She's got this illness where her body will like, shut down to where she can't get out of bed. It can make it hard for her to stand for a long time or even write with a pen."

Mason tapped at his phone with one hand while taking a swig of coffee with the other. "Aidan made her a special mage staff. Lightweight and ergonomic."

I'd never considered the nuances of role playing, or how physically demanding it could be. "That was thoughtful."

Aidan pushed a toast crust around on his plate with a fork. "I had the materials anyway. It was nothing."

Dan put up his hands, holding up seven fingers. "We went through this many prototypes before we found the right combination of materials."

So, more than nothing. "Do you ever build props with real mechanics? With moving parts?"

Aidan looked at me. "I suppose I could. I'd probably need a 3-D printer. Or, you know, someone who knows a little about mechanical or electrical engineering."

I stilled. *I* knew a little bit about mechanical and electrical engineering. Aidan didn't know that. No one at this table knew that.

I could tell them, but that would pry open even more things I'd been hiding. Ugh, it was such a chore to hide parts of myself, but I'd been doing this so long I didn't know how to stop. Somewhere in the middle of my old and new Lila personas, the real me was trapped and trying to break free.

The conversation moved on. Eventually, we paid and made our way out to the parking lot. Even though I was only a short drive home, I couldn't be out too much longer without a chain of alarmed texts from my parents.

We walked as a group and reached Aidan's truck. A healthy film of dust and grime coated the truck with the words *Me land But* on the rear passenger window. "What's that all about?"

Aidan rolled his eyes. "It said *Medieval England or Bust.* Dan changed it. He can't resist a butt joke."

Dan patted his pockets. "Speaking of butts, crap. I left my phone on the table."

"I'll come with you." Mason followed Dan back inside the diner.

Which left Aidan and me standing alone together. We weren't standing as close as the night before, but the *aloneness* sensation was as clear as the stars in the sky.

"Thanks for sharing about your role playing. There's so much about that world I don't know."

Aidan leaned against the driver's side door. The grimy, gross door. He sprung forward, dusting off likely not-inexpensive faire clothes. "Thanks for coming out. I was hoping you would."

"It wasn't Mason's idea?"

"Uh, yeah. Mason...and mine."

"Right. Well, thanks for thinking of me."

"Kind of a trend lately."

"Oh?" I managed in a nonchalant tone.

He grinned. "Yeah. I think about you a lot."

Internally, I squealed. Not only at what he said, but how he said it, and the way he looked saying it. Gone was Aidan's hardened stare, his firm set jaw. He looked relaxed, even happy. I fought against the explanation that *duh, we were off work, of course he'd act more relaxed and happy*.

Only Aidan aimed that relaxed and happy toward *me*.

The leather ties on his vest begged to be tugged. I wanted to use them to tug him closer.

He moved closer. "Lila."

I held my breath having no idea what to do next. What to feel or what to think. The buzzing cars on the nearby highway faded into the night. Nothing else mattered right now except the way Aidan looked at me.

He looked at *me*. Like he saw me.

Aidan practically drifted forward, reminding me of this hot ghost in one of Mom's beloved holiday movies on cable. I blinked and suddenly he stood one short reach away.

"We should hang out again," he said.

"Okay."

"Really?"

I laughed, welcoming the release. "Yeah. I'm up for it." I wanted to hear more about his weapon crafting and the LARPing adventures. I wanted to tell him about robotics and *The Expanse*—the things I'd held back because I thought I had to.

My mind returned to Summerfest, to our brief moment holding hands. To those moments that seemed to happen more frequently where we found ourselves alone together.

I wanted more of those moments.

I liked this Aidan who looked at me like nothing else existed. I'd never experienced attention like this before.

Closing the gap, it all happened at once. Our hands connected as a magnet force drew us closer and our lips made contact. Warm and cool together, his taste melted into me. A lightness that felt bright as Fourth of July fireworks.

Aidan was kissing me on a perfect summer night.

Chapter Seventeen

♥

To Do List - Revised:

~~make cookies for 4th of July work potluck~~
~~brownie mix (with sprinkles?)~~

- grab a pudding 4-pack

Perfect summer nights turned to working heat-filled days, though the imprint of Aidan's lips still lingered. As did the memory of Dan and Mason crossing the diner parking lot moments after Aidan and I had parted. Our kiss became our secret. I liked having a secret if it meant sharing it with someone. Sharing it with *Aidan*.

That was new. I had a lot to obsessively think over while I worked today.

On schedule for the Independence Day holiday, I stayed a few extra minutes in the break room before my shift, admiring the food spread. My coworkers knew how to Potluck with a capital P.

Joe held open the break room door for Kara. "I'm just saying, the kids here have an edge." Joe made eye contact with me. "What's up, Lila? We were just talking about you."

I grabbed a star-spangled napkin matching the frosting on a patriotic cake. "You were?"

Kara *tsked* at Joe. "Don't cause trouble."

Joe slid into a seat across from me. "You're going for the bonus money, right?"

I nodded.

"You know what the other kids are doing?"

"By kids, do you mean Mason, Dan, and Aidan? Because all of them are interested in the bonus money."

"Joe's old, Lila," said Kara. "Anybody younger than him is a kid."

"Hush, Kara. You're old, too." The two of them laughed.

The guys hadn't revealed clues about their own proposals. "Nobody is discussing details. At least not with me. What have you heard?"

Joe sat back. "Dang. I was hoping you would tell me."

Kara laughed at Joe from across the kitchen. "Struck out!"

Joe looked back at me. "All I know is, Daddy needs a new deck."

"You know you can't build a whole deck for what they're giving out," Kara fired back. "Especially after taxes."

He gave her an indiscernible look. "Let a man, dream, alright?" He shot up from his seat and loaded a plate from the potluck buffet.

This was about to get seriously competitive. I needed to bring everything I had to this project or I wouldn't stand a chance. Since my idea would cost money over bringing savings, I needed to create a vision. A vision where more money could be made after changes and investment in the business itself.

Out on the floor, I found the golf range packed. I barely had time to think the next two hours. Scratch that—I had thoughts. First, a beach with a crisp, cool breeze off the ocean as I read a stack of library books. Then my mind drifted to a foot massage and one of those fancy umbrella drinks. The drink could be Kool-Aid and Sprite, I didn't care, but the little paper umbrella was vital. Aidan materialized in a beach chair beside me, talking about dragon factions.

"Lila?"

"Huh?" Oh. It was actual Aidan beside me. I'd spaced out, leaning against a support pillar in a recently cleaned golf bay.

We hadn't talked about our kiss yet. I glanced to either side checking for eavesdroppers. My head spun and I palmed my forehead.

"You should drink some water," Aidan said. "You look dehydrated."

How could I be dehydrated when I was so sweaty? I took a step and my head practically drifted up like a mylar balloon. Ah, yes. *That* sort of dehydrated, where my reserves were depleted and my brain went loopy.

Hands went to my arm. Aidan's hands. I blinked to clear the fog. "You're right, I'm lightheaded."

I sat in the nearest chair and ice water appeared in front of me.

Aidan parked himself at the table by me. "Drink slow at first."

I drank half the water. I should have taken it slower, but whatever. "Don't tell Jen."

"Like I'm going to tell Jen you almost had heat stroke. She'd take you off the schedule."

A clammy chill settled against my skin. I'd gone through this before when my family took a day trip to an air show and we walked a mile back to the car to save on parking.

"Besides, Jen isn't here—she doesn't have to work holidays like us." Aidan scanned the bays and signaled to a server. "Have you started an idea for the bonus yet?"

Apparently, everyone had the bonus on their mind today. "Why are you asking? Looking for intel?" I couldn't help the snap in my voice, heat stroke or not.

He shrugged. "Just asking."

Aidan traced a finger along the edge of the table. He was suspiciously quiet.

"What?"

He looked everywhere but me. "Nothing."

"Hey." I pointed at him, feeling my strength regaining. "Remember honesty? You're not being honest. Spill."

He leaned his elbows on the table, his shirtsleeves riding up to reveal those lean arms. "One more shot to tell me."

A different sort of chill washed over. "What are you talking about." I couldn't even make it a question. Just a wary demand.

"I was in the basement. Looking around."

I remained still. At least I tried. Being lightheaded made it difficult to tell if I swayed or if we'd been transported to a cruise ship that dipped one way then the other. I channeled coolness in vibe and in temperature. "And?"

"Things were moved around. I found a gap in the junk pile where it looked like something used to be but is no longer there."

He wouldn't. He wouldn't dare.

"Didn't anyone wonder where you'd gone?" I asked. "Seems odd for a shift leader to be rooting around in storage during peak hours."

He levelled his gaze at me. "Lila. I know."

Until he said it, I wouldn't let a breath of it leak. I suddenly became aware of my heart thrumming like techno beats. A swirly sensation rocked my brain. Aidan now had my back—my literal back—as he moved to steady me.

"Hey, I'm already sitting down," I said, but the words felt heavy.

"Here. Drink more water." Aidan moved the glass toward me. "Let's get you to the break room."

Aidan slung an arm around my back and supported me for the short walk. The break room being fully interior and air conditioned, I instantly felt cooler.

He sat me in a chair and squatted in front of me. His eyes filled with concern. "Are you okay?"

I nodded. I still felt weird, but not as loopy. I drank more water.

He dashed out of the break room and returned a minute later with Kara.

She laid the back of her hand to my forehead. "Feels clammy. Drink that water and rest up a bit." She looked at Aidan. "Can you wet a rag for her forehead? Lying down may help too."

"I'm fine." I waved them off. "Thank you for the concern. I'm okay."

A cool wet rag was procured for me regardless. After pressing it to my head and assuring Kara I would survive—

no really, I swore I would be okay—she returned to work, leaving Aidan and I together. Alone.

I steadied my breathing. My heart switched from techno beats to more of a steady lullaby.

Aidan wrapped ice cubes in a new rag and handed it to me. "Feeling any better?"

I pressed the new rag to my head and yanked it back. So cold. I held it to the back of my neck instead. "Yeah. Just a little embarrassed."

"It happens to the best of us."

"This happened to you?"

"I said the best of us. It happened to Mason."

I laughed. "He is kind of the best of you guys."

He lightly pumped his fist in the air.

"What?" I asked.

"I made you laugh."

"That was cause for a victory fist pump?"

"Absolutely."

The boy was strange. And I didn't hate his brand of strange.

"I wanted to make sure you were actually feeling better. You seem to be steadier and more focused, so that's a good sign."

"I'll be back on my feet in a minute."

His shoulders relaxed. "Good."

"I'm guessing you'll want to talk about, *you know*."

He raised a single brow. "Oh, will I?"

I fanned myself with my hand, which just made me feel hotter. "About the other night."

"Which night?"

I couldn't help rolling my eyes. "You're really going to make a girl who nearly fainted say it out loud?" I glanced to the door which remained closed. "Our *kiss*," I said in nearly a whisper.

He grinned. "I'd love to talk about that. I just have another pressing matter first."

What could possibly be more pressing than our lips? "Yeah?"

He looked me in the eyes. "I know you took the robot."

I definitely had a problem. Aidan had helpfully left me to my own devices after dropping his knowledge bomb about the robot, but now that my dizziness from the heat had passed, I needed to not only return to work, but face Aidan again.

Aidan, who I'd kissed. Aidan who knew I'd taken the robot from the Teed Off! storage.

Back on the floor, I found him lurking by my supply closet. Almost like he'd been waiting for me.

His expression softened when he noticed me. "You look steadier. I can cut you early if you're okay to drive home. We're busy, but we have coverage."

"Are you going to tell Jen?"

"About the heat exhaustion? I can if you want, but you wouldn't get in trouble or anything. Or did you mean about *us*?" He flashed a grin.

"About the robot," I said through my teeth.

"So, it's true. You took it."

I jerked back. "You said you knew I'd taken it."

"Now you've confirmed you did."

"I've confirmed nothing." We both knew that was a lie. But whatever. "So, what are you going to do?"

He scanned his clipboard. "I can't imagine what you'd want with an old animatronic. I'm curious. Why did you take it?"

"I'm not confirming or denying anything." I held my chin up. "I had an idea. It's too complicated to explain."

Aidan opened his mouth to speak, but two adults with a tangle of kids between them circled around us. One kid whined he was bored already. An older boy grabbed a club and cracked it against a chair.

Aidan's eyes popped wide. "Hey—uh, we have kiddie clubs somewhere—"

"I'm eight!" the boy yelled back. "I'm not a *little kid*."

"Brayden get back here!" a woman called over. When Brayden didn't get back to anywhere, she stomped over and snatched the club from his hand. "You said you were old enough to handle this."

The kid folded his arms against his chest. "I thought we were going to the golf place with the trees."

The mom made an exasperated sound. "I don't know what that means."

Aidan held out his arm to the woman and gestured to the golf club. "I'll take that. He means the miniature golf course. It's north of here about twenty minutes." He gave the name of the town. "Shady Pines Miniature Golf. It's the only one around here."

Brayden perked up. "Can we go there, Mom? To the place the guy said?"

Just then a crash sounded two bays behind us. The woman's eyes fell shut. She sighed the sigh of someone who needed a vacation somewhere tropical. Alone.

She opened her eyes and looked at Aidan. "Thanks." She grabbed her son's hand and spun on her heel. "Rick? We're taking the kids and leaving. Whatever just broke, we'll need to pay for it."

Aidan and I exchanged *eek* expressions.

"I should probably go see what that crash was," I told him.

My heart raced with possibilities on my walk to the crime scene. That family's little calamity was the exact reason Teed Off! needed a more kid-friendly course. Smaller clubs, kid food, and fewer breakable items.

Aidan followed. We discovered broken shards from a fallen plate and a drinking glass nearby a large man holding a flailing child.

"Sorry about this," the guy said, looking as much like he needed a palm tree getaway as his wife. The kid kicked his legs in the air and wailed.

Poor kid. He needed to go somewhere he could run around.

I fetched the broom and dustpan while Aidan stood guard to block any guests from the area. We cleaned efficiently and swiftly, assuring the family it was an accident and there was no reason to pay for the broken dishes.

The family left. "Does this happen a lot?" I asked Aidan. "Kids breaking stuff here by accident?"

"Sometimes. We've got plastic cups for kids, but yeah, they knock into things or they hurt other people swinging the clubs."

I looked across the open bay to the pristine green. "You said the nearest mini-golf is in a different town? That seems weird. Shouldn't Ginsburg have one?"

"There isn't even a mini-golf at Midwest Wild Adventure," he said naming the theme park on the outskirts of town—the opposite direction from where I lived.

Business opportunity! flashed in neon in my mind.

I pressed my lips together to squash my idea from bursting out. I *really* wanted to tell Aidan about my mini-golf idea.

But I couldn't. Aidan was my competition.

Then again, he already knew I'd taken one of the robots, even if I didn't admit it. If he returned to the basement and looked closer, he'd figure it out. He could rat me out to Jen any second. Telling him about my plans would at least show him I didn't mean any harm.

"Are you okay?" Aidan asked. "I'll get you water." He started for the break room.

"Aidan." I caught his sleeve. His warm skin sent an electric jolt through me. I retracted my hand but stayed close. I hadn't thought this far ahead and stared at him.

"What is it?" His voice came softer now.

The background faded. The noise, my rattling thoughts, everything. Aidan looked at me with care and concern. With something more I couldn't name.

"Do you want to come to my house?" I blurted. "I'll show you what I'm planning. If I can trust you won't say anything to anyone."

Aidan took a second to respond. His cheeks flushed which sent my own blush in action. "You want me to come over?"

This was a stupid idea. "Yes."

"Okay."

He *agreed*? Now what? "Cool. How about tomorrow?" My mouth just kept on moving.

"Sure." His grin showed less smirk and teasing than earlier. More genuine. "I'm looking forward to it."

Stupidly, so was I.

The next day, I woke up at eight in the morning. Eight-oh-two to be exact. I took a shower and did my hair. A little hair spray because that's what I did to my hair even though my hair looked the same either way. Mascara.

Okay, who needed mascara on to work on a robot?

No, I was putting on mascara because Aidan would be here. In my house.

My brilliant idea to invite Aidan over was actually happening. I could say the heat had scorched my judgment, but the truth wasn't buried too deep in my brain folds. I wanted to tell Aidan about my plans because I thought he'd understand. He had crafting skills from his work with the LARPing group. He knew just about everything about the golf range. He even knew about a mini-golf place in another town.

If I really thought he'd tell on me to Jen, I wouldn't have said anything to him. The weirdness between us had definitely changed over the past weeks. Changed enough that we'd *kissed*.

Aidan's reaction would let me know if my idea had any legs, robotic or otherwise, or if this idea would waste my time. Then it wouldn't matter if we competed for the money. I'd return the robot under cover of night in a new set of trash bags and be done with the whole thing.

I was about to text Aidan not to bother coming—I had his number now which felt new and exciting, like kissing him all over again—when the doorbell rang.

I pounded down the carpeted stairs to the foyer, skidding to a stop. I needed to chill. I'd been home alone with a boy before. Plenty of times. Maybe, three times. The first time, Dad came back from work twenty minutes later. Another time, Matt and I had an hour to ourselves, where we'd pigged out on Oreos and watched YouTube. The third time, we'd made out and it was amazing. At least I'd thought it was at the time.

I opened the door.

Aidan wore his Teed Off! polo since he was scheduled to work later today, thus our before-noon meeting time. The polo fit him well and he had on gray pants with lightly worn cuffs. The rest of him appeared freshly scrubbed, polished, and eager.

He adjusted the backpack slung over his shoulder. "Hey, Lila."

I stood aside to let him in. I channeled calmness, recalling the Cyber Tai Chi course I took when I was twelve (terrible name, lasting instruction). Leading him farther in, I stopped when we passed by the kitchen. "Soda? LaCroix? Water?"

"Maybe a *pop*." He said it funny, like *pahp*, with a nasally tone.

I laughed. "Why did you say it like that?"

"Oh, making fun of myself. It's a Midwesterner thing."

"I've grown up saying both soda and pop. My mom says pop—she was born here. Dad says soda. He grew up first in the Northwest, in Oregon, then he lived in Texas. I've lived in Texas." *I've never talked so much.* "So, um, something to drink?"

Aidan nodded and grinned. He was teasing me with that grin. I loved it. I hated it. I hated that I loved it.

I took out glasses to fill with ice. "We're refined in this house. None of that can drinking."

Aidan opened one soda and poured it into a glass. I did the same with the other. Here we were, a mess of awkwardness because I had zero plans for how to act around him while we weren't at work. Why had I invited him here? On my turf, where I was prone to blurt out strange things?

"Did I tell you what Dan said to a rude customer yesterday?"

Work-talk saved the day. I listened intently as Aidan acted out the scenario, ending with a perfect impression of Dan backing away saying, "It's a trap!" in the Admiral Ackbar voice from *Star Wars.*

My anxiety now pretty much gone, I stood. "Okay. Follow me."

We descended to the basement to the workroom area, beyond the pine-knotted divider wall Dad swore he'd demolish some future weekend.

"Whoa. This thing is *massive.*" Aidan ran his hands along the workbench.

"Oh, yeah. Mothra. The mother of all workbenches."

He shook his head laughing. "You have a name for your workbench?"

This was the type of thing I usually kept for family ears only. "Uh, yeah. The thing about old houses, according to my parents, is people leave behind huge furniture pieces too difficult to move. Mothra will be here even if the rafters burn to the ground."

Seemingly carved from a tree rooted through the floor, the thing wasn't going anywhere. Ancient but functional fluorescent lighting had been mounted overhead.

I flicked on the light. "Anyway. You're here for the grand reveal." I removed the light cloth I'd laid over the robot. She lay face down with the back panel still open.

Aidan peered into the robot. "Wow. So, you're doing some kind of robot surgery, or what?"

"I checked the wires for corrosion. They look pretty clean despite the age. I found schematics online—from the same company at least to get started on troubleshooting. My Grandpa will help me, he just hasn't had time to give her a look."

The room grew quiet. I refused to pull my gaze from the workbench or I'd end up looking at Aidan. I couldn't handle his reaction. Even though I'd invited him over for exactly this reason.

"It's weird, isn't it," I said in a rush. "All of this. It's weird and you're probably wondering why in the world I'm showing you this."

His voice came soft. "You fix robots. Where did that come from?"

I didn't think, just answered. "Middle school robotics club."

I finally dared a look at him. His face seemed curious and interested. Not disgusted or weirded out. I'd hoped he would understand given his own interests, but to actually show him this piece of me was another thing altogether.

"So, what happened?" he asked. "Did you lose interest?"

"Sort of. There isn't a robotics club at our school." Except that wasn't the reason I'd stopped. "Anyway, when I saw the robotics in the basement, a spark lit me up. I had this idea come together and thought my old skills could be useful. You know, for the bonus money. It's a mini-golf course."

I filled him in with my idea to draft a business plan and how I'd do a live demonstration of the robot once I got it working. The range could display the robot as an ode to the old course or actually use it on the new one.

"So." I clasped my hands together. "Big, impossible, dumb idea, huh?"

Aidan appeared to absorb what I said. "You're excited to work on this. It's more than the money."

"No, it's for the money. I need the money. I just need you to tell me if this is even worth trying."

He scratched his chin, then folded his arms, studying the spread of tools on the workbench. "You're right, the idea is *big*. But you have a good point. The range has a history with the old mini-golf. There's been talk of adding more food options and specials to attract kids and families. What if they expanded the whole range itself?"

"Right!" I nodded. "Exactly."

"Only you don't need to fix a robot to do that as your idea."

I opened my mouth to contradict him, but stopped. How about honesty? "Okay, here's the thing. I haven't worked on a project like this in a long time. I want to see if I can still do this. I sort of decided at some point it was kid stuff and moved on."

"Building a base for an electrical engineering career is kid stuff?" He gave me a teasing look. "I'm a nearly-eighteen-year-old who dresses in costume and runs around the woods acting out a fantasy world. And I do that with grown adults. I'd hate to give that up."

The real truth, the real me, existed one more layer down. One more back panel to pry open. "I guess I just wanted to not be the geeky robot girl when I moved here. I didn't want to spend all my time doing this stuff instead of making friends." Whew, this was hard to say out loud.

"Does Matt know?"

I could pretend I didn't know what he meant, but I did. I studied the shag carpet. "No."

"You didn't want him to know you liked robotics. You didn't want any of us to know."

I shrugged. "Something like that."

He made a *hmm* sound. "What changed?"

I turned and leaned my lower back against the workbench. "Everything."

That wasn't really an answer, but Aidan didn't seem confused by it. "I get it. Well, for what it's worth, thanks. It's cool you trusted me enough to tell me all this."

I practically floated from the weight lifting off me. "I... really wanted to tell you. Especially, after hearing how you craft weaponry."

He beamed. "*Craft weaponry*. You make it sound legit."

"The way you and the guys described the process, it is. You're modeling real swords and knives, but adapting the design for your activity. That takes skill."

Aidan ran a hand through his hair, stepping back and looking around the room. "It's not a big deal."

"Why did you come here?" I asked. I still couldn't quite believe how Matt's ex-bestie stood here in my basement seeing my exposed wires for what they were.

Aidan stood still again. "I'm curious about the robot. And about you."

From the closeness of his voice, I swore the windows fogged. And we weren't even in a car.

I started talking and quickly. "I bookmarked a website about vintage electronics. I've taken a bunch of notes." I tapped a notebook I'd grabbed the other night to continue my plans. "Then I found this tribute site to old-timey miniature golf courses with way more detail than anyone should know about miniature golf courses. You know, a little light bedtime reading."

Aidan fanned himself with his hand. "Stop, you're turning me on."

"If old tech and mini-golf turns you on, do I have some schematics that may blow your mind." I waggled my eyebrows.

OMG, were we flirting? Did anyone seriously waggle eyebrows when flirting?

"I never knew the word schematics could sound...sexy."

My hands shot to my face to cover it. "I've made this so awkward!"

"Lila, it's fine." Aidan was laughing.

I peeked out from my hands and, dear God, he had a dimple. Right there on his left cheek. He had to smile pretty big for it to show up, but there it was. I never cared about dimples before, but his face, the way it transformed from the scowl into something so bright and genuine, he was not the same Aidan I used to know. I hadn't known him at all.

"I have an idea if you might indulge me," he said.

"*Indulge.* Quite possibly a line of chocolate bars targeted to women in those overly sensual commercials." I winced—still not beyond the awkwardness. "Did I say that out loud? I could swear I did not actually say that out loud."

Aidan clasped his hands in a knuckle-bearing knot, leaning elbows against the metal-edged worktable. "Please say more things out loud you think are only in your head."

I rolled my eyes. "Whatever. You said you had an idea."

"Right." Aidan gently tilted the robot to view the front, then rolled her back. "What about an apron or a smock? Something to add texture. Waterproof material for outdoors."

"Oh cute. Like, to fit around the robot girl? That could work. I'm not really into sewing though."

"If you want, I could make it."

"What do you mean, make it?"

"Make as in sew." Aidan swallowed, each side of his mouth warring with the other, one side tugging up, the other drawing down. "If you wanted me to repeat, I am offering to hand sew a doll apron for your retro robot girl."

I let out one single *Ha*. "You make your own Ren Faire clothes, don't you?" I should have pieced that together by now.

"No, I'm not good enough. Not to assemble actual clothes I'd wear in public." He scrolled through his phone's photo gallery. He faced the screen toward me. "Accessories, mostly. Leatherwork I learned in Boy Scouts. Sewing is something I'm working on. My grandmother has a thrad machine."

"Is that an advanced type of sewing machine—a thrad?"

"No. It means *thoroughly rad.*"

I narrowed my eyes at him. "No. Unacceptable. I will not accept that term in any form, even related to a beloved grandmother's prized sewing machine."

"It's a Dan word. Come on, you love thrad. You're going to work it into a full sentence, aren't you?"

"Never." I steadied my own lips from smiling. "Nope."

"I like the idea of crafting something out of materials." He leaned in to look more closely at the tools beside the robot. "Of being a maker of things. *Useful* things. This concept of crafting, of creating with my hands—that's what I want to do. That's what you're doing."

"I never thought of it as creating but more like deconstructing. You have to take it apart to figure out how it works."

"That's the thing, though, right? You deconstruct, then you construct again. You see how it works, and you build. You make the thing your own thing."

"What kinds of things do you want to make?"

"I'm thinking about trades and crafts. So less a specific object, but the medium in which you make it. I don't care that much about making a clay pot, but I want to learn to use a potter's wheel. The skill of manipulating the clay at the wheel, the glazing, and using the kiln. I want to know how hot you need the kiln. You know what I mean?"

I nodded, enjoying the rhythm of his speech as I studied the robot's innards under the task light.

"Dan made fun of me for this, but last year at the Ren Faire, I spent an hour at the blacksmith talking with the couple who run the shop. They're both actual blacksmiths —it's not a gimmick for the faire. They can shape iron and shoe a horse." He cleared his throat. "There may not be a high demand for smithing these days, in an urban setting, but these are skills I'm interested in."

"Mechanical engineering. You can invent, explore, and get paid real money while doing it."

Aidan leaned against the table at an intentionally crooked angle to get my attention. "I want to *shoe* a *horse* with my *bare* hands." He flexed his fingers for emphasis.

I laughed.

Awkward flirting aside, this felt almost normal hanging out with Aidan. I offered to get us some snacks and returned downstairs to the workshop. We dug into my parents' CD collection, all carefully sorted in boxes waiting for those coveted media shelves that would one day build themselves.

Aidan checked the time on his phone. "I've got to take off. Figure out which apron you want for Gertie."

"Gertie?"

"She needs a name. I was surprised you didn't have one for her."

Her cherub cheeks had an unnaturally rosy glow, almost like smeared marker for cheek coloring. Poor thing. "Gertie is perfect. It feels both old and fresh. Fitting for an overly precious robot girl."

"I was hoping you'd like it." There he went again, with the boyishly charming grin. That blasted dimple.

Because Aidan had an uncanny effect on me, I went ahead and said the thing itching beneath the surface. "If you're helping me with this, isn't it a conflict of interest for the bonus?"

His smile fell. "It doesn't have to be."

"Because there's no way I'd win?"

"I didn't say that."

It was possible we were destined to offend each other.

I chewed at the inside of my cheek. "What are you doing for your project?"

His face further shadowed. "Look, I don't want to get in the way of your idea and would expect the same for me. You're right, we're still competing."

"You swear you won't tell anyone about this?"

He seemed to relax. "There's nothing that says we have to keep our projects a secret, but yes, I will keep this between us. Just make sure you clear the robot thing with Jen at some point. She probably doesn't know that stuff is down there at all."

We made our way upstairs and outside to Aidan's truck.

"My parents think I lack focus and follow-through," he said as he unlocked the driver's side door. "I need to show them I'm not a quitter. I'm committed to the bonus and want the money for a project of my own. I want to craft for LARPers who need adaptable accessories. I want to build a workshop. Obviously, I think you should go for the money too. You're doing something that matters."

"My only other option is liquid soap."

"I'm going to pretend you didn't say your back-up idea involves liquid soap." He checked his watch again. "We can talk more later. I think you should give this your all. It's a great, ambitious idea."

He reached across to me, his hand trailing down my arm before he disappeared into his truck and backed down the long drive.

Ambitious, yes. And now our competition had an added layer. Our own emotional wiring twisted within it.

Chapter Eighteen

♥

Lists to make:

- Robot parts needed
- Robot parts cost analysis
- Robot parts cost vs. what I owe my parents
- Liquid soap efficiencies

Back on shift together, Aidan swung by where I'd just finished mopping the hallway. "I have something to show you out front."

His tone sounded suspicious.

"Is this a prank?"

He returned an exaggerated sigh. "I won't live those down, will I? Not a prank. I have something for you in my truck. Isn't it time for your break?"

I wiped my forehead with the back of my hand. I was definitely due a break. I fell in step beside him out the doors of the golf range across the lot.

Aidan opened the passenger door of his truck with a knowing smile cued up. He handed over a bright white and red checkered piece of shiny cloth. "Do you like it?"

I unfolded the fabric. "An apron for Gertie." I looked over the garment, admiring the straight and even stitches on the waterproof material. "This looks great." I pointed to the little tucks in the skirt part of the apron.

"Your basic pleats."

"Now there's something I know nothing about. Basic or advanced pleats."

"I'll teach you pleats if you show me how to solder wires."

The way he said wires, hanging on to the *s* a second longer, made my neck tingle. "Deal."

"Oh—and I have this." He handed me another item.

"Is this a bow for Gertie's head?"

He offered a confident chin nod. "I know what's up. Real men sew hair bows."

I snort-laughed.

"That's my new gamer tag on Xbox," he said. "No, I'm kidding. It's too many characters to fit the tag."

"Don't downplay your skills. It's cool you can sew. It's a relevant trade."

We headed back inside and the cool rush of air from the lobby sent a chill across my skin.

Aidan spun to walk backward. "Opening weekend of the faire is coming up. Are you interested?"

I missed going to faires. "I'd love to. Count me in." Then again, money. "How much is it again?"

"I can get you the discount ticket price—that's like twenty bucks. Food and some of the attractions cost more, but the joust and stage shows are free. I can float you cash."

"I don't know. There's parts for Gertie to buy." I made a grunt of frustration. "Why does everything cost money?"

"Yeah. That's a thing. Seriously, it's not a big deal to cover you for the faire."

It was a big deal to me. Owing money when I already owed my parents so much—and their loan—not going to happen.

"I'll think about it," I told him.

We both ended our shifts midday and met in the break room as we clocked out.

Aidan leaned a shoulder against the wall beside the timeclock where we swiped our badges. "I have an idea. It involves a road trip. A short one."

"A road trip?" Who could resist a summer road trip? Not me. "Where to?"

"Shady Pines Miniature Golf. You know, for research purposes."

My excitement surged and lost momentum in the span of a blink. "Isn't that a conflict for you?"

"It's two coworkers checking out the competition. Besides, look." He held up his phone with a *Buy One Ticket Get One Free* offer. "I'll buy mine and yours is free."

I clipped my badge to an inner pocket of my bag. "I don't know. First the apron and now this—you might be helping me too much for the competition to be fair."

Aidan shook his head. "Forget about work then. Let's just go because it's fun."

Like a date.

"Like a date?" I asked.

His eyes glinted as he searched my face. "Do you want it to be a date?"

I paused my breath. I did. Very much so.

I nodded. "It's a date then. Not business."

He looked me over again in that way that took all of me in. Only this time, I didn't feel awkward and I didn't straighten my hair or worry about what clothes I had on.

Aidan opened the door for me. "Fair warning, I will conquer all if we putt the nine holes."

"*Putt* the nine holes?" I gave him a gentle shove. "Oh, you're on."

Out in the lot, I made my way to my car. "Should I drive since you're getting me into the mini-golf for free? Goldie could stretch her legs."

"Is Goldie your car?" He stopped walking and squinted. "But your car is green."

Right, he didn't know. Might as well spill the rest of my geekery. "It's short for a longer name. The Heart of Gold."

"Did you say—"

"Heart of Gold, yeah—"

"Like from *Hitchhiker's*—"

"It's what we call my car."

He laughed. "Of course, it is. You quoted *Hitchhiker's* that one day, about the meaning of life, the universe, and everything. And used it as an *insult*." He slow-clapped four times. "Nice."

"I guess you bring out my geekier tendencies."

"I don't know if you meant that as a compliment, but I'm taking it that way. By the way, you look nice."

I unlocked the car doors and let mine hang open to air out the stale heat. "I'm wearing mop water pants."

"Funny, I've heard mop water pants are this fall's fashion trend."

"Ha. Hardly."

"I've gone through a pair of khakis already this summer. I don't know what it is about the driving range, but I'm constantly filthy when I get home."

I grinned at the word *filthy*. It was one of those words that sounded like its meaning. *Filthy* tasted grimy and dirt-filled on the tongue. "You probably wanted to kill me when you caught me in the back room with all that old junk."

"By the time we hit the basement, my khakis were late to end stage. The bottoms shredded, a pocket coming loose. Grease stains so old they'd set up a 401k. I'd say they were a lost cause by the time I found you."

I liked the way he said *I found you*. That's how this summer felt—like I'd been plucked out of some other life.

"Oh, I just remembered I'm low on gas," I told him. I mentally calculated how many trips I could make home and back to the range without filling up when I'd definitely need to fill up for a drive out of town.

"I'll drive, no worries." Aidan headed to his truck. "I just filled up yesterday."

Stupid money always being an issue. I pushed the annoyance aside. This was supposed to be fun. A *date*.

As we drove away from the range, we talked who worked next shift and our next days off. Talking about work felt easy. With a few exceptions, talking about a lot of things came easy with Aidan. I decided to tell him about my dad discovering my car at a construction site, and the improbability of it turning out to be a decent car, and yet it had. With minor fixes, of course.

"No offense, but your dad kind of scares me."

"From what you saw when he picked me up that one day, you were meant to feel fear."

"Right. Teenage boys are the worst. Coming from an expert."

We arrived at the course, where outlines of jaunty wooden pine trees shot up from the sign with a cartoonish grizzly bear face as the mascot. The theme was woodsy and outdoorsy with expert landscaping filling in around the putting greens. No robotics.

We exited the truck and headed for the entrance. "This looks nice. I don't think I've been here since I was a kid with my grandparents," I said, checking out the décor and layout. "Points for originality if we use old-timey robots at our course."

"I thought you said no business?"

I stopped walking. "Sorry. I totally forgot."

"It's okay if you want to talk about it. I told you I'd keep your idea a secret from everyone."

But it still felt weird. "I'll just observe silently."

We progressed through the first few holes and finally I had to admit, I wanted to dish about the layout of the course. "See how they have those last two holes join up? That could save on space and allow more room for scene setting with robotics."

"Would it help if I took pictures?"

It was one thing for me to geek out over the course, another for him to assist in my documentation. "I'll use my own phone. First, let's do a selfie."

I gestured for him to join me in the frame as I held up my phone. He slid in and made a face where his eyes bugged out and bottom lip curled in.

"Hey." I swatted him after seeing the pic. "Okay, one more." This time we both made faces. I showed him the pic and we laughed.

"Your face is *terrible*," I said through my laugh.

"This face and my master key ring is how I get all the ladies."

We walked to the next hole, alternating who shot first. "So, why is it you don't have a girlfriend?" He kept cracking those ladies' man jokes, and yet.

"Oh, you know. The way of the faction leads to hefty sacrifice."

I hit my green golf ball and sent it careening across the curved course. "What about Allison?"

"From the LARPing group?" He looked back at me, the early afternoon sun causing him to squint.

"Yeah. Or is she way older, like the Ren Faire queen?"

"No. Not much older." He set his golf ball against the artificial turf. He tapped the ball, sending it to the guard rail where it angled toward the hole, but an inch too far to the left. "We sort of dated. She graduated and wanted to start fresh for college, so we ended it. We weren't serious, but we're still friends."

His experience sounded immensely different from mine, and not horrible. "That's good. I'm glad exes can be friends."

Aidan gave me a sharp look. Then again, the sun was fierce and hitting the hottest part of the day.

"One last putt." I nodded toward the end of the course.

We logged five and six shots each on the last hole, ending the overall game in a tie. We stashed our clubs at the exit and made our way through the noisy but thankfully air-conditioned arcade attached to the course.

Aidan held up a quarter. "Do want to play golf *digitally?*" He stood beside an ancient arcade machine with a golf theme. "We can cover all golf formats."

"I'll pass. Besides, I think you have to get tokens to play."

Aidan made a show of flipping the quarter in the air, catching it, and slipping the coin into his pocket. Not going to lie, it was hot. He owned the dorkiness without hesitation. He didn't seem dorky at all. Just, Aidany.

Back outside in the heat, I looked back at the cute wilderness-themed golf course. "I should force my family to come out here. We haven't been doing much together since my grandmother died. I forget sometimes how much that's changed us. How it's still changing us."

"That was only a few months ago, right?"

"Yeah. *Way to be a downer, Lila,*" I said, chastising myself in a dopey voice.

"I lost my aunt to cancer two years ago. Lots of things remind me of her."

"Wow, I'm sorry."

"I wish I could have been there for you. After your grandma."

"Oh." My first instinct was to wave him off, tell him it was fine, or add how he and I had hated each other then, so being supportive wouldn't have made sense. I liked the idea of sharing grief with someone. The littlest things reminded me of Grandma.

"There's a rose bush by the door." I pointed back to the mini-golf entrance. "I can't see a rose bush and not think of her. Grandma Rose. She loved roses."

He didn't say anything, following my gaze. Almost like he was taking a moment of silence for my grandmother. My breath hitched. He hadn't even met her and here he was showing her respect.

"My aunt swore like a sailor. I learned every good curse word from her, and some of them weren't even real ones. She was an expert at making innocent words sound dirty."

I couldn't help it, I burst out laughing. "That's a unique thing to remember about a person. And by unique, I mean totally fitting."

"Because I say creatively dirty things?"

"You use descriptive words."

We returned to his truck, the A/C turned to full blast, which barely made a dent in the hot, trapped air.

I looked over at Aidan. He glanced my way for a second, then forward as he drove out of the mini-golf lot. "Can we stop somewhere else? It's on the way back to Ginsburg, but off the back roads."

"Okay." A low current of anticipation ran through me. "I love back roads. I used to study maps. Seeing how the roads connected in real life always fascinated me."

"Lila, the cartographer. I used to draw out my own video game levels on graph paper. Kind of like a comic strip where each panel would show progress in a level."

"Oh, that's *cute*."

"Cute? My game was a space station where the player arrived and everyone was already dead. Just bodies. Dead bodies everywhere."

Yikes. "Have you thought about doing video game design?"

He turned onto a two-lane road bordered by browning grassland on either side. "Game design is more Mason's thing."

"It's funny, you all have your things and always have to point that out. Dan does LARPing with you but says it's your thing. You helped him with his story, but you say writing is his thing. Now Mason with the gaming."

"I think we all learn from each other, but we respect each other's expertise. Now I know, anything mechanical I should ask you."

"I don't know about that."

"I do."

My skin warmed at the idea of Aidan thinking he knew me. How he'd unmasked these smaller details about me, and bigger ones too, without me realizing it.

"Here it is." Aidan slowed and turned into a rocky drive. A pumpkin farm with hayrides and a corn maze was set up for summer with a small petting zoo and horse riding for kids.

"Horses...and little chickens!" I plastered my face against the window looking at the animals. Nine-year-old Lila re-activated.

He parked and pointed out the front window. "There are walking paths here. Too hot for this time of day, but the gift shop has a good selection of candy."

"Because of course you come to a farm for candy."

We walked the outer perimeter of a weathered fence edging the stables. We hadn't paid for the petting zoo part, instead inching as near to the animals as we could for free with the intent to stop by the gift shop for their apparently great candy selection.

"I used to *love* horses." I gazed at the silky brown mane of the horse across the field.

"I gathered from your reaction when we pulled up." He leaned his arms across the top rung of the fence, watching the deep mahogany-colored horse saunter toward the shade of a tree.

"It's sort of an expected thing if you're a girl. I read multiple sets of books about girls and horses when I was younger. I had horse collectibles. They sort of materialized."

Aidan laughed, that rolling, easy laugh of his. "I didn't know girls and horses was a thing."

"I thought everyone knew girls and horses was a thing."

"I have a brother. Also, a mother determined not to gender childhood. Humanities professor," he added.

He held his phone up and snapped a few pictures. "I should get a real camera. One with an adjustable lens. Except, then I'd have to learn how to use it."

"You mean one with the f-stops?"

"I think so. I don't know what the settings are called."

"Your aperture setting is how much light is let in, and then there's focal length. A sharp picture needs more light. You need a tripod to do it right."

"How do you know this?"

"I read up on it one summer."

"So, what you're saying is, you're good at everything. I should hand this over to you." He held out his phone.

I gave him an exaggerated eye roll.

With Matt, I would have worried I came across as a know-it-all explaining things to him. With Aidan, I wanted to share.

He took in a breath, letting it out slow. "Being out here, I feel like we could do anything."

"We?"

"Did I say we? I meant me. You obviously know how to do everything already."

I made a bug-eyed look at him and he laughed. It was now an official goal to make Aidan laugh.

My gaze fell to the open prairie beyond the fence. The grass, the earth, the animals, all had the scent of heat warming their outer layers. A natural, organic smell as a perfect companion to the view.

I let myself absorb the sun and the moment. Another one to collect for my Experiences of Summer list. "Earlier, you said you found me. You were talking about finding me with the mini-golf stuff in the basement, but it felt like—"

"Like finding you. Finding each other."

"Yeah."

Our gazes connected. The outline of him sharpened, like seeing Aidan for the first time. Any association with school or work broke off. This here was stand-alone Aidan. Not part of a series or entourage Aidan. Our future sorted itself in front of me. Making things together, discovering hidden places. All of it fell in order, only the details were fuzzy. In a breath, it all blew away and scattered into a different future. The future could be anything, going any direction into art or robotics or working on my golf swing (why not?), and all of it was mine to discover.

The air around us stilled. I let my thoughts fragment and fall away. Aidan was close. This was now. This was us.

He skimmed a hand across my cheek and into my hair. Every nerve in my body danced. His lips fell to mine and I caught them. I caught all of him, every piece he was open to sharing. He tasted like mint and sky and summer. A moment I would catch and hold onto, into my being. This was more than any list could capture.

We broke apart.

He tucked a strand of hair behind my ear. "I've been wanting to do that...again, for a while."

"I've been wanting that...again, too." I created the same pause he had. Our first kiss felt almost accidental and like it might not happen again. This time, I knew we'd plan sequels.

Without speaking, we headed to the small store front by the petting zoo entrance. We loaded up on old fashioned candy and a caramel apple each. I let Aidan pay. I only had one crumpled dollar bill and some change, and he insisted we experience the full array of treats. I couldn't think of much else beyond the impression of Aidan's lips against mine.

We retreated to the truck, rolled down the windows to air out the heat, and promptly made out.

These kisses were less sweet and more, what was the word? I didn't know. Words failed. But I really liked the taste.

Chapter Nineteen

♥

Things that did not make my Experiences of Summer planning list:

- Kissing my ex's best friend
- Paying so many taxes
- (but mostly the kissing part)

I promised Natalie we'd hang out. I had so much to tell her.

Aidan. Our kisses. My lips still tingled from the memory. If I didn't tell *somebody*, I'd implode.

Natalie waited for me at her favorite coffee shop, sitting at an outside table beneath a scrape of shade from a spindly tree. "Hey, girl." She was one of those annoyingly punctual people (which for all my planning, I was not, thus my annoyance).

"Hey." I slid into a chair. "Sorry about having to work today, but I can't say no to more hours." I wore my work polo because I was just that cool. I hefted my backpack with my lunch and work shoes onto the seat beside me. "So, I have to tell you—"

The door behind us swung open, sending out a burst of air-conditioned splendor and loud boy voices.

"I'm telling you, man, he can still get traded. Oh, hey, ladies."

I looked up to see Brandon and another guy who stood a head shorter but was equally as broad shouldered. I shot a look to Natalie who brightened at the sight of them.

Brandon pulled out the chair beside me, plucking my backpack off the seat and setting it beneath the table. "Hey, Lila. What's up?" He nodded toward the other guy who had black hair swept to the side and wore a crisp white T-shirt set against copper-toned skin. Every ounce of his attention focused on Natalie. "This is Manuelito."

The guy shoved Brandon at the shoulder. "I go by Manny, dude, you know that."

Brandon snickered. "Just messing with you."

Natalie's pupils may as well have been heart-shaped. "Good to see you again."

Again? Who was this guy?

"Manny, this is Lila," she said. "So glad you could make it."

So, this wasn't a Natalie and me thing after all.

Brandon set down a drink in front of me, already sweaty at the sides. "I got you that icy tea lemonade stuff Natalie drinks. She said you'd like it."

Natalie beamed. "She *loves* it. Don't you, Lila? It's all we drink in the summer."

It was all *she* drank in the summer. I liked it fine. But he'd bought this for me and I wouldn't act ungrateful. "Thanks. That was really thoughtful of you."

Brandon and Manny resumed talking about basketball. I looked across the table at Natalie. *What gives?*

She scrunched her shoulders, all smiley, signaling with her eyes at Brandon and Manny. She waited for a pause in their conversation. "Lila and I were just saying how we'd *die* to get courtside seats to a Pistons game."

Manny snapped his fingers. "My uncle Julio knows a guy. Name a date and we're in."

Except I would not die for such seats. Nor would I get marginally ill for seats at a basketball game.

The conversation continued and my phone buzzed.

Aidan: *Thought of you today.*

A photo of a rose blossom appeared beneath his message. The area around it faded in soft focus, almost muted, so the bright red of the rose stood out even more. Everything around me dulled. A rose, like my Grandma Rose.

I love it, I typed back.

Aidan: *Working today?*

Me: *At 2. Headed over soon.*

"Lila." Natalie's voice sliced through my thoughts.

"Huh?" I set the phone face down, gritting my teeth as it vibrated again.

"We were going to hang out anyway this weekend, right?" Natalie was saying to me.

"Uh-huh." I pushed Aidan from my mind. The rose image, his excited expressions when he talked about creating. The taste of his lips. I pinched myself under the table. "Yes, I'm all about hanging out." We'd talked about a sleepover night. Just the two of us with ice cream and YouTube and charcoal face masks.

Natalie held my gaze another second. I sent back an apologetic look. We only had an hour together and I'd been texting someone else. Then again, she'd invited Brandon and Manny. Who were still talking about basketball.

"You'll come with us, won't you, Lila?"

I stepped out of the Cage, the ninety-plus degree temperature testing my patience and the limits of my Secret Outlast XTend deodorant. Those limits were fully extended in this heat.

Dan and Mason stood on the opposite side of the fence, waiting. Hounding. They'd been pitching me all afternoon.

"Listen, I don't know," I said. "You might have to convince me I'm Ren Faire-worthy." I wanted to hear Dan and Mason try to sell me on the faire, even though I planned on going. Their excitement built up my own anticipation. Besides, not sharing I'd already been to a Ren Faire in my Past Lila life seemed harmless. Unlike the fact Aidan and I had made out until our lips were puffed, and neither of us had bothered to share that detail with anyone. Aidan hadn't spilled to Dan or Mason. If he had, it would be instantly obvious. I knew how to read them now.

Dan opened the gate for me. "One: giant turkey legs."

The three of us traveled the fenced walkway, returning to air-conditioned relief.

Mason held up two fingers. "Two: they serve a fake ale in a frosty stein that makes it feel like you're drinking real beer."

"That doesn't sound very Renaissance—"

"Do not speak ill of it!" Dan exclaimed in an English accent.

Aidan approached, and before he could speak, Dan pointed at him, saying, "Three reasons Lila should go to the Ren Faire, and you're three—go!"

"Honorary Dragon Faction."

"I get to be in a faction? First time?"

"Honorary," he stressed, holding up a hand. "Also, reason number three-point-five, opening day is Saturday *and* I checked—we all have the day off since we worked the Independence Day holiday."

Nala passed us with an empty serving tray hugged against her side. "What are you kids up to? Pranking each other with exploding golf balls? *Again?*"

Dan and Mason exchanged guilty glances.

"We're going to the Renaissance Faire," I told her. I caught Aidan's eye. He smiled back, not bothering to look away or play it cool.

"Ooh, Ren Faire." Nala paused to give me her attention. "I went there once. Those knights who do the joust?" She fanned herself. "*Smokin.'*"

Dan shrugged. "Knights are overrated. I prefer the bard. That's what I am. A storyteller."

Mason waved him off. "Whatever, dude. Court jester is where it's at. History's original stand-up comics." He tapped an invisible microphone. "Is this thing on? I just took a pilgrimage by sea, and I've got to say, I've had better food in a dungeon."

"Boo!" Dan mimed flinging fake rotten food.

"Are you all dressing up?" Nala asked.

"Well…" That was an absolute level-up in geekdom. I'd already been thinking through possible costume ideas, but in Ren Faire as in life, I desperately needed fashion consultation. Wait—there was an idea. I could invite Natalie to the Ren Faire. Bridge our interests. We'd barely been hanging out and were talking about a sleepover anyway. This would be perfect. Ren Faire in the day, face masks and snacks at night.

I headed to the supply room where I fired off a text to Natalie.

Me: *I have SUCH a fun idea. Let's go to the Renaissance Faire. Opening weekend is this Saturday!*

Me: *Don't be weirded out - Aidan, Dan, and Mason will be there.*

I got back to work until my break rolled around. Checking for texts, I headed to the break room. Nothing from Natalie yet.

In the break room above the food table hung a bulletin board with policies bordered by staff photos. Nala and another server sticking their tongues out at the camera. Joe and guys from the kitchen wearing Detroit Tigers caps. A group I didn't recognize except for Jen in the middle, holding balloons and wearing party hats.

A photo of Aidan, Dan, and Mason caught my eye. Another photo tacked above it had an edge hanging over part of the picture. I slid the second photo aside, revealing Matt. He looked off camera while the other guys were visibly laughing. A month ago, Matt would have looked to me like the responsible one, having better things to do than pose for a pic with these cronies. Now it seemed he wanted to be somewhere else. Like he'd already checked out.

My phone buzzed in my pocket.

Natalie: *This Saturday is the lake house. Remember?*

Lake house?

I typed back a reply asking for details.

Natalie: *Brandon and his boat. Saturday. We just talked about this.*

I searched my memory.

Me: *Isn't Saturday our sleepover?*

Natalie: *I knew you weren't listening.*

Crap.

She was still typing.

Natalie: *Come on, Lila. It will be fun. Brandon has been asking about you.*

Ugh, the Brandon thing. Okay, so he was nice (according to Natalie), decent looking (according to others), and a great guy to hang out with for the summer (per Natalie). Maybe I could have him rub sunscreen across my back as we—sailed? Motored? What kind of boat did he have?

It didn't matter. I wanted a fake sword, a giant turkey leg, and a seat at the joust. I wanted enchanted fairy folke to braid my hair. I wanted a guy in tights to say to me, "Good morn, M'Lady."

I wanted that guy to be Aidan.

Jamming a handful of sour cream and onion chips into my mouth, I let the artificial flavors coat my tongue. I hated disappointing people. Hated it.

My break ended and I reluctantly returned to work. Dan passed by me on my way to restock bathroom supplies. "Huzzah!"

I sustained my smile until I'd passed, not letting him in on my mental anguish.

Natalie wanted me to make the best of the summer. Maybe I needed to figure out summer in my own way. Making plans was the point here. Sure, these plans were outside of what she'd been thinking, but I could convince her to hop on the Ren Faire wagon. Worse would be if I was still holed up in my blanket cave, crying over old photos and mainlining Netflix original content.

Honesty. That was the word of the summer. I texted Natalie.

Me: *I'm sorry. My mistake to agree to the boat thing. I thought you meant the sleepover. I promised I'd go to the Ren Faire. Can we do lake day another time?*

The little dots indicating she was typing a response danced along my screen.

Natalie: *You're really hanging out with your ex's friends over me?*

I read the message three times. Another time. Each read through, the last two words *over me* struck deeper. What did it mean that I wanted to hang out with Matt's friends more than my own best friend?

Anything I wrote back would sound like an excuse. Natalie already thought it was totally weird I worked where Matt used to. That I'd befriended his buddies. Saturating myself in Matt's old life all while trying to get over him probably seemed pretty bonkers. I got it, I did, but it wasn't like that. The only people here who even knew I'd dated Matt were Aidan, Dan, and Mason. Jen, the kitchen crew, and the servers had no idea I knew Matt at all.

Which was a little strange, come to think of it. Hadn't Matt ever mentioned me? *My girlfriend Lila and I...* Lila wasn't exactly as common a name as Sarah or Emma. It proved yet again that Matt and I were never the Matt and Lila I'd thought we were.

Me: *I'm sorry. I don't mean it to be that way.*

Natalie: *So you're coming to the lake or not coming?*

The phone grew hot in my hands. The two options meant two different paths.

The supply room door swung open and Jen peeked inside. "Lila, there you are. I need you and your mop in the second-floor bays."

Me and my mop to the rescue. I slid the phone into my back pocket without responding.

As I finished with the spill, Aidan stopped by. He sprung over, like his legs were made of wire coils. "I have costume ideas to run by you. *On the cheap*. You don't have to go all out to rock a casual Renaissance cosplay."

He stood close, a reminder of his touch, our secret. Okay, secrets plural. First the robot, then the kissing.

I looked beyond him to a cluster of female customers wearing sashes. One sash read *Tee Queen*. "I...I can't go Saturday. I'm sorry. I forgot I had plans."

Aidan's smile hung on a few beats before my words caught up. "What do you mean? You have the day off."

All my energy seeped out, sinking me into the floor. "I forgot I told Natalie I would do something with her. I asked her to come with us, to the faire, but she made other plans for us. I'm so sorry."

Aidan slid one palm across the slick table. "No, I get it. You made plans with her first. It's a bummer, but I get it."

He knocked a fist on the table once and turned away. He looped back. "Don't think you're off the hook. The faire runs through Labor Day."

He flashed a smile hitting me at the knees. Him being so understanding only made me sink further.

It was a bummer alright, a bummer of my own choosing. Each choice had negatives in some way. At least choosing the lake, I wouldn't disappoint my best friend.

Instead, I'd only disappointed myself.

Chapter Twenty

❤

Lake Day Packing List:

- Sunscreen SPF 50 - waterproof
- Sunglasses
- Swimsuit - tankini? (Ask Natalie)
- Flip flops
- Towel
- Hairbrush
- Change of socks
- Phone charger
- Trail mix and granola bars
- List notebook
- Backpack

That Saturday morning, Natalie and I headed to Brandon's house, where a group of us planned to meet first, then drive up to the lake together. In the opposite direction from the Ren Faire, I couldn't help note.

The lake house plan turned out to be for the best. Who could turn down a whole day of free fun? Not this gal.

Besides, I could follow the faire fun on Instagram. The guys said they'd post updates. Mason had a surprisingly high number of followers being tapped into the gaming industry crowd, sharing about video game and app development in his captions. Dan mainly reposted memes from sci-fi TV and movies (including content about all the fierce women on *The Expanse*!). Aidan's account included a mix of Ren Faire posts, photos of his family dog (Bean—a dachshund—the cutest) and landscape shots. Soft willows by a pond and a snap of early sunset.

Sigh. F-stops. Aidan's kisses.

I needed to fill in Natalie on the Aidan development, but at the right time. Which was not now since we were parking on the street in front of Brandon's house.

"Oh my gosh, won't this be *fun*?" Natalie said for at least the third time since I'd picked her up. "I'm *so* glad you came."

I shook off my Moody McMooderton attitude. Grandpa always said the key to a good life was knowing somebody with a boat. All of the summertime perks with none of the licensing and maintenance hassles.

We made our way up the drive. Brandon and Manny waited for us, talking and basically looking cool.

Natalie squeezed my hand. "Do I look okay?"

I scanned her for a nanosecond. "Of course."

Natalie was the epitome of outfit of the day: beach edition. Oversized sunglasses, hair piled in a messy topknot, an over-sized slinky tee draped over a colorful bikini top, well-worn jeans cuffed at her shins, and flat sandals with jewels matching the colors on her beach bag.

In my plain shorts and T-shirt, I felt like the Before to her After in a makeover montage. Would I ever get over not feeling like I measured up? This was getting old.

"He's so..." Natalie trailed off, her attention on Manny.

Manny wore a loose black T-shirt and board shorts to match his easygoing stance.

"Perfect for you?" I asked.

She elbowed me, but her smile didn't waver.

"How do you know him again?" I asked.

"Hey, ladies," Brandon called over, cutting off any response Natalie might have. "We're waiting on a few folks."

Behind us, Grace and Holli Hayes joined the group along with Olivia and a guy named Greg who sometimes sat with our group at lunch. We were all West Ginsburg High students with the exception of Manny.

Everyone piled into a glistening SUV, leaving me and Holli standing awkwardly in the driveway.

"Aw, man. I counted wrong." Brandon hopped out of the driver's seat. "Lila, you can sit up front with me. Manny, bro, you need to take your own car. Take Greg with you."

Manny stood from the passenger seat, leaning over the SUV's roof. "And leave you with all the girls? No way, dude."

"Bad deal," Greg agreed.

"I can drive," I offered. "I'll take Natalie—" Natalie shook her head an imperceptible-but-to-me nod. Fine, Ms. Heart Eyes wanted Manny time. "Or, whoever."

Brandon looked back at the guys. "For real? Neither of you will drive? You're going to make Lila?"

If I drove, there might be time enough to get home early and catch up with Aidan and the guys, or work on the robot. "It's not a big deal."

Holli volunteered as tribute and joined me at my car.

"Sorry about this," I told her as she slipped into Goldie's passenger seat.

"Fine by me. My sister's making me do this anyway."

I considered telling her I too was a victim of someone else's persuasion, but I wasn't a victim. I'd chosen to spend time with Natalie today. Then again, here I was driving without Natalie or any of the friends she promised we'd have fun with. Instead, I ended up driving Grace's younger sister.

We left Ginsburg and headed north. Holli navigated from the GPS on her phone, chattering about running and a young adult fantasy book series she loved.

Stretches of forest and farmland passed with occasional isolated houses winking from their spots off the highway. Eventually, we arrived at the lake road turnoff, finally stopping at a driveway in front of a small gray house with the garage facing the street.

I parked in the driveway beside Brandon's SUV. Holli and I walked in through the open garage to a kitchen that overlooked a living room area. Floor to ceiling windows covered the wall farthest from us facing a cobalt blue lake.

"Lila." Brandon slung an arm around me like this was a thing we did. "What can I get you?"

The unprompted touching could have made me flinch but didn't. I could maybe see what Natalie said about him being cute. Gelled hair aside. "Pop. A soda. Anything."

I thought of Aidan saying *pahp* in a nasally voice and smiled to myself. Brandon walked off to the kitchen and I pulled up Instagram. Dan's feed featured a video of Aidan's truck with a banner on the back of their LARPing faction logo. A hip-hop song played over the top of the clip.

Natalie sidled up to me. "He asked about you on the ride over."

I blinked at her. He...*Brandon*. There would never be a great time to do this, and I couldn't let her think I was interested in him. I just wasn't. Not after what Aidan and I had started. "I need to tell you something. It's about Aidan."

She let her head fall to one side. "Aidan *Pemberton*? Is he making you feel bad for existing again?"

"I told you we cleared things up. Things have... progressed."

Meanwhile, Natalie gazed at Manny who looked all broody near a potted plant. Her head snapped back to me. "Has Aidan been giving you a hard time? I knew working at the golf place was a bad idea. I can still ask around for job leads."

"I don't need another job." I didn't bother hiding my exasperation. "The job is fine."

She flinched. "I was only trying to help. Look, can you forget about work and Aidan for one day? Have fun. For me. I know it's hard, but give it a try?"

In a flash, I thought of freshman year, eating lunch alone at a table of misfits with their social shields activated. One table over, Natalie sat with a group who I'd later learn all knew each other since elementary school, including Olivia and Grace. Natalie and I had been paired as science partners, and later that week she asked if I wanted to sit with her group at lunch. The social invitation that changed everything. I'd graduated lunch tables.

I owed Natalie so much. I had a social life because of her. Giving this party a fair try seemed to mean a lot to her, and she meant a lot to me.

"I'm going to get out of your way so Brandon has room." She shot me a sly grin and glided over to Manny, who immediately perked up at the sight of her. I mean, who wouldn't.

"What's going on, Lila?"

Brandon stood in front of me now, holding out a fizzy drink. "It's a sparkling water thing. My mom has cases of it. Natalie said you liked this stuff."

I eyed Natalie across the room. She sat on the armrest of an overstuffed chair, looking intently at Manny as he explained something. "How do you know Manny?"

"We go way back. Our parents are friends. He goes to Saint Anne's."

The Catholic high school in Ginsburg. "Okay, cool." But how did Natalie know Manny? She'd never said. How had I missed that she knew this hot guy from another high school? I'd been working too much, that's what. Now, I barely knew my own best friend.

I didn't have anything else to offer on the subject of Manny or Catholic school. In fact, I had no idea what to talk to Brandon about, period. "So, this house is pretty great."

"Yeah, yeah." He gestured toward the windows and the lake. "My parents want to move here after my younger brother graduates."

We talked about the joys of moving, since I'd done it so much, and all the places I'd lived. Brandon had a way of hanging onto each word, and then suddenly we were discussing another topic entirely. I intentionally did not act flirty and maintained distance between us. The last thing I wanted was to make him think I was interested in him as more than friends.

"Do you want to go out?" Brandon looked at me, waiting on an answer. "To the lake?"

Of course, he'd meant the lake. Just that pesky pause in there to throw me off. "I'd love to."

Brandon rounded up everyone and we grabbed our towels, sunglasses, and granola snacks (that was me) and headed out to the rocky shore where a simple wood-planked dock jutted into the water. An open-top speedboat bobbed beside the dock.

More kids joined us from the house and boarded the boat. Brandon got in and showed us where the life jackets were stowed.

Natalie bumped me at the shoulder. "Safety precautions. You've got to love that."

Okay, so she knew me well.

Once everybody boarded, Brandon reversed from the dock and turned the boat toward the wider section of lake. The deep blue waves moved in a soft rhythm beyond us.

Everyone talked at once, so I took another quick check of Instagram. Dan's feed included a pic of the obligatory giant turkey leg, plus a group of costumed fest goers holding up mugs and singing. Mason's showed part of a parade, a dude in chain mail holding an axe, and a group shot with himself, Dan, and Aidan. I zoomed in on Aidan to inspect his costume.

I switched over to Aidan's profile, realizing I'd been saving his for last. His sole photo so far featured a garden gnome. The gnome peeked out from flowers and glass balls set on pewter pedestals, its little gnome eyes mischievous and curious. It almost looked alive.

"Earth to Lila." Natalie tossed her wadded-up T-shirt at me. "Brandon asked if you wanted to steer."

"The boat?" Obviously, the boat. "Um, sure."

As the boat idled, Brandon slid aside, moving a hand to my back to guide me into the white captain's seat. The word *captain* was literally stitched across the leather chair back.

"Here's the throttle. Just go like this." He covered his palm over mine resting heavy and kind of sweaty. "Natalie said you drive that golf cart with the cage on it. I've seen that thing. People are still hitting golf balls while you're in it?"

"It's not so bad." I let out a nervous laugh. "Natalie sure has been telling you a lot about me."

He leaned closer but kept his focus on the water. "She and I have been friends a long time. I trust her."

I trusted Natalie, too. Clearly, she wanted this thing with Brandon to happen. Why couldn't I see what she saw in him?

Because Aidan's clouding my vision. Aidan, who had messy ties to my ex. Aidan who still competed against me for the bonus money. Aidan was...complicated. He didn't feel complicated when we were together. Only now, with the surrounding blue sky and calming water, could I see more clearly how complicated we were.

Brandon glanced at me. His hand over mine pulled back to slow the throttle. "Easy, right? You're a pro."

Brandon would be the simple choice.

I smiled, because I knew he wanted me to. It was easy when I remembered how this worked.

After lapping the lake, Brandon slowed the boat and dropped the anchor. The guys peeled off their shirts and swung their legs over the edge. Greg cannonballed into the water, followed by Brandon who dove in a practiced arc.

I couldn't turn down swimming in the lake. I tossed my own T-shirt aside and pulled my hair back into a ponytail.

"Are you going in?" Natalie asked, a lazy arm lingering dangerously close to Manny's bare back.

"I think you're good right here." Manny slid his arm around her shoulders and she eased back. Their bodies, hers tanned against his bronze coloring, so artfully casual. Every day with Matt I'd worked to be the image of Natalie and Manny in front of me. I studied her, but I would never be her.

Suddenly, I felt completely okay with that.

If Matt had been here, I would have waited to see if he wanted to swim. Even if he'd told me to go ahead without him, I wouldn't have. I knew I wouldn't have. Pathetic.

"I'm going in the water." A declaration. I would live this summer the way summer was meant to be lived. Wet hair, sandy toes, and bug bites. I straightened my arms in front of me and dove in.

The lake water rushed cool over my skin, the cold jarring in the best way to shock my senses. I needed a full reset.

This lake was it. I would come out of here a changed person.

Brandon swam over. "Are you cold?"

"I'm good. I could stay out here for hours."

Holli splashed in and disappeared. When she surfaced, she swam toward Olivia and Greg. I flipped to my back to float and watch the clouds.

Brandon treaded closer. "You're a good swimmer. Why aren't you on the school team?"

"I'm more of a one sport gal. It feels enough to play softball."

"I hear ya. Some kids have no life besides school sports. No time for this." He head-nodded toward the boat, where Greg climbed up again for another go at a cannonball. Greg bombed into the water, sending sheets of lake water every direction. "Seven at best." Brandon waved him off. "So, you almost left for the summer, huh?"

"Yeah. It's kind of crazy to think I could have been thousands of miles away in another country, and then, I'm not." Because I'd decided it. Maybe the lake didn't need to change me. Maybe I'd been changing since that day, since that decision.

Matt may have decided to date Megan without breaking up with me first, but I'd been the one to walk away. I'd taken the steps to move on. I wasn't waiting in the boat for a boy who wasn't coming back.

A laugh escaped my throat.

Brandon looked around. "What's funny?"

I laughed again. What else could I do? The old version of me was so predictable, so pathetic. If I didn't laugh, I'd tear out my hair. "I don't know. Life is weird."

Brandon watched me. "I was thinking, maybe when we get back, we could talk some more."

We were talking now. Oh—*talk* talk. Yikes. Infinity yikes. I needed to stall him. If I could talk to Natalie—

A sense of calm rose up, like the water smoothing over my anxiety. I knew what I needed to do.

"So, I sort of started seeing someone. From work."

A flash of hurt crossed Brandon's face. "Oh."

"It's new. It's not exactly defined yet, but I thought you should know. I haven't told Natalie—it's that new. I didn't want you to think—"

"It's cool." Brandon kicked off with his legs and circled back, his long arms reaching through the water and sending ripples my way. "Thanks for telling me."

Wow. That hadn't been too bad.

"Whoever it is—they're lucky."

"Thanks. That's sweet of you."

Brandon spun around and squirted water from his hands at Greg.

One down, another one to go with Natalie.

Eventually, we returned to the house a wet and hungry stampede. A stocked fridge supplied ingredients for burgers, but no one wanted to put it all together, so Brandon ordered pizza.

I excused myself to change into dry clothes, finding a small bedroom with two twin beds.

A knock sounded at the door. "Can I come in?" Natalie.

"Sure."

She slipped inside and closed the door. She rifled through her beach bag and pulled out a tank top. "Brandon is having his friends pick up firewood so we can do another bonfire."

Bonfires typically happened at night. "Are we staying that late? I'm getting kind of tired."

"Lila. I thought you were *in* for today." This time, her typical emphasis came off accusatory.

"I am. I'm here."

She rocked a hand at her hip. "For all of it."

"I only said I was tired. I clean and stock all day at work. It's tiring." I flipped my hair over, wrapped a towel around it, and squeezed out the water.

"Sorry you had to miss the festival thing, but this is *way* more fun, isn't it?"

"I would have had fun at the Ren Faire, too."

"Except it was with Matt's friends. I still don't get that whole situation. It's like the Stockholm thing. You know, when the *captive* starts to *befriend* the captors—"

I yanked the towel from my head. "I do not have Stockholm Syndrome. I do not have captors. And they aren't Matt's friends. They barely talk to him anymore."

She dawdled by the dresser and picked up a snow globe with a miniature beach scene in the glass. "It's because he's in Brazil. When he comes back, they're going to go right back to him."

"You don't know that."

"That's what they do. They *follow* Matt. They're his, what did you call them? Like, his minions?"

"Cronies," I answered, a sense of shame rising around the term. I stared at the blue bed comforter until the pattern blurred.

She sank to the bed across from me. "I don't think hanging out with them is a good idea. You're constantly hearing about Matt and these things he did while you were together. That *can't* be good for you."

"Matt is barely ten percent of what we talk about. Anyway, they're mad at Matt. They feel betrayed. They're mad because he hurt me, and because he'd been ditching them too."

Natalie grabbed her sweatshirt and slipped it over her head. She fluffed her hair out from the collar. "You'd rather be hanging out with them. You've been distracted all day."

"I'm having a good time. I loved swimming in the lake."

"And Brandon?"

"He's a good guy, like you said."

She shook her head, a quiet laugh rippling out. "I have said that, about *ten times*, haven't I?" She sighed, leaning back on her elbows. "You know I'm only pushing the Brandon thing because I want what's best for you. Brandon would never cheat. I think he's *exactly* what you need this summer."

"Except..." I owed it to my best friend to tell her I had feelings for Aidan. Those feelings had evolved to some pretty hot kissing, all of which made me miss Aidan and not being at the faire with him all over again. "Aidan and I —"

Knocking rapped against the door. "Is Lila in there with you, Natalie?" Brandon spoke through the door, hesitation in his voice. "We didn't know where you two went."

"Yes." Natalie hopped up to get the door, but turned back to me before opening. "Are you staying?" she mouthed.

I wasn't lying when I told Natalie I felt tired. It wasn't only because of my job. All of this time hanging out took so much effort. Being social came easily to Natalie. For me, this was work.

For pizza. I'd stay through pizza. "Okay."

Natalie opened the door and Brandon peeked in, looking past her to give me a quick nod. "Chris and them wanted to know what beer you want."

My internal alarms activated. This night was turning into something I hadn't expected.

"Oh, I'm good. Lila and I don't really drink." Natalie swept her hair back in her specifically Natalie way. "Thanks."

He took off, leaving the door open. I sprung toward Natalie. "Chris who? More people are coming over?"

Natalie's expression settled on practiced patience. "I told you Brandon's friends were bringing firewood. And look, we don't have to drink. What's the problem?"

"I thought you meant Greg and Manny were the friends. Not different friends. And what's the deal with him, anyway?"

"With Manny?" Her eyes grew starry. "I don't know. It's probably nothing."

"It looks like something." Something she'd forgotten to talk to me about at all ever. "Where did you meet him?"

"Oh! We met kind of by random chance over spring break. He came into the vet clinic one day. I was surprised to find out Brandon knew him. It's been *so fun* to reconnect."

My shoulders eased. "I'm happy for you if you like him. He seems like a decent guy."

"Really? You don't think he's too cool for me?"

I snorted. "Too cool for you?" What was she talking about? "You're too cool for me and here we are."

She waved me off. "Whatever. Okay come on." She started toward the hall, but my feet weren't moving.

I needed to clear the air on Aidan. "Wait, Natalie. About Aidan. I like him. I really like him."

She stood halfway out the door and leaned against the door frame. "I know what this is. It's situational. You *work* together. He's there, and he's in Matt's circle of friends. They're familiar, so you *think* you like him." She shook her head. "You have so many more options. Just wait until the other guys get here. Maybe it's not Brandon, but someone —"

"No." Natalie needed to hear me. Old Lila would have gone along with whatever Natalie said. Pretending I didn't care about Aidan wasn't fair. Not to me, to Natalie, or to Aidan. "It's not about options. Aidan gets me. I can be myself. I don't have to act." Aidan had uncovered the real me, beneath the artificial layers reinforced by my sheer will. Yet here I was, keeping my true self tucked away from my best friend. "I pretend a lot. I don't even think you know me as well as you think."

Her lips parted. "What do you mean? Are you saying *Aidan Pemberton* knows you better than I do?"

It was exactly what I had said, but not at all what I meant. "No, that came out wrong. I try hard to, you know, fit in when I'm with you. I try to be the person I think you would like."

"So, now you think I can't figure out how to like my own friends?" Her voice rose.

"I was only trying to be honest. I want you know me for me. It's been...difficult."

"Well, if I'm so difficult to be around, maybe you should go and hang out with Aidan." She pivoted toward the kitchen.

A hollow pang hit having nothing to do with hunger. Hello, Universe? Could I rewind and start over? I should have prepared better. I hadn't planned it out right and now look what happened.

I jammed my wet swimsuit into my backpack. When I'd first met Natalie, I hadn't been special or cool, even with carefully chosen outfits copied from *Teen Vogue*. Even if I'd pretended to be who I imagined she liked, Natalie wouldn't have hung on all this time if she didn't at least like me a little bit.

I couldn't leave yet. Not until I talked to my best friend.

The pizza arrived, followed by kids I recognized from classes and parties over the past year. Another group came afterward, and another.

Greg found me in the kitchen eating a slice of sausage and onion pizza. "Hey, Lila. Can you move your car to the street?"

I finished chewing. "Why?"

"Some of my boys want to stay the night. They want to park in the driveway." I must have been taking too long to answer because he huffed and held out his hand. "Keys. I'll move it myself."

I'd be leaving soon anyway. "The keys are hooked onto my backpack." I pointed to the guest room.

Music blasted, and red cups materialized. Chips and sodas were cast aside for cases of beer and liquor bottles on the kitchen island. I grabbed two carbonated waters for later. Natalie and I made a pact not to let each other get drunk at a party. Too many horror stories. Maybe that would change someday for each of us, but for now our pact worked.

I caught a glimpse of Natalie on the back deck, her arm looped through Manny's. She tipped her head back laughing and disappeared in a mosaic of faces, walking toward the water.

I could chase after her or...make the most of this experience. I resisted checking my phone and found Holli in the side yard. I joined her for a game of bags—aiming beanbags toward a board with a hole in it—playing against Brandon and Olivia. We finished a game and switched teams, so Brandon and Olivia on opposing teams stood on one end together. They kept bumping against each other and giggling. His hand lingered on her arm. Looked like Brandon had moved on already.

Something loud thudded from inside the house.

Brandon chucked the bags to the ground. "That can't be good." He bolted.

Holli rubbed at her arms. "I'm going to get my long sleeves. Want to come?"

I scanned through the crowd on the deck and in the yard. "Yeah. Natalie must be inside. I want to see her before I take off."

Inside, an armchair lay overturned as someone pretended to surf on it. The small living room filled with bodies to max capacity. Many faces I didn't recognize. Where was Natalie?

I headed to the kitchen right when the door from the garage opened. I stopped. Time stopped.

A large figure stood at the door. Disheveled, easy-going, and utterly impossibly present.

"Lila? What are you doing here?"

Matt. He was here. In this house.

He was back.

Chapter Twenty-One

♥

List of things to say to Matt when I see him again:
  (written hours after breaking up)
- Have a nice summer? (in snarky tone)
- You trashbag
- Got typhoid? (assuming his travel vaccine hadn't worked)
- How dare you. Never mind, don't care

Matt was *here*. Standing mere feet from me when thousands of miles should have separated us.

He stared at me. I stared back. He stared some more.

People around us were staring. Whispering.

Matt twitched. His gaze darted around the room. He looked back at me. "You're at Brandon's." He spoke slowly, either to help himself understand or to inform me on my surroundings.

"I'm here with Natalie." Wait—I didn't owe him an explanation. "What are *you* doing here? The trip doesn't end for…another few weeks." Funny, I didn't even remember how many days were left since I'd stopped thinking about the trip.

His gaze shifted again, taking in the kitchen and living room beyond it. "I didn't tell anybody except my parents. I texted a few guys a couple hours ago. I got in this morning after an overnight flight." He rubbed at his face, his eyelids droopy. "Things weren't working out in Brazil."

Things weren't working out? *What things?* Where was Meghan? Never mind. It didn't matter. At least now I had an official reason to leave this party.

I heard snickering and Matt's face flushed. He lowered his own voice as he approached me. "Hey, can we talk somewhere?"

Now he wanted to talk? My palms were drenched, like personal hand-shaped saunas were attached to them. My heart, a freight train barreling toward my ribcage.

Brandon edged through the crowd to face Matt. "Where's your new girl? Or did you ditch her like you ditched Lila?"

Matt's bottom lip curled, his face twisting into a grimace. "You don't know what you're talking about."

"Who even invited you?" Grace Hayes demanded. Her petite frame matched Matt's height from her attitude alone. "You treated Lila like trash, and now you show up here like everything's cool?"

A Grace Hayes allegiance. Who knew?

Never one to miss a spotlight, Grace angled her way farther into the kitchen and into Matt's space. She gave him a thorough stare-down. Her long, electric plum-colored hair swung around bare shoulders from her strapless top. Grace was gorgeous and fearless. "You are such a douche-poodle."

That got everyone within earshot laughing.

Matt's face reddened.

I stood there, speechless. It was like I'd turned to stone and my brain dissolved into pebbles.

"That's not what happened," Matt said through clenched teeth. "I'm here to have a good time like everybody else."

"I don't know if I want you here." Brandon moved forward, his broad shoulders menacing when he put grit into his step.

Matt shot me an irritated look. "What do you mean? I knew you guys before she ever did." His usual over-confidence appeared significantly sapped. He pouted, a look I knew well. It used to be cute.

"Lila, are you okay?" Natalie's hands clasped my shoulders from behind, her lavender scent surrounding me. "You don't have to talk to him."

A rush of relief came over me. Natalie was at least willing to be here for me in this super weird moment.

"Thanks," I told her.

Manny moved past Natalie, his hands carefully shifting her aside, to stand next to Brandon. "It doesn't sound like you're wanted here." He cracked his neck. "Is there going to be a problem?"

"You're *kicking* me *out*?" Matt's gaze flitted from Brandon to Manny, then to me and the rest of the staring faces. Brandon's friend Chris held up his phone, filming.

Matt turned back at me, seeming to search my face for understanding. "Lila, do you want me to leave?"

Brandon looked back at me. Scratch that. *Everyone* looked at me.

Oh no. No, no, no. For someone highly skilled at blending, this was my worst fears come alive. Add to that, confrontation. Strike me down, I was out. Dead.

All sound vanished except for tinkling glass bottles and distant outside voices. Sand coated my throat. Matt—the guy who'd been my everything, the proof of social boot camp achieved—waited on me to kick him out in front of all our friends.

No, not all our friends.

You deserve better.

I deserved a guy who wouldn't humiliate me, multiple times, in front of people whose opinions I cared about. Stupid as caring what they thought may have been, I did care.

Brandon opened the door to the garage. "This is my house. My rules. I think you need to go."

One time, I saw my dad get beaned in the face by a two-by-four on a job site. The whole end of the wood beam swung right at the back of his noggin, by accident from one of his crew. Dad had this dazed look, like he couldn't make sense of reality. That was what Matt looked like right now.

Immediately, Olivia and Natalie corralled me into the room with the twin beds. How dare Matt put me on the spot. The nerve of him showing up here. What was up with leaving his trip early? It was everything I needed and wanted to hear, only I didn't feel satisfied.

Olivia left to get me water. Natalie leaned close. "I'm sorry about earlier. I don't get what you said about pretending and all that, but I don't want to be mad at you."

A small sense of relief took some of the stress away. "Thanks. We should talk more. Later."

Olivia returned, and I managed to appease them enough to let me sneak away to the bathroom. Alone. I needed a break to think.

I closed the bathroom door. Okay, not what I expected from tonight. I didn't even want to *be* here.

Which reminded me—I hadn't checked in with Aidan and the guys in hours.

Twelve new text messages.

The first three were all about the faire. Then:

Aidan: *I just got a call. Don't know how else to say this but Matt's back.*

Aidan: *He didn't say why. We can talk later if you want.*

Aidan: *Sorry if this ruins your plans. Just wanted you to know.*

Gah, if only I'd checked my texts. I could have prepared. I could have bolted before Matt showed up. Aidan didn't know Matt was coming to this party. Aidan didn't even know there was a party. For all he knew, I'd headed home after a day at the lake.

The remaining messages included two from my parents, reminding me of my curfew, and the rest from Dan and Mason.

Mason: *We've got your back*

Dan: *We'll tell Matt your a Cage Fighter. Driving the Cage like a champ!*

Dan: **you're*

Dan: *I won't actually tell him that*

Which reminded me Dan and Mason were clueless about my status update with Aidan. Unless Aidan shared our news today at the faire. I hoped he had—it would be a relief.

Knowing they had my back with Matt home early, and a thumbs-up to move forward with Aidan? Perfect.

I tucked my phone into my back pocket.

When I emerged from the bathroom, half the party had moved back outside. Natalie sat on the couch in the living room. "Are you leaving?" she asked me.

"It's getting late." I checked her expression. She was either playing down the tension between us or she and I really were back to normal. "You want a ride home?"

She chewed at her lip. "I could go, sure."

She didn't want to. "I can go back myself if you have a ride."

Before we could go any further with that conversation, Brandon burst through the door from the garage.

"Hey, guys? Listen up." He tapped a button on his phone and the music in the house stopped. "The cops are here."

Chapter Twenty-Two

♥

Things I DON'T plan to ever get:

- A bad tattoo
- A perm for my hair
- A failing grade
- A police record

The cops breaking up a house party had to be on somebody's summer list, but not mine.

My mind raced through possibilities. Breathalyzers. Calls to parents. Citations. *Arrests*. Let's just say there was enough alcohol in this house to fill an above ground pool. Okay, a kiddie pool. Still.

Brandon pointed at us. "Everybody stay here, stay quiet. Manny, tell everybody outside to shut up and stay low. I'll be back." The door closed behind him, leaving the rest of us to shrink back from the windows.

Outside, a few risk-takers took off running across the yard, cutting through neighboring lawns.

Only the kitchen's under-cabinet lighting remained on, casting a dim glow through the half-empty liquor bottles covering the kitchen island. We were so screwed.

After ten minutes, Brandon returned. "Alright, fam, let's keep the noise down and we're good."

Manny hoisted himself from the floor where he'd been sitting with his arm around Natalie. "They're not coming in?"

Natalie sighed with relief. "I don't even care why, I'm *so* glad."

"I care." Manny held up his bitten-down nails.

Brandon rinsed his hands in the sink, as if he'd only come back from wheeling out the garbage. "My parents and everybody on this lake pay the cops' salary. They're not coming in here."

Manny peered out the kitchen window. "If that was it, I need to hang out at white kid parties more often."

Brandon gave Manny a light shove. "Come on, we're all cool here. It doesn't have to be like that."

He shook his head, chuckling. "I'm not kidding. If this happened in my neighborhood, no way would the cops leave because we asked them. Once, my cousin got arrested for sitting on a curb. There were empty beer cans in the gutter. The cops said they were his. No proof, no nothing."

Brandon didn't have a response.

Not that I wanted any of us to get citations—or worse, arrested—but Manny had a point. We weren't merely lucky to get away with this party. Every one of us was underage. We'd been allowed to get away with this.

A group of kids moved through the kitchen, leaving. Out back, the deck had cleared. A lot of people had made a run for it.

"Let's get out of here," Natalie said to Manny. She looked at me. "Lila, can you drive us back to my house? I can take Manny back from there."

I grabbed my bag and keys, my curfew inching closer. "Absolutely."

Olivia gathered her bag and towel, holding it in a bundle in front of her.

"For real?" Brandon blocked our path to the garage. "Plenty of party left. Olivia? Come on."

"Sorry. Maybe another time." She moved past him.

Grace floated by with a red cup. "I'm staying. Holli, you have a ride?"

"I'll take her," I told Grace. I tossed Brandon a weak smile. "Thanks for earlier. With Matt. Making that decision."

He waved me off. "No problem. Sorry he showed up here."

I followed my friends through the open garage to the driveway. I stopped. "Where's my car?"

"Greg moved your car, remember?" Holli said, because apparently Holli paid attention.

"I know, but he said he'd move it to the street."

I trotted to the end of the drive, squinting through the dark both directions. Only a few cars remained on the street and none were mine. My heart crawled up my throat. I circled back. My car had to be here. Somewhere.

"Greg!" Natalie yelled toward the house. "Where did you park?"

Brandon came out. "I thought you were leaving."

"My car." I kept my tone even, trying to breathe. "Where is my car?"

Chris, the one who'd been recording Matt's meltdown, walked over. He held out his phone. "Hey, is this it?"

The screen showed the bumper and license plate for Goldie. The video zoomed out as a tow truck backed up and hitched onto her.

"A *tow truck*?"

Brandon swore. "It must have been before the cops came. I didn't see anything."

I pointed at Chris. "You didn't think to tell us cars were being towed?"

Chris shrugged. "I made an announcement in the house about it."

Probably when I'd been outside. "Let me see that again."

The video showed my car beside a sign. I stomped to the street. "There's a No Parking sign *right here*." AT ANY TIME covered the bottom half of the sign.

"I'm sure it was a misunderstanding," Natalie said, her voice swallowed by the night. Or my rage.

"Why not a ticket? Who tows a car immediately?" I could not believe this. "Why are these other cars still here? Why only my car?"

"Beats me. These rich people do what they want." Chris looked at Brandon. "No offense." He gestured to the house next door, a three-story modern home with meticulous landscaping. "They probably have their own deal with the cops about how to treat house parties."

I looked past him to the neighbor's house. Tire tracks ground up the grass beside the curbless street. The tracks clearly led into the neighbors' yard. Cars had been parked *on the lawn*. I spun around. "*Where is Greg?*"

Brandon winced. "He texted. He took off with some other guys."

Beautiful. Just beautiful. "So how do I get my car back?"

Manny shook his head. "You have to call the impound lot."

Okay. I'd gone to one of those with Dad to pick up a car for his crew member.

"Lila." Natalie moved in front of me. It was possible I wasn't seeing anything in my peripheral other than the clear-as-water No Parking AT ANY TIME sign. "Let's figure out how to get home."

"I'm not leaving my car."

"The lot isn't open," Manny said, scrolling through his phone. "I did a map search and the closest one is here." He showed me the screen, but the map meant nothing. I didn't know this town. "It says closed by 6 p.m. Saturday."

We were well past 6 p.m. How it made sense to be closed but still tow cars was beyond me. Manny had the phone on speaker calling the listing he'd found.

What would I tell my parents? I could say Goldie broke down, but Dad or Grandpa would insist on taking me to pick her up, and how would I explain the towing?

Manny gave me a thumbs-up. "The voice message says open tomorrow at nine." He hung up and looked at me. "Give me your number and I'll text you the info. You can pick it up tomorrow."

Tomorrow.

"You guys can crash here," Brandon said.

Stay here? No way. "I have to get home. My parents expect me."

"Same," said Holli.

"Me three," Natalie added.

Brandon scrubbed the back of his neck. "Well, I've been drinking, so…"

Of course. Brandon couldn't drive. *Of course.*

I marched over to him and held out my hand. "Give me the keys."

Chapter Twenty-Three

♥

Notes from *Teen Talk: How to Make (and Keep!) Friends (library paperback, borrowed Freshman year)*

- *Ask how your potential friend is doing before talking about yourself*

- *Trust your new friend with a small task - then they will trust you*

- *Follow the rules and trouble won't know where to find you*

- *Get plenty of sleep - start each day at your brightest*

I wished I could say I couldn't sleep. Last night's face-plant into my pillow apparently knocked me out so hard I'd slept through my alarm. No, check that. No alarm set. I rolled over and squinted at the clock. One hour before my shift at the golf range started.

I checked my phone.

Manny: *Did you get your car?*

I squeezed my eyes shut again. My car. No luck waking in an alternate timeline. My car sat imprisoned in an impound lot thirty-some miles away. I'd managed to evade parental questioning last night after Natalie dropped me off. By this time of day, they'd notice my car was missing. And I needed a ride to work.

This day was starting out amazing.

After showering and dressing in my mostly-clean work polo, I carefully approached the stairs and braced for impact. I reached the bottom of the stairs only to be greeted by silence.

"Hello?"

Nothing.

I dashed to the kitchen and opened the door to the garage. Empty. My parents were gone.

A note in the kitchen said they were meeting for brunch with friends and would stop by a home improvement show at one of the nearby community centers. Work stuff.

At the bottom of the note, as a P.S:

Did you leave your car at Natalie's? XoXo

So, they'd noticed my car was missing but assumed the best. That bought me time. I tapped the link Manny sent last night for the tow lot. Getting there today was crucial. My parents wouldn't suspect—hold up. My breath caught as I read further down the screen.

"You're joking," I said at my phone. It cost *one hundred and twenty dollars* to get my car back? Over *one hundred* dollars to get my car when it never should have been parked illegally to begin with. I slammed my phone on the dining table. This was so unfair.

If I'd had Greg's number, I would have called it and put the speaker next to the garbage disposal when he answered.

I needed to get to the tow lot. Somehow.

Speaking of getting somewhere, the kitchen clock told me I had fifteen minutes until my shift started.

Looked like my ride was tomato red.

I mentally sorted the best options for getting my car out of impound.

Natalie had a church thing all day with her family. I had Olivia's number now, but it turned out her parents grounded her for coming home smelling like a distillery after someone dumped their drink on her by accident. I would have tried Holli, but she wasn't old enough to drive. Grace? I didn't have Grace's number. To be honest, even if I did, I doubted she'd be up for it. On the ride back last night, since we'd all had to leave with me driving Brandon's SUV, Grace belted sea shanties the whole way. She was probably still asleep with a wicked hangover to look forward to.

Softball friends. I imagined going through my team list asking any one of them to drive me north to an impound lot. Were any of them at the friend level one could ask to drive to an impound lot in a dinky lake town they'd never heard of? My breath came shallow. *Super awkward.* But I might not have a choice.

I stopped by the Teed Off! kitchen, parking my cart beside the entryway as Joe opened the door.

"Is that your scooter out there?" he asked. "Looks vintage."

"Yup, all mine. Just call me the Tomato Tornado." I winced at my own Dad Joke.

"You and ketchup—kind of a thing, huh?" He chuckled.

I hadn't even connected the scooter and my not-love affair with the red sauce. Somehow, ketchup mocked me even outside of work. "I've been having car trouble."

"Need me to take a look? I'm pretty handy."

"Uh, no but thanks." No way would I ask Joe to drive me to the tow lot. He had a family to take care of when he wasn't here running the kitchen. The last thing he needed was an irresponsible kid asking him to fetch her car from impound. "Thanks for the offer. I've got it covered." Hopefully.

"There she is."

I turned at Mason's voice in the hall behind me. Beside him, Aidan held his arm out toward me. A small burlap bag tied at the top with a black and white patterned ribbon sat on top of his outstretched hand.

"For you, M'Lady," he said, nodding toward the bag.

M'Lady! I couldn't help a squee. "Really? For me?"

Aidan's eyes met mine. A burst of heat flowed through me.

I plucked the gift from his hand and tugged the ribbon apart. Curled inside lay a piece of leather with designs imprinted on it. Thin leather strips hung off one end and looped through a closure. A wrist cuff. Detailed into the leather, the outline of a dragon.

The cuff was exactly the type of craft I loved. Unique and handmade. "Thank you so much. I love this."

Aidan smiled the smile that turned my knees to goo. And then he kissed me. Right there in front of Dan and Mason.

I couldn't even kiss back. "*Aidan.*"

"It's cool, Lila," Mason said, grinning. "We know."

"High five." Dan waited for me to accept the hand smack.

I stared at Aidan. "You told them?"

Mason laughed. "Give us some credit. It wasn't hard to figure out."

"They asked me what was going on between us." Aidan had his hands shoved into his pockets, his cheeks flushed. "I hope you're not mad."

"Mad? No." Relief. So much relief. "I'm glad you guys aren't mad."

We'd come so far, the four of us. I laughed thinking how I'd dreaded working with them weeks ago. My laugh strained and detoured into a mangled groan.

It was happening. My throat constricting, my lip trembling. I was about to lose it.

"Hey, what's wrong?" Aidan inched closer.

"It's nothing. I'm fine."

I wasn't fine. I was freaking out. I couldn't hide, unless I ran and—

"We don't mind you and Aidan are hooking up," said Mason.

"It's not that—"

"Jen's coming," Dan said in a breath. He and Mason took off. Jen took a turn toward the golf bays, walking away from us.

Aidan still stood in front of me. "What's going on?"

It was no use keeping this in. I had hours to go on my shift. "It's my car. Last night...didn't go as expected." I told him about the party and its clearly inadequate parking situation and Greg who failed to read signs. "It's my own fault. Anyway, my car is in impound. I'm trying to figure out how to get it."

The look on Aidan's face was not clear to me. Part confusion for sure, another part steely and closed off, but a touch of something else. Understanding—sympathy maybe? He blinked and his expression shifted to a confident resolve. "We should go now. I'll tell Jen it's an emergency."

"What?"

"I'm taking you to get your car."

"I have to work. You have to work."

"The impound lot will charge you more the longer your car sits there. Your shift ends after eight. It will be too late."

Aidan headed toward the golf bays, to where Jen disappeared.

I abandoned my cart. "Aidan. We can't leave."

He didn't stop walking. "Are your parents taking you later to get your car?"

When I didn't answer, he turned to look back at me. My response evident in my near tears and panic.

"Look," he said. "I've done this before. Believe me— sooner is better. Take the cart back to the supply closet and I'll take care of Jen."

Whatever taking care of Jen meant, the end result brought me to the passenger seat of Aidan's truck.

The air in the truck cab hung thick with heat and silence. Aidan turned to me as I moved toward him. All at once, our lips came together in a frantic kiss.

Aidan pulled back first. "I'm glad you're okay."

"Matt's back," I blurted.

Obviously, no guy ever wanted to hear about the ex who came before him, especially after a kiss like that, but my blurting tendencies around Aidan were uncontrollable.

"I know. You responded to my texts."

I hadn't said much, but I'd wanted to let him know the messages were received. Just too late to matter.

"The party. He was there last night. With everything else I didn't get to that part."

Aidan stilled. "Matt came to the lake? You *saw* him?"

I nodded.

He looked dazed. "What happened?"

I explained how Brandon kicked him out and Manny had his back. "The overall vibe toward him was pretty hostile."

Aidan leaned back at an angle. "How did Matt take it?"

"Not well."

He started the truck and drove us to the highway. We didn't speak. I knew Aidan wasn't mad. Not at me. He was probably stewing with emotions, same as me. I smoothed my fingers across the leather cuff on my wrist.

Aidan pointed to my backpack. "Do you have cash? If you don't, we should take the next exit and stop at the bank."

"Okay, sure." No point in getting all the way there and having the tow lot reject my debit card.

Aidan turned at the next exit. We found a branch of my family's bank in the retail strip a mile down. I got out to use the walk-up ATM.

I clicked account balance. My parents had locked down my college savings, so I only had access to my checking account. Thankfully, they'd told me to wait a few pay checks before making payments back to them for the trip. The ATM spit out my cash. I cringed at the balance.

Returning to the truck, I slammed the door shut. "Sorry."

"It's okay."

We took off again. This time I couldn't think of anything to say. He was being so nice. And why? What had I done for him?

"You don't have to beat yourself up, you know."

I shoved the cash into the pocket of my backpack. "How do you know what I'm thinking?"

"Lucky guess."

As much as I hated to say it, I had to say it. "We should talk about Matt."

He sighed. "Yeah. I've been avoiding texting him back. I don't know what to say."

Silence took over again until Aidan broke it with the stereo. Familiar female vocals sang out.

"Hey, is this—?"

"Utra," he finished for me. "I've been listening to her. You're right about the quantum physics poetry. It's cool."

We talked about music until the lake exit. Aidan tapped his phone and the GPS chimed in with where to turn. We reached the lot in minutes.

"You don't have to come in with me," I told him. "I can take it from here."

He gave me his best stink face. "No way. I'm coming in."

I got out and stood in front of the one-story building and its weathered sign for Peterson's Auto Lot. Something nagged at me, deep down.

I turned to Aidan. "You're not annoyed at me."

"I'm not. What do you mean?"

"This is the very definition of inconvenient. You left work and even covered for me with Jen. We had to stop at the bank because I didn't even bother to plan ahead and get cash and you don't seem even the slightest bit annoyed."

He scrutinized my face, even though I didn't think I was talking in code. "I wouldn't have driven you here if I was."

Matt. That was it. Matt would be annoyed. He would have complained the whole way here about how unfair it all was. Easygoing Lila wouldn't have bothered Matt with something like this anyway. She avoided complications.

Aidan's hand found mine. "Look. This is a dumb thing. It sucks that it costs money. I know that's hard for you right now."

Aidan couldn't have been more different than Matt. How had they ever been best friends? And how had I never seen their differences?

Inside, we tapped a bell at the desk until a bored guy sauntered over. I gave him my name and make and model of the car.

He hit the keys on a grime-coated desktop PC. "That'll be one-eighty."

"You mean one hundred twenty," I corrected. "That's the price on your website."

He tapped a laminated sheet taped to the counter. The plastic corners curled at the edges. "Overnight storage cost."

I gripped the cash in my sweaty palm. "But this here, the one-twenty, is the cost of one day in impound. Yes, it was stored overnight. One night included in the tow fee." I tapped his laminated sheet back at him.

"I said one-eighty." The guy didn't look so bored now. He scrubbed a hand over his ruddy face. "How 'bout I cut you a deal for one-sixty."

His "deal" was still forty more dollars than the website and his lousy laminated sheet. "This is ridiculous." I made a point to shove my cash into my pocket. I spun on my heel and pushed open the greasy glass door, expecting any second to hear *"Miss? Go ahead and pay us the one hundred twenty."*

No voice called after me.

Gravel crunched underfoot as Aidan caught up. "Lila. We have to pay them or you don't get your car back."

I only had an extra eight dollars from before the ATM stop. "I don't have enough."

"I do. Come on."

I grit my teeth and followed Aidan back inside. One hundred and sixty dollars lighter in cash, we walked out with my keys biting into my palm.

The lot guy moseyed past us and opened the lock on the chained gate. I spotted Goldie two cars in and ran to her.

I hit the auto-unlock and yanked open the passenger side door. My glove box hung open with papers scattered on the seat and floor. A towel and water bottle were tossed on the back seat. "Hey. It's a mess in here."

Aidan joined me. "Look through everything. Make sure you're not missing personal property."

Murder, murder, murder. I took a breath and combed through the mess.

Aidan crouched in the backseat. "I found a notebook. Is there anything else important you would have left in here? Anything valuable?"

Cars buzzing past on the busy street faded to a drone. A cold sensation pressed against my chest.

The trunk. *The trunk, the trunk, the trunk.*

I scrambled backward out of the car. *"Ow."* The back of my head made contact with the door frame. Wincing, I hit the trunk unlatch button beneath the driver's seat.

Aidan popped up still in the backseat. "Lila?"

"Gertie." Her name fell out of my mouth.

"Gertie?"

"In my trunk."

"Why is Gertie in your trunk?"

"To take to Grandpa's." I rubbed my head to dull the sting, but the worse sensation came from my gut. "He has a better workshop than we do with more tools. I planned to take her there the other day, but we had to switch times. I just left her in the trunk."

How had I forgotten about the girl robot and her shiny pink face? She'd probably rolled all over the place after the tow truck hoisted and dragged my car however many miles. Driving my car to the lake had been a last-minute choice. Gertie was supposed to sit secured in my trunk at Brandon's until visiting Grandpa tonight.

"She better not be dented." I flipped the trunk open and gasped.

Aidan slid beside me. "I just see a blanket and more notebooks."

I stared into the space where I absolutely, definitely had laid Gertie the robot, tucked between an old sleeping bag and reusable grocery sacks.

Aidan looked at me. "The trunk is empty."

Yes. Yes, it was.

Chapter Twenty-Four

♥

A list I didn't make:

- What filled my trunk

"You're sure you left Gertie in here?" Aidan asked me.

This was ridiculous. This could not be happening. "I think I would remember whether or not I'd packed an animatronic mini-golf robot in my car." How could a robot disappear? Who would even want it? I couldn't replace a vintage mini-golf robot.

I spun around. "Hey!"

The impound lot guy slouched over his phone, waiting on us to close the gate.

"I *said*, hey! You!"

He tapped a rusted metal sign affixed to the chain link fence.

PETERSON'S AUTO IS NOT RESPONSIBLE FOR LOST OR STOLEN ITEMS

"Not responsible?" I marched toward him, arms flailing. "That's exactly what you're responsible for. Moving my car to your *secure* lot. Why even bother with this lock?" I kicked a rock at the gate.

Aidan waited a few paces back. "Lila, come on. We'll figure this out after we get out of here."

"Listen to your boyfriend," the guy said.

Fabulous. Way to introduce *that* conversation into the middle of this.

Aidan placed a hand at the crook of my arm. "I promise, we'll figure this out."

"These tow trolls. They had my keys. They could have sold Gertie for scrap metal."

We both fell silent. Aidan closed the trunk and shut the rear door. "I'm sorry."

"Don't be sorry. This is my fault. Greg was an idiot for moving my car to a no parking zone, but I'm the one who let him. This is on me." I was like a bowling ball let loose, leaving a flattened path of destruction. "Now I owe you money."

"Don't worry about it." He smiled weakly. "It's a shame Gertie's apron is gone. I was proud of my pleating."

I'd been so careless. Now Aidan's efforts had been wasted too. And I owed him that money, regardless of what he said.

He reached for my hands. "You okay to drive?"

Besides being blinded by rage? Sure, I could see well enough to get home.

I closed the trunk, realizing I'd never dropped off those old notebooks to the dump. How was that for symbolic? I literally hauled my baggage with me.

Aidan returned to his truck and I reunited with Goldie. I steeled myself against my emotions. I refused to cry right now.

We made our way back to Teed Off! where I had my scooter to deal with.

Aidan parked beside me at the edge of the lot by the dumpster. We met at the back of his truck. "I think you should head home and take the rest of the day off," he told me.

"I can't. I need the money." My shoulders slumped at the thought of going back in there to mop and clean. My bones ached.

"I can ride Red Fury to your house later, since you've got two vehicles here."

"Red Fury?" He was trying to make me laugh. Almost succeeding. "I don't know. I can't think straight."

He moved closer. His touch rested cool against my skin. Steadying. Looking up the extra inches he had on me in height, his eyes met mine. Deliberate, confirming.

Aidan had this way of looking at me like he saw all of me. Seeing me and accepting. Freak outs, mishaps, and all. I ran my fingers along the back of his neck and pulled him into a kiss.

Every kiss with him felt new and different and familiar all at once.

"I sure know how to romance a pretty girl," he said after pulling back. "A little sunshine and some dumpster."

"At least I'm not under it looking for my helmet. What were you doing with my helmet that day anyway?"

A shadow crossed his face. "I'd just gotten the master keys from Jen and was unlocking the bin—it doesn't matter. I'm sorry. I was never mad at you, you know. If anything, I was…jealous."

"Jealous? Of who?"

He leveled his gaze. "Who do you think? He had a girlfriend who would do anything for him and he threw it away. While I admittedly considered you a little pathetic—"

"*Hey.*" I swatted him.

"*—at the time,*" he added. "Even then, he didn't deserve you. You were the one to show me how much Matt changed. He didn't care about any of us anymore. He only cared about fitting in with people he thought were cooler."

Kind of like I had. More like, exactly how I'd *planned.* "I chased popularity too."

"Look where it got you. Making out by a dumpster in the parking lot of your crappy summer job."

"Who's making out?" I made a show of looking around. "I see no making out."

He kissed me again. Deep and meaningful, this kiss wasn't messing around. Aidan liked me. He truly liked me. And the best part? He liked me for me. Lila Actual.

"You've got to me kidding me."

I shirked back like I'd been stung. The voice spun dread through my veins.

Matt. Matt *again.*

Aidan and I froze in a half embrace. I stood there speechless. No speech to be had.

"So, this is how you really spent your summer." Matt's dry tone came fully loaded with anger. With hurt. "You couldn't have me, so you had to steal my best friend."

Chapter Twenty-Five

♥

Potential Date Options with Matt:
   (fall of Junior year)
- *Movie (obviously)*
- *A party at a senior's house*
- *College campus party (#goals)*
- *Apple picking and corn maze*
- *WinterFest concert downtown (tickets on sale Oct. 15)*
- *Ice skating (over the holidays)*
- *A cooking class*
- *Learn about Portuguese food (as prep for possible study abroad trip?) (too dorky)*
- *Hike or bike a trail*

   I fumed all through the remainder of my shift because yes—I returned to work after picking up my car. Like I'd told Aidan, I needed the money. My parents wouldn't expect me home for another few hours.

   I fumed all night after I got home. I didn't steal Aidan from Matt. It wasn't nearly the same thing as what Matt did to me with Meghan. Everything had been going well—mostly well—until he'd shown up again.

At work the next day, I continued to fume over Matt. I'd say I was running on fumes, but that implied a nearly empty tank and my rage at Matt fueled me.

Jen appeared in the lobby in front of me as I walked in. "Lila. I need to speak with you in my office."

I took a breath to center myself. I needed to get my act together.

I followed her and froze in the office doorway. A visitor sat in a chair facing her desk.

Jen closed the door behind us. "I understand you know our former employee."

The visitor turned and grinned. A wicked, unfriendly grin.

"Hey, Lila," said Matt.

I did not like this. Not one bit. Matt home early, for inexplicable reasons, and here on my AstroTurf. I knew it was bad news when we ran across him in the parking lot yesterday.

It took a second to register another guest also sat in the room. "*Gertie.*" I clapped a hand over my mouth. *Never allow me to play poker. Ever.*

"You named that thing?" Matt laughed. "What were you even doing with it? Playing dress-up?"

My vision narrowed. Gertie's handmade apron was flipped up on one side, as if smashed at a clumsy angle by something heavy.

Jen moved to her side of the desk but remained standing. Power move. "Lila, Matt tells me this is property of Teed Off! and that it was found in your car. Can you explain?"

My brain couldn't process quickly enough. "*Found?*" I lasered a glare at the guy I'd once shared my hopes and dreams with. At least the socially-approved ones. "You *found* this?"

He shrugged with an all-too-cool-and-collected expression. "More like I recovered stolen property. It was left unsecured."

In my *locked* trunk? I stared at him as the pieces tumbled into place.

Matt had taken the robot. Matt, at the party. The Matt who'd been scorned after being kicked out.

Greg moving my car. Greg apparently not locking my car. Matt must have looked around in it for some gross and invasive reason. Because I'd humiliated him.

"The tow truck." I pointed at him, my hand trembling. "You. Tell me it wasn't you."

"I wouldn't know anything about a tow truck." The malicious gleam in his eyes told a different story.

That was why it had only been my car towed. I'd been targeted. "You absolute trash barrel."

"Lila," Jen cut in. "You haven't answered me. Clearly, you two have a history. You'll have to deal with your baggage on your own time. Now, explain."

I swallowed. "I...the robot is for my proposal. For the bonus."

She raised a brow. "You simply took this from the business for your own personal use?"

"My intention was to fix it. Use her as a showcase piece to the mini-golf I was proposing." This was not at all how I'd planned to share my idea.

"A mini-golf? That was your proposal?"

"I found this." Matt handed Jen a notebook. The one with my sketches of the course and robot schematics. Wait, I thought Aidan had found that notebook in the backseat. No, must have been a different one. There were so many.

Jen sifted through the plans, but not long enough to take in any detail. She let the notebook fall to her desk. "Why didn't you come to me for permission?"

I bit down on the inside of my lip. "I'm sorry."

"This idea is hugely out of scope for what we're looking for in an employee workplace proposal."

Matt snickered.

I bit down harder, tasting copper.

"I'm afraid I have to disqualify you from the bonus, Lila."

I couldn't have heard her right. A numb sensation washed over me. I wouldn't even get a shot. The whole proposal, scrapped.

She folded her arms. "Additionally, because of the theft, I also need to let you go. Collect your last check on Friday."

My breath was stolen. "What? No! Jen, I'm so sorry. This is a misunderstanding." I jumped out of the chair, desperation leaping forward and taking me with it. "Please, give me a chance to make it up."

She let out a sigh. "My hands are tied. If employees are caught stealing, we cut them loose."

Except I hadn't been caught. She'd been *told*. "So, you're going to take his word for it? That he happened to find the robot in my car?" This was a total last-ditch effort. Jen only knew about the robot from what Matt told her.

Matt held up his phone. "I have proof." His screen showed my car with the trunk open, the license plate clearly visible, and the top part of Gertie sticking up.

Any last retorts dissolved. He'd stolen Gertie from me, only Gertie had never been mine to steal. No matter how I spun this, I was in the wrong. Now, it cost me my job.

Matt rubbed his hands together. "Jen, I'm ready to get back to work. I'll pick up the slack." He eyed me with vicious grin. "Sorry this had to come out, Jen."

He didn't look one bit sorry.

"Since I have seniority," he added, "you could switch out Mason from registration and add me."

The nerve. The very nerve.

Jen shook her head. "Don't get greedy, kid. You're not calling the shots."

Any victory at that jab faded fast. I'd been fired. *Fired.* I'd never failed so badly at anything in my life.

"I'm sorry," I squeaked out. Jen probably saw me as some immature teenager with sticky fingers and a vengeful ex-boyfriend. I handed over my supply room keys. "I liked working here. You were a good boss."

Jen's face flickered with a hint of softness. She held out her hand. "Your badge. If you have personal items in the break room, we can stop there. Matt, you can go."

I avoided looking at Matt, the scuffing of his feet toward the door grating my nerves like sandpaper against an open cut. We emerged from Jen's office. I kept my focus on the floor.

Mason stood at registration, busy with customers. I glanced back just as he looked up and noticed us. His mouth dropped open. *"What's going on?"* he mouthed at me.

But we'd already progressed to the door of the staff break room.

Please be empty, please be empty.

"Quick, hide, the boss is coming," Joe said as Jen entered ahead of me, followed by a round of laughs.

"Lila, I have stew saved for you—" Kara's words cut off when she saw my face.

I took my lunch from the fridge. My jacket from a locker on the far wall.

"What's going on?" Joe looked from Jen to me. "Are you okay, Lila?"

The break room door burst open. Matt sauntered in. "Guess who's back." He held his arms open, grinning.

"Matt, I told you to go." Jen's words came out pinched.

He barely concealed a smirk. "Didn't mean to intrude. Just wanted to say hi to the gang."

A dense silence curled around us.

Matt looked at me. "Leaving already?"

I summoned hot ash and scorching liquid tomatoes to rain down on him. Only none of that happened. Just the faint buzz of the overhead fluorescents made any sound.

Chet pointed between the two of us. "You two know each other?"

Matt perked up like a wilted plant after a spring shower. "Lila didn't tell you? Lila used to be my girlfriend. Kinda funny how she ended up here, taking my spot after I left. Taking a few other things, too."

Joe, Kara, and Chet watched me, waiting for a response. My face felt like fire. "You're the *worst*," I said to Matt through my teeth.

"Okay everybody, mind your business," Jen barked. "This isn't an episode of *Riverdale*." She banged the locker shut and walked toward the door. "Matt. You first. Go."

Matt turned backward and hit the door open with his back. Grinning the whole way.

I didn't have it in me to explain. Not with Jen holding the door, waiting to walk me out. For good.

Chapter Twenty-Six

♥

Save the Summer List:

- Get job back
- Apologize to everyone
- Learn how to not suck

I'd blown it. This whole summer ended up one colossal nightmare.

Lost my boyfriend.

Lost big money from canceling the trip.

Lost my shot at the bonus.

Lost the job to pay back my parents.

Lost the respect of my work friends.

Lost trust with Natalie.

This was what I deserved for going off-list. From the night I threw Matt's medal into the fire, I should have known I was careening toward a fatally planless path.

Once home, I closed myself in my room. My parents weren't around, but an open door offered an invitation I wasn't interested in giving.

I collapsed onto my bed and shot up again. Paced the room. Whatever I'd eaten earlier turned to acid in my stomach. *Fired.* The look on Jen's face. I'd let her down. I'd let myself down.

I fell back on my bed, letting my adrenaline discharge. I curled into a ball and faced the wall.

My phone buzzed beside me. It buzzed again, so I answered.

"I heard what happened," Aidan said before I fit in a hello.

I'd only been home ten minutes. "From Mason?"

"Yeah. I'm on my way over."

"Don't." I curled tighter. I didn't know where to start. What to say.

"This is obscene," Aidan filled in for me. "There's no way you should be losing your job over this. I'm going to Jen. I'm going to tell her I approved for you to take the robot out of the basement."

I bolted upright. "You can't, Aidan. No way."

"I figured out you took the robot and didn't ask you to take her back. I *named* her."

Well, that part was true. "Don't risk your job because I did. I should have asked Jen in the first place. Or made my proposal about liquid soap."

I expected a laugh, even a pitying one, but Aidan didn't laugh. "I'll be there soon."

I stared at the ceiling until I heard a car door shut outside. Then, the doorbell.

Still wearing my stupid green work polo, I made my way downstairs and opened the door. Aidan burst forward, taking me into his arms.

He pulled back, looking me over. "I'm so sorry."

A cloud hung over my head I couldn't step out from. "I don't know what to tell my parents."

Sunlight stretched around him from the open door. "I'm going to fix this."

He'd moved into my role—fixing what shouldn't be fixed. "Cute. Nice try, but no."

"It's not *cute*." He shifted and the sun's glare hit me. "He did this. Matt did this."

Yes, yes, he had. "But—"

"No, Lila. Do you see what's happening? He's getting back at you. He's put everything into building his reputation. He won't let this go. And then us. Seeing us together."

I walked to the front living room. The formal one no one ever sat in except special company. And those boxes of our stuff Mom had been sorting. "I don't care about Matt."

Aidan followed. "He'll get as many people on his side as he can. He manipulates. He drops people when they don't act the way he wants."

"But I don't *care*." Repeating the words forced the meaning deeper. The more the realization sank in, the more the tension loosened from my shoulders. I simply *did not care* what Matt planned to do. Or what he thought, or how he felt. I laughed in one hot burst. "It doesn't matter. All I want is to talk to people at work—Nala and Joe and the lunchroom crew. I want to tell them I'm sorry for screwing up. And for not being honest about knowing Matt. And to Natalie. I messed up with her too. I was trying to be honest, but it all came out wrong. I need a chance to explain and apologize."

Aidan threw up his hands. "It's completely stupid for Jen to let you go when I helped you, and even stupider to give

Matt his job back. You know he's not going to clean any toilets."

He didn't know Matt tried convincing Jen to switch him to registration. "That's his problem. I'll have to find another job. It sucks, but I'll find something." Paying my parents back would take forever, but that was reality. I shouldn't have banked on a shortcut with the bonus, and even worse, taking Gertie without asking. "Aidan, you have to promise me you won't go to Jen."

"What are you talking about? The only reason I didn't go right to Jen is I came here first. To see if you were okay." His breathing came hard. He watched me, waited for me to concede.

But I wouldn't. "Don't go to Jen. It's not what I want."

He folded his arms, shaking his head. "I don't get it. It's like you want Matt to get away with this."

"No, that's not it. This whole summer I've spent dealing with life without Matt. I realized I missed out on life *because of* being with him. I need to be done, officially, of reacting to Matt. Of basing any of my life around him. Getting re-hired at Teed Off! puts me back in Matt's territory. That's the last thing I need."

Aidan was quiet as he took in what I said. He paced the room, then stopped. "I don't want to work at the range anymore. Not if Matt's there. Not if I have to lie to Jen about how I helped you."

"You're going to quit? Because of me? Don't do that."

"Are you hearing what I'm saying?" He looked at me, hurt flashing in his eyes. A desperate, pleading look. More than that. Demanding. Insistent. "I'm trying to protect you. I don't want to work there after what just happened."

"But your parents—"

"I won't disappoint them. They already think I'm a quitter."

He wasn't fooling me. He cared what his parents thought and he cared about his job. This sacrifice, it was all to make up for mistakes I needed to own myself. I couldn't let him take this on.

"Aidan, you can't quit because of me." A current of anger pulsed through me. Anger at how I'd let my life end up here. "This is my problem to solve. Not yours. You still have a shot at the bonus money. Don't lose out on that."

He studied the patterned curtains. "I don't get it. Jen doesn't know what actually happened. Don't you want me by your side in this?"

I took in his face, his solemn expression, and considered all he'd done in helping me shed layers. I was so close to fully stepping out from old fake Lila. There were too many threads that needed tying before moving forward with Aidan.

"I think we should take some time to ourselves," I said. "It's best if I figure this out on my own."

The full impact of what I said sent him stepping back. Like the force of my words physically moved him. "You're...you're ending it? Ending us?"

Take it back, take it back. My heart squeezed, aching on all sides, the hurt coursing through my body. "For now."

His face twisted and he turned away. "I don't understand."

I could tell him I needed him, I wanted him, which I did, but...but I couldn't. He was too willing to set his life aside and it made me angry. I couldn't explain it. He shouldn't fix this for me. I wouldn't let him.

I squeezed my eyes shut to get the words out. "I think you should go."

And then he did.

Chapter Twenty-Seven

♥

Save the Summer List (Updated):

- ~~Get job back~~
- ~~Apologize to everyone~~
- Learn how to not suck

Let's just say, things were not awesome in the Vaughn household.

Not only did I need to fess up to my parents I'd lost my job, but I had to tell them why. Talking around the reason would not fly. As Dad predictably blew a fuse that I hadn't asked for permission to borrow the robot, I was then questioned about my car.

"I suppose it's a good time to talk about this." Dad unfolded a thin yellow sheet of paper and tossed it on the dining table in front of us.

The copy of the impound lot receipt. He must have found it beneath a notebook in the passenger seat, not hidden at all.

Yeep.

I opened my mouth, but silly me, that had been a rhetorical question. "Your car was in impound? In another county?" Dad did not blink. He was good at that not blinking thing. "What on earth did you do up in a lake county where you couldn't drive your car home? And how *did* you get home?"

"I—"

"You *lied* to us," Dad said in his coldest tone. "Repeatedly."

Mom shook her head, tsking at appropriate times.

Since he wouldn't be happy with any of my responses, I angled to get in a question of my own. "I know about the loan. Why didn't you tell me the business has been struggling? Is that why you've been selling our stuff?"

They looked at each other. Mom spoke first. "Our company paperwork is our business. It is not your concern how we handle our money."

"But if we need money that badly that I need to work minimum wage to pay you back, I think I deserve to know."

Dad pressed his fingers to his forehead. "You deserve food, shelter, and safety, which we provide."

"And love," Mom added, though Dad seemed questionable on that at the moment.

"But you weren't honest with me either." I pressed my luck hard with this stance, but if we were having this out, it all should come out. "It doesn't excuse me keeping things from you, but you kept things from me too."

Dad appeared to have an inner battle playing out and I couldn't tell if he was on the losing side or gaining ground in combat. Mom placed a hand at his back. He muttered and shook his head.

Looking at me, his spoke clearly but more softly. "Things have been hard. Your trip was a stretch for our finances, but we want you to have opportunities. Lila, you need to learn there are consequences to your actions. You will still pay us back half that money. You're also grounded other than work. Until you find paid work, you'll help us clean up the basement and do yardwork at Grandpa's."

I hated that I'd hurt them when I'd only been trying to help. I'd made some dumb mistakes along the way, but I guess that's what I needed to face now.

He nodded at the chair in front of me, so I sat. "Now, about honor."

I settled in for the long haul. Dad loved a good lecture on honesty and honor. I had a lot of listening to do.

"Lila!" Mom called to my room where I'd finished showering after a morning babysitting one of her work friends' twin daughters. A reasonably easy forty bucks once I got the six-year-olds on board with creating a water park in the backyard with a hose, trash bags, and a dusty sprinkler.

"Is it Natalie?" I shouted back down the stairs. I'd been expecting her to call, but my phone was charging downstairs.

After I'd sent Natalie an email explaining my original Social Bootcamp plans, we had a big, long chat involving two awesome boys—Ben & Jerry. (A video chat, since I was grounded from any in-person fun.) I told her I'd gotten carried away with creating what I thought was a likable identity because I believed my actual self wasn't likable enough. It sounded obviously dumb when I'd said it out loud, but maybe because I knew now it didn't matter. Natalie liked me for me.

I thundered downstairs where Mom held my phone as it connected to the kitchen charger. By penalty of Dad Law, we were not to remove that charger from the outlet by the refrigerator. "This thing's been buzzing on the counter the past ten minutes."

I checked messages. A number I didn't have a contact listing for and...Dan?

Dan: *Call me when you get this.*

I nearly hit the call icon when the phone rang in my hand.

"Dan, I'm going to need more context—"

"Lila, it's Jen. From Teed Off!"

"Hey, Jen. Uh. Hi."

"I'm sorry to bother you. If you're free, can you stop by the range?"

My heart dropped. I quick-turned my back so Mom couldn't hear me. "Are you filing a police report? I'm again, so sorry about the robot. It was my fault for not asking if I could take it." I'd started an apology letter, but got stuck on whether I should mail it or drop it off when I picked up my check. My last check.

"It's not the cops. We've had an interesting turn of events after the bonus proposals were presented today. I think your presence will make things more clear."

Nothing was clear on my end.

"Please come down if you can."

Part of me wanted to say, screw it. But loose strings. I jumped in the car and made it over in less than five. I shut off the ignition and stared at the front entrance.

It had been two weeks since my firing. Two weeks of trying not to think about the friends I'd made, the familiar schedule. Aidan.

I hadn't seen or spoken to Aidan in two weeks. By my own choosing. I was miserable.

Mustering every scrap of inner confidence I could wire together, I got out of my car and crossed the lot.

Inside, an older couple stood in the lobby wearing brightly colored polo shirts and casual knee-length shorts. Smile lines deepened by sun and age formed as the two laughed and talked to staff. They definitely owned a boat.

Jen met me at the door. "Lila, thanks for coming. I know this is unpleasant after what happened. These are the owners of Teed Off!, Bob and Tess. Please be assured, we only want to hear more from you."

I nodded, though I didn't feel assured. I just wanted to get this over with.

Jen steered me in front of the owners. "This is Lila Vaughn. She's the one who came up with the miniature golf proposal."

I whiplashed toward Jen. Why did Bob and Tess know about my proposal?

Bob rocked back-and-forth in his loafers. The leather kind with those little ties around the edges. "We forgot all about those old miniature golf parts in the basement. I figured Tess had 'em cleared out."

Tess swatted his arm. "You know I wouldn't throw anything away. It's history."

"Let's move toward my office." Jen waited on the owners to walk ahead.

"We love the innovation that's come out of the employee bonus contest," Tess explained as we walked. "We started rewarding new ideas with money after one of our own suggested energy efficient rated fixtures. They saved the facility more money than we expected."

Bob nodded at Tess. "This year's winner, Joe Morgan, had a wonderful idea for efficiency in the kitchen with a newly designed prep station."

Joe won. Great news. Still, what did any of this have to do with me?

Tess sat in the nearest chair. "When that boy brought up the mini-golf, we were intrigued. Then, well, I'll let Jennifer tell you the rest."

My head felt like the inside of a broken blender.

Jen handed me papers. The schematics and a printed copy of the proposal slides I'd drafted. "Are you the author of these notes and plans?"

"Yes."

"Where did you get the notes for the robot?"

"I wrote them myself. The schematics I found online from a vintage robotics forum. The users there helped me with questions." Bob and Tess watched Jen, and she nodded toward them. All this silent communication reminded me of my parents. "I thought I could restore a robot and show it off for the presentation. It was a stupid idea, I'm sorry."

"You chose this idea because you were in robotics club," Jen added. "Like you had on your resume."

I kept my breath steady. "Yeah."

"Thank you for confirming, Lila. Matt approached Bob and Tess with your proposal as a potential business venture."

My jaw hinged open. "He what?"

Bob placed a hand at the back of Tess' chair. "A shame that boy had to lie and take credit he didn't earn."

That jerk. That weasel. Words failed. He truly had it in for me.

I looked at each of them. "I'm so sorry. I'm sure this has to do with our...personal issues. He's upset with me. It's a long story." This was worse than explaining my breakup to my parents. Worse than Dad threatening to go to Matt's house to straighten him out. Which I wouldn't actually mind right now.

"You have quite the loyal following here, Miss Vaughn," Tess said to me. "One young man spoke up right away when he saw this fellow presenting your idea to us. What was his name, Jennifer?"

"Aidan," she answered.

My breath left me. Aidan was still protecting me even though I'd pushed him away.

Jen continued. "Aidan had photos of you and him together at a miniature golf range where he said you'd been doing research together. He told us he discovered you'd taken the robot and didn't turn you in since he believed you had good intentions. He explained it in detail."

"That left the other fella Matt downright stewing," Bob mused, chuckling to himself. "Quite a ruckus started. He accused the other boy of stealing his girlfriend. It was like one of those reality TV shows with everyone talking over each other and pointing fingers."

"That Aidan boy, he offered to take himself out of the running for the bonus," Tess added. "That right there is a young man with integrity."

"But we couldn't let him do that," Bob said. "In fact, his idea to update the registration software will be implemented too. Instead of maintaining two incompatible systems for registration and payment, we'll streamline to one product. We'll come up with a way to compensate him."

My attention ping-ponged between them. I couldn't believe Matt tried to pass off my proposal as his own. I couldn't believe Aidan offered to take himself out of the bonus, but ended up winning respect and probably some money too.

"Many of your colleagues came forward to say what a hard worker you'd been." Tess smiled at me. "They talked fondly of you."

My heart swelled at how my coworkers came to my defense. And Aidan.

Bob leveled his gaze at me. "We don't condone theft, but your heart was in the right place. Since you were borrowing, not stealing, we asked Jennifer to give you your job back."

I swung to Jen, who smiled, less formal now. "With the owners' approval, yes, you can return to work."

"Wow. Thank you." I leaned against the door frame, gathering myself. "I appreciate this so much."

Tess stood and joined me by the door. "Everyone makes mistakes. It's how you handle the consequences that matter."

I thanked her again. This was a lot to take in.

"Matt is no longer employed at Teed Off!," Jen stated evenly. "I swear, I may never hire another teenager."

"It was nice to meet you, Lila." Bob held out his hand for a formal handshake, something I'd done countless times during my parents' military service. "Tess and I were thinking. Since you're a student, we could lend you the animatronics if you'd like to work on them for a school project. They're only collecting dust."

I was so relieved the cops weren't involved and I had my job back, I hadn't expected anything else. "That's super generous. But I'm not in robotics club anymore."

"Our grandson in Ohio is part of a county-wide robotics team," Bob said. "Their robots fight each other."

"Isn't it the coolest?" I blurted.

"Did you know there's a regional club that includes Ginsburg?" Tess asked. "I bet they'd love to have you."

Life sure had a funny way of coming full circle. "Sounds like a plan. I'll return the robots to you in working order. Maybe we can do a display in the lobby and show pictures of the old mini-golf course."

Tess' eyes sparkled. "What a great idea for the next anniversary."

I left Jen's office practically hovering.

"Lila," Mason called over from registration. "Are you back?"

Dan popped into view on the other side of him.

I let out my breath in a whoosh. "I'm back."

High fives all around.

Dan leaned across the desk, keeping his voice low. "Did you know Matt tried to get Mason moved from registration? He told Jen there'd been a complaint."

Mason scoffed. "What is *up* with him?"

"He's fired, that's what."

"He is?" Dan and Mason said at once.

"Is that not common knowledge? Jen told me."

Dan scowled and dug out his wallet. He slapped a twenty-dollar bill on the desk.

Mason scooped it up and slid the bill into his back pocket. "Less than ten days."

"You had a bet riding on how long he'd last?" I couldn't help laughing.

"It's just business," Mason said with a straight face.

I nodded toward the staff hall. "Besides the Matt drama, how did the presentations go?"

Mason tapped his cell phone against the desk edge. "My pitch was an app with Teed Off! discounts and mini-games. A puzzle golf game with different point tiers."

That sounded awesome. "I'm sorry it didn't win."

Mason shrugged. "Thanks. Everyone wanted Joe to get the money."

"Yeah, now he can build his deck."

Mason and Dan exchanged looks. "Don't you know?" Dan asked.

"Know what?"

Mason greeted a customer over my shoulder. I stepped aside to the end of the desk where Dan slid over to meet me. "He's building a ramp from the back door to the house. For his son."

I must have looked totally lost because Dan continued. "His son uses a wheelchair."

I knew Joe's son's name was Joe Jr. and he played Minecraft and Super Smash Brothers and collected bugs in the summer. "I didn't know about the wheelchair. Why would he say he wanted to build a deck?"

"He didn't want sympathy points. He wanted it to be fair."

I could see his point. Now that I was employed again, I could ask Joe more about his family. If he was willing. I'd lied to him about knowing Matt. Maybe he and the others wouldn't want to talk to me, even if they had stuck up for me to Jen.

"My proposal was a social media campaign with a choose your own ending fantasy story," said Dan.

"I like the idea of having a story. Did the fantasy tie into golf?"

Farther down the desk, Mason mouthed, *don't ask.*

Dan gave an overview involving dragons and a planet that mined the material golf balls were made of, which he'd had to look up.

"I heard Aidan's idea will be implemented too," I said, since I wasn't sure how to follow up dragons and golf ball mining. It felt weird talking about Aidan after I told him I needed space. And yet, Aidan had been the one to stick up for me and call out Matt on his lies.

Dan nodded toward the golf bays. "He's here, covering your shift, actually."

I stepped back. "I'll call Jen later and see when she wants to add me to the schedule." My head spun. Seeing Aidan would only add to the spin. "I'm going to take off."

I walked out of Teed Off! in a daze, ready to shut myself in my room and reconsider life, my existence in this universe, Simulation Theory.

"Hey, Lila. Can we talk?"

I reached the bottom steps and came face-to-face with the person who started it all. Matt.

Matt stood at the foot of the front steps out of view from the main doors. His name, once painful to say, now tasted dull against my lips.

Immediately, his hands went up in defense. "I only want to talk."

A rush of anger hit me square in the chest. "Matt, you got me *fired*. You told on me to Jen, laughed about it, and tried to pass off my business proposal as your own. You got my car towed. You owe me money."

His confidence flickered. "You have to admit, it was pretty weird finding an old robot in your trunk."

He wanted me to admit it was "weird" he stole something from my trunk?

His hands shot up again. "Okay, I get it. You're mad. I guess I just reacted. People were pissed at me. I didn't mean to get you fired. Not really."

I breezed past him. Only my chest did this tugging thing. He was a loose end. I had a chance to say what I needed and finally, forever, be actually finished with him. "You want to talk? Fine."

Matt chuckled. "You seriously couldn't find a different job?"

I wasn't interested in catching up on our summers. "What do you want?"

He flinched. "Can we sit?"

Matt sat on a stone bench, his legs wide and taking up space. I took the bench across from him. Direct sun nailed me in the eyes while his offered shade from a tree. "So, things got kind of crazy since I came back. The lake house, the stuff with that robot."

I waited.

"I shouldn't have done you the way I did. I should have told you earlier about Meghan."

I said nothing.

"I know I said we were drifting apart. I'm sure that's been bugging you since I left." He blinked a few times. "It was lame how I brought your grandma into it. You were sad when she got sick and all, so of course you were going to be distant or whatever. Coach was riding me about the team, and then the Brazil trip. There was so much they wanted us to do to prepare. I took those extra language lessons with the tutor. It was a lot. Meghan, she understood."

For a moment, Matt appeared as wavy lines. Heat or visible rage, too soon to tell. Beyond us across a strip of parking spaces stood the dumpster. With a little combustion, it could symbolize this conversation.

"Once I got down there, I realized Brazil was a mistake. Being in another country does that to you. Everything is so different. I didn't have anyone to lean on, you know? I thought Meghan would be that person."

"And?" I found myself asking.

"And...Meghan wasn't you." Matt looked at me, his eyes soft at the edges, his lips lightly parted. "She didn't listen to me the way you do. She didn't know all the things you used to pay attention to. She was all about meeting the locals. She'd go on day trips without me. When you and I planned for Brazil, we talked about all the stuff we'd do together."

A picture formed in my mind. I had the impression this picture did not match what Matt put together.

He inched forward on the bench and reached for my hands. I scooted back. Matt coughed and rubbed his hands together to play off my rejection. "Meghan couldn't compete with you. I don't think any girl can."

They were dream words. Words I would have written as a spell and shed blood for as a freshman. A boy flying home early from his summer abroad to tell me I was the only girl for him? What could be more perfect?

"I want you back, Lila."

I didn't know what he expected me to say in response to his *no girl can compete with you* speech. All is forgiven? Let's go out again? I can't live without you?

I took a steadying breath. "You cheated on me. You only fessed up because you were caught. You embarrassed me in front of my friends and cost me my job as revenge. You cost me money."

Matt blinked. He shook his head, like he was emptying sand from his ears. He sprung from the bench. "Revenge? How about hooking up with my best friend?"

I shot up too. "Aidan?"

"Yeah, Aidan. He won't answer my texts. He won't talk to me."

"Your best friend title might need to be amended."

"Amended—what? What are you *talking* about?" Matt stomped away and circled back. "Look, I told you I was sorry for how I treated you."

"No, you didn't. You talked around an apology. And let's go back to Meghan. The only thing you feel bad about is how she didn't one hundred percent focus on you like I did. This is where I come in with my one and only apology." The boldness inside me grew unshakable. "I'm sorry I was such a good girlfriend. I was so good, I tricked you into believing you had to do absolutely nothing to gain my devotion. You could have spat on me, and I'd wipe it from my face and tell you how great you were at spitting." For shame, if that wasn't a sad reality. "I wanted so much to live this fantasy of having a boyfriend, I worked constantly to make sure what we had seemed perfect. Imagine my shock learning we weren't perfect. You're right on that. We hadn't been okay for a while."

He clapped his hands once and pointed at me. "See? I knew it. You're jealous about Meghan. You only hooked up with Aidan to get back at me. Man, I can't believe Aidan fell for it."

"Fell for it? Why, because Aidan couldn't like me for me?"

"You're driving around with some old robot in your trunk. Throwing my swim medal in a fire. What's gotten into you?"

All of the hurt, the concealing, the managing my every action to be who I thought he wanted, the suppression roiled beneath my skin, searching for escape. I'd pretended too long. I'd held back too long.

"What's gotten into me is what I should have done a long time ago. I deserve better, Matt. I deserve better, and I found it. I found Aidan."

My heart cracked open. I'd given him up. I'd told Aidan to keep away because I'd been such a mess. I might deserve better, but I wasn't sure I deserved Aidan.

"Aidan saw through the person I was trying to be to the person I am," I continued. "He deserves better than how you treated him, Matt. You used him. You used Dan and Mason. They were your friends when it was convenient. Friendship isn't always convenient. Neither are relationships." I willed my tears to stay put, needing to purge this frustration. "I'm not sorry I found you with Meghan. I should thank you for waking me up. So, in the end, thank you, Matt. Thank you and goodbye."

Matt let out a dumbfounded laugh. "Thank you? *Goodbye?* Have you even been listening?"

"I don't know, have you?" Aidan appeared on the sidewalk.

I did a double take. How much had he heard?

Matt's jaw tightened. "Stay out of this, Pemberton."

Aidan stopped a mere foot from Matt. Fully removed from Matt's shadow, he created his own. "If you're mad right now, I'm sure it's because Lila told you the truth. There's no elaborate scheme here. She's been happy without you. People here like her. We're the friends you ditched when cooler people invited you out. The friends you asked to lie for you, to cover up how you'd been cheating."

"Dude." Matt backed up, laughing. "You both are *out of control.* You're jealous. Look, I get it. I took off and—"

"You don't get it." Aidan advanced, gaining ground on Matt's retreat. "You viewed Lila like your personal servant. I always wondered how you could end up with a girl so many levels above you. I knew you'd trash it someday. I only hoped Lila would notice and break it off first."

Matt scowled. "Yeah, well, she writes lists about how annoying you are."

My heart stopped. Lists...my notebook with the mini-golf notes. I'd been so scattered with my list making lately, grabbing whichever notebook I had available. The loathing Aidan lists, they covered multiple books.

Matt saw my hesitation and latched on. "Didn't think I'd read through your stuff, did you? Yeah, Aidan. She says you don't have a personality. She calls you a cronie. You're getting played."

"That's not true." I didn't dare make eye contact with Aidan. "Well, technically, it's true but I wrote those before I knew you. The real you. Back when you stole the scooter helmet and pranked me with ketchup."

Matt laughed. "Dang, I would have liked to see that. She has other weird stuff in those notebooks too. Like, practicing how to be popular." His expression grew smug. "I have to say, I liked seeing my name so many times. I should've grabbed them all and started a book club."

No. No, this was my nightmare. A never-ending one. I'd left my whole history of lists exposed in my trunk.

Finally, I ventured a look at Aidan. He stared, seething at Matt. "I saw the list myself. I don't care. I did lack a personality sometimes, trying to figure myself out. I did prank Lila and stole her helmet. We've talked through those things already. That's what mature people do. They call each other out when they've done wrong. They listen to each other. And then they change."

He was right, we had talked through it. He'd seen the real me, and he still stood here by my side.

Mason and Dan stood in the path now, shoulder to shoulder.

"We're not cool with how you wanted us to lie for you," Mason said to Matt. "We know you talked crap about us to your swim team friends."

Matt laughed with a heavy note of sarcasm. "Great, so Mason and Dan are your little lap dogs now?"

Dan's expression was void of emotion. "No lap dogging here. We were averse to conflict and didn't know how to bring this up."

"Averse to conflict? You guys are something else. Did you all agree to hate me after I left?" Matt's sarcasm eroded into bitterness. "I'm the jerk, huh? None of you cares what I went through in Brazil?"

"Did your phone fall into the ocean?" Mason faced his phone at Matt. "The last message from you came the day you got on the plane. *Don't let fools talk smack about me after the party.*"

Matt's face twisted. "So, you guys are mad I didn't *text* you? I was in *Brazil.*"

Aidan stood rooted to the spot beside me. "We don't hate you, Matt. We expect better. Call us when you're ready to be better."

Matt sneered, but the bite in his features was now flattened by hurt. He shook his head, making a point to laugh loudly in one more sarcastic burst.

One more thing. "I hope you gave Meghan an explanation."

His face scrunched in confusion. "Why?"

"Because she deserves better."

Still confused, he shook his head. "I see how it is. Whatever." He turned and walked to his car.

We all watched him, saying nothing, as Matt opened his car and got in, then drove away.

Mason let out a low whistle.

"Well, that went swimmingly." Dan kicked a loose stone into the shrubbery.

Aidan stared after the dust cloud from Matt's car. "He needed to know he hurt us."

"From the second he started talking, I knew nothing changed," I said. Yet everything had for me. This wasn't about Matt anymore. "Thanks, you guys. It means a lot that you supported me, and spoke up for yourselves."

Mason waved me off like it was nothing while Dan ran his fingers up and down the cord of his lanyard. This had probably been hard for both of them.

I turned to Aidan, my heart nearly bursting. "Thank you. You...you're here. You stuck up for me with Jen. And now... did you hear—"

"Everything," he finished. "Well, everything about me. Before that, Matt was whining about you driving around with a robot in your trunk."

"Which is the real lesson of the summer. Never drive with a stolen robot in your trunk."

He held up his pointer finger. "Never drive with a stolen robot in your trunk to a lake house where your jilted ex shows up, gets kicked out, and steals the robot in an underhanded jealousy attack."

"Why is it only exes are ever jilted?"

"Hard agree. Seems like a word that should be mainstreamed more."

"You read the list about you. About how I loathed you. You didn't say anything. Why?"

He shrugged. "Like I said, some of it was true. I had changing to do too."

"When did you see it?"

"At your house. There was a notebook open on the workbench. You went upstairs, and I flipped ahead on your plans. On the back of one of the pages..."

My eyes fell shut. "I'm sorry."

"If I thought you still believed those things, I wouldn't be standing here. Neither would you."

What a strange summer this turned out to be. Totally against plan. And maybe that was a good thing. Maybe going off book was what I needed to do more often.

I placed my hands at Aidan's shoulders and ran them up the back of his neck, looking into his brown eyes.

Aidan kissed me. I leaned into him, kissing him back. Sweet, warm, and a comfort.

"We're gonna, uh, take off." Mason's statement was followed by the scuffling of feet.

Aidan broke away. "Was that okay? You said you needed to figure things out and I didn't mean to push—"

I kissed him again. "Yes. Yes, it's okay."

He brushed his lips against my forehead. "Thanks for sticking up for us. For all of us."

I twined my fingers through his, memorizing the feel of his hands. "Thanks for doing the same for me with Jen and the owners. Speaking up won me my job back. And, I hear you might be winning some bonus money after all."

Aidan's cheeks reddened. "Yeah, the owners asked what I'd do with the money if I'd won. I started to tell them I'd save it for college, but told them about my cosplay weapon crafting. They asked a lot of questions. Which was cool that they seemed into it all."

"So, you're going to do it? Invest in making more prop weapons for people who need modifications?"

He nodded. "Yeah. My parents are actually impressed for once. Only it's more about my idea to streamline the registration and payment software. They think I should pursue IT information systems." He rolled his eyes.

"At least they see you committed to a project. That's a win."

He kissed my forehead.

The small gesture sent a buzz through me. "I'm sorry I pushed you away."

He squeezed my hand. "You don't have to end things to give each other breathing room."

"I think the time might have been good for both of us."

"*You're* good for both of us." He said it like an insult, but I knew better. That grin and dimple gave him away.

"You are ridiculous. Never change."

I slid closer, thankful for the shade overhead. I could stay here all day.

We kissed again. I breathed into him, letting go. This moment mattered. Not what happened yesterday or what would happen next. Just us, here, right now. Us, who we were now and whoever we wanted to be.

Epilogue

♥

I bit into the juiciest, most tender turkey leg I'd ever feasted on. Okay, to be honest, I hadn't feasted on many turkey legs. Maybe not any unless dry Thanksgiving turkey counted.

I grabbed another napkin and dabbed at meat juice trickling down my arms. "Huzzah!"

"Huzzah!" Aidan saluted with his own drumstick, courtesy of Ye Olde Renaissance Faire.

"You guys are *so* weird." Natalie gestured at us with her veggie pita sandwich.

Aidan planted a greasy kiss on my cheek. I squealed and landed an equally greasy kiss right smack on his lips.

"Get a hut," Dan called out. When none of us laughed, he threw up his hands. "You know, like, get a room. With a thatched roof."

I shook my head. "Nope. You missed the runway on that one. Sailed right past."

Lady Ariana, sitting beside Dan, batted at his arm and giggled. No surprise there. The girl giggled at anything Dan said.

She may not have been the queen, but her cousin was a member of the royal court with inside access to the guild and the guild after-party. After meeting in the central square when the parade dispersed, Ariana and Dan kept on talking. Hours later, they'd become inseparable.

I bumped Natalie with my shoulder. "In another hour, we'll have you dressed up like it's 1599."

"I was thinking something like that." She pointed at a young woman passing our picnic table in a flowy skirt, fairy wings, and slipper shoes with ribbons crisscrossed up the leg.

"The fairy look is cute." I could easily picture Natalie wearing a similar outfit.

"Not the fairy. The other one."

I craned my neck. "The archer? With the cape? Definitely cool."

The woman wore a long brown cape with a hood peeled back and had a black leather quiver for arrows slung over her shoulder. Natalie the archer? Sure, I could see it.

My own costume was a DIY mix for the budget-thirsty—a handkerchief skirt I'd created from a YouTube video by tying together strips of fabric from an old sheet, a hand-tooled leather belt (thank you, Aidan) with loops to hook my custom tankard (for free not-actually-beer refills) paired with a simple tank top. The handmade corsets in the Ren Faire shops were tempting but needed to wait until I didn't owe my parents money.

Manny returned carrying two bags. He dropped a kiss on Natalie's lips, sending a blush down her neck. From one bag he pulled a crown of dried flowers, placing it gently on her head.

Natalie gasped. "You went back for it." She adjusted the crown and threw her arms around him.

"Get a cottage!" Dan shot me and Aidan a look. "Better?"

I tossed a curly fry at him.

Mason returned from his quest for different food options. Two familiar faces joined him.

I waved. "Hey, Holli. Tala."

Holli Hayes and her friend Tala Ramos each carried their own fry basket. Tala and Mason walked awfully close.

"How's your summer going, Lila?" Holli asked. "I mean, since..."

"The lake house party?" I grabbed Aidan's hand. "Not all bad."

Holli blushed, looking down at her fries. I'd forgotten how shy she was.

"Take a seat. Join us," Aidan said to Holli and Tala.

"Actually, we've all got to get going if we want a good view at the joust." Mason glanced to Tala. "If you're into that."

Tala's face lit up. "There's a lady knight this season. Which sounds lame now that I said it. There shouldn't have to be a separate distinction for *lady* knight."

Mason did a subtle chin nod toward Aidan. "We're pretty tight with the guild. We'll be partying with them later. Maybe you can meet the knights."

Aidan shot him a look. "We're not actually—"

I jabbed him in the side. "Don't crush his game."

"Game? What game?" he muttered.

"Mason totally has game. Look at him."

Mason had on a fitted navy blue T-shirt and jeans frayed in strategic, designer places. With spiky styled hair, he looked more like an off-duty model than a part-time cosplayer like the rest of us. Mason was doing his own thing, and that was cool too.

The way Tala looked at Mason, Aidan could have been a knight of the joust himself and she wouldn't have noticed.

Holli watched them with a wistful look. "I don't want to tag along or anything."

I stood and held my hand out. "No way. You're coming with us."

"You're sure?"

"Absolutely." This didn't have to turn into a couples' thing. We were all friends here.

"The faire should make a fast pass app like they have at theme parks," Aidan mused. "You could check in for the joust for priority seating."

"Sounds like tech for the privileged class," Dan quipped. "For a simple peasant like me, the joust should remain free. As free as can be."

Ariana giggled.

Aidan shot me a shadowed smirk.

"She's sweet," I said to him. "And adoring."

"Kind of like how you were with me when I found your scooter helmet."

"Watch it, Pemberton." I tossed my food trash and reapplied SPF Chapstick. "We just sold that scooter for a cool nine hundred bucks. I'm finally making a dent in what I owe my parents." Minus the money I'd owed back to Aidan, which I'd insisted on.

Our newly larger group assembled, ready to head to the joust. Aidan moved into my view. "Hey. Stay there for a sec." He lifted his camera—a separate one from his phone—tweaked the lens, and clicked.

I stood a little longer than comfortable since Aidan tended to take a lot of shots at once. "Done?"

He turned the back of the camera toward me to the digital display screen and backtracked through the photos. "Here it is."

I smiled, but not directly at the camera. Behind me, perched on top of a row of wooden lattice, sat a bird. A bronze-chested robin, its little beak pointed upward. "Aw." I looked at Aidan and smiled. "Pretty."

"So are you."

I slipped my hand through his. "You sure can be sweet. Sometimes."

He breathed, sending his minty scent my way. "When you start at negative credit, you can only go up."

"I wouldn't say negative."

"You called me a cronie. You loathed my existence."

"I can vouch for that," said Mason. "Let's not pretend you could stand being around us."

In less than two weeks, school would start. If summer could bake in what we had here, right now, keeping us solid when the leaves fell, I would be the happiest of happy. I could only hope.

Old Lila would have it all planned out. School clubs, weeks of outfits, and social strategy. Instead, I had my friends. I didn't need to pretend to be some fake version of myself.

This summer wouldn't have been as meaningful if I hadn't planned on doing something else entirely. Giving up the trip, walking away from Matt, digging through the driving range basement—all of those experiences kept me moving forward. Flaws and all.

I took Aidan's hand, a cool comfort in the August heat. He squeezed back.

"I could see you as an archer," he told me. "Ooh—maybe an archer in the queen's guard. We can draw up a character sheet for you."

A blank slate to be whatever I wanted.

"You know, I'm cool with my hodge-podge." I twisted so the layers of my skirt danced around me. "It's not anything special, but it's me."

Aidan trailed his fingers up my arm to my neck, sending a chill through me. "You're beautiful in whatever you wear."

Heat rose in my skin. Not just my skin, but deeper, all through me. I liked this version of Lila, with her future open and her friends beside her.

Aidan held out a hand. "M'Lady."

My very own prince of the faire.

What's Next

♥

Thank you for reading! Reviews help readers find books. Please consider leaving a review on your favorite retailer.

Next in Series: Sunset Summer
Read on for chapter 1 of Holli's story!

Sunset Summer

♥

Following the legacy of a popular sister wasn't easy. In my case, following the legacy of Grace Hayes, the Grace Hayes, was like sifting through the wreckage of a wayward party barge.

And that right there proved how much I knew about popularity and parties—I'd just described a party as a barge. I barely knew anything about boats.

For my entire existence, I'd been known as Grace's kid sister. The one with the weird name. Holliday, or Holli for short, which wasn't so weird in my opinion. Even though some kids started a movement in third grade to call me Chris, short for Christmas. You know, because Holliday = holiday = Christmas. Thankfully, that faded by Easter and none of them thought to call me East. Or worse, Eggs.

Grace's notoriety as a capital P Party Girl had spread over the years across town. The Catholic high school kids knew about Grace from the students who'd been sent there after being permanently suspended from our school, West Ginsburg High. Grace had often contributed to their suspension in the first place, sentencing them to finish school under God's watch. Our sister school, East Ginsburg, knew about Grace because she'd dated a Whitman's candy sampler of their football team, hockey team, and baseball team. She left her mark on all three sports seasons.

Even Grace graduating couldn't stop her wreckage from capsizing my life. My summer plans now thoroughly shredded, I faced endless weeks in exile. All Grace's fault.

See, there was this party.

"Holli, wake up," Grandma's voice jolted me awake from the front seat of my grandparents' minivan. In place of the van's comatose digital clock, a wristwatch affixed to the dash blinked eleven-twenty a.m. "We're almost home."

Home. Their home, in Deer Cove. Home to my grandparents and no one else I knew. A tiny beach town along Lake Michigan and a ninety-minute drive from Ginsburg where I lived. Ginsburg, where every plan I'd made for this summer lived.

Out the van window, a laundromat slumped next to a bait and tackle shop. Even the exit to Deer Cove was a blink-and-you'll-miss-it afterthought.

I leaned back against the headrest, my mind drifting back to where I'd resisted the whole ride. To my sister. My last glimpse of Grace as I'd loaded into the van, she'd given me an indifferent nod. Grace with her arm angled into a sling and bandages covering the stitches above her eye. She'd come out of the accident banged up but not beaten down. In fact, she may have had another party lined up that very night. Not that my parents knew.

And stupid me, I still felt bad for her.

Even though she was the very reason for my lockdown with the grans while she remained free back home. Funny,

I'd heard firstborn kids were supposed to get the harsher rules and punishments. But she wasn't the one being sent away for summer.

Grandpop turned after the retro Sunset Inn sign on the corner of their property. Grandma considered the sign's cartoonish cursive back in style: the top of the "S" like it was drawn around an egg and the bottom curled under like a cat's tail.

Truth? The sign looked old. Worn. Tired. Like this town.

But my grandparents owned the inn and were proud of it.

We rolled to a stop and I heaved open the van door. I wasn't ready to give up on my summer. Once things cooled down, it should be easy enough to convince my grandparents to let me go home. I just needed to play this right.

I was good at playing the good girl. Intentionally doing bad things risked me breaking into hives. Seriously, that happened *more than once*. I wouldn't wish full body hives on anyone. Even Grace.

Well, maybe Grace. After her arm healed and the stitches came out. Then it was hives ahoy!

Grandpop grabbed for my suitcase, but the weight yanked his arm down. He made an exaggerated face. "Lead boots back in season?"

"Ha-ha," I spoke the laugh. Still, I felt bad he had to carry my baggage. Both literal and figurative. "I've got it." I took the bag and tipped it to the roller wheels.

"Take everything to the sewing room." Grandma nodded toward the other side of a low fence from Sunset Inn's rental cabins. Their pale blue house reflected wide open sky, but the siding was tinged gray with grime. Curtains in the front windows hung half drawn. Paired with the worn front door, the house scowled.

Inside, I found the room where Grace and I always slept. Bolts of fabric and department store sacks with knitting yarn crowded around the lumpy pull-out couch. I opened the door to the small closet. Neatly labeled boxes took up one side from floor to ceiling. Sewing supplies in plastic bins and a pegboard on the back wall covered the rest. No clothes bar or hangers.

This was so not going to work.

I checked my phone for texts as a distraction. My heart dropped. One lone bar of coverage hanging on with a half-hearted flicker. Maybe it was better this way. The post-party damage had already been done.

See, there was this party and...*sigh*.

I'd called my best friend Tala in a panic yesterday as I packed, telling her the news I'd have to delay the movie theater job we'd applied for together until I figured this all out. And I had to ask. "Are people talking? About the party?"

"Like, rumors?" She made a low-key comment in Tagalog, something she did if she needed a couple of extra seconds to regroup. And because she knew I couldn't understand. "There are always rumors."

"About my sister?" About me?

I'd avoided all my online profiles. I'd only texted Tala to say we'd had an accident, but I was okay.

"People always talk about Grace."

They did. And now after this disastrous party, I'd be talked about too. And not in a way I wanted.

Tala knew everything about me. More than my sister did these days. Back in second grade when we met, we'd bonded over ballet (which I wanted to be good at but never was) and our shared obsession with this book series *The Trash Can Alley Kids' Mystery Club*. She was Team Tin-Can Annie, and I was Team Sammy T. Sleuth. Tala always got me. She always saw what I couldn't see in myself.

Grandma appeared in the sewing room doorway. She stood shorter than me with soft brown hair threaded with silver. Freckles and sunspots dotted her white skin from years living steps away from Lake Michigan, the selling point to Sunset Inn. One block from the beach.

"Hey, does the attic still have the daybed?" I peered into the hall to the narrow door at the end leading to the partially finished third floor.

Grandma made an *mmhmm* sound. "It's messy. We can take a look."

Her version of messy varied greatly from my personal definition of a mess. I followed her up the steep stairs to the old attic playroom.

Grandma crossed the room and hefted open a window. "We'll need to air this out. And clean up this clutter."

Sure enough, "messy" and "clutter" to Grandma consisted of two neat stacks of boxes on one end of the room and an old bookcase with some books knocked over on the shelves.

On the other side of the room, my aunt's old dollhouse stood angled in a corner. A daybed and dresser sat in the middle of the room.

The walls sloped to mirror the roof with two windows Grace and I called look outs. We used to imagine the room as our castle.

"I'll take it," I said, trying to sound like an eager buyer. This was definitely not as terminal as the sewing room.

"Let me fetch a box fan from the shed." Grandma looked at me. "I'm glad you're here with us, Holliday. Now wash up and come eat lunch."

Up early this morning and over an hour drive later, it was only lunchtime. On day one.

Downstairs in the kitchen, a grilled cheese sandwich and soup waited for me. The comfort food settled my nerves.

Grandma pointed to a note on the table in the eat-in kitchen. A schedule. "Here are your cleaning shifts."

Just like that, I was now an employee at Sunset Inn. "No interview? That's nepotism for you."

Grandma did not crack a smile at me cracking wise. Then again, I wasn't exactly here on vacation.

I looked over the schedule. This was steady part-time work. Unpaid part-time work. Definitely not like making popcorn at the movie theater sharing a shift with my best friend.

Grandma's ancient cell phone startled awake with a weirdly hyper ring. She answered, talked for a minute, and clicked off the call. "That was the community center. You can enroll today and start your service hours tomorrow."

My skin prickled with heat. "But we just got here. I haven't even had my new employee orientation at the inn."

She still didn't smile at my clearly brilliant wit. "You've been here enough times you know the drill at the inn. If you get an early start on those service hours, you can show the judge you're responsible."

She didn't know it yet, but I wasn't planning on sticking around long enough to enroll anywhere. Tala and the movie theater expected me. The cross-country team expected me. The team I'd just been named co-captain of as an incoming junior.

"I really don't think—"

"Holli." Grandma's voice came sharp. "This isn't your time or place to think anything. We agreed you'd come here and do your community service hours. End of discussion."

I hadn't agreed to anything. I'd been told.

The conversation with my parents rewound in my head. I recalled a lot of yelling and demanding. No actual contract to negotiate. I'd never seen them so mad, and Grace once stayed out all night and came home with a lip ring.

I ate my grilled cheese in silence.

The silence last ten seconds.

"This is very serious, Holli." Grandma rested her elbows on the table and looked me over.

It was mildly terrifying.

"Your sister's blood alcohol level was far above the legal limit. And for a seventeen-year-old, that limit is zero."

Obviously, I knew this, but when Grandma began a lecture, best to wait it out.

"The only thing worse than my oldest granddaughter failing a breathalyzer was discovering my second oldest granddaughter had been the one driving her intoxicated sister. On a *learner's license*."

She wasn't wrong. I'd been the nearly sixteen-year-old (just a few more weeks) who'd done her good girl best by driving her drunk sister home from a party the cops busted. Scratch that—*attempted* to drive her drunk sister home.

I'd crashed the car. My perfect daughter record tarnished.

And I'd hurt Grace. I'd physically hurt her. As much as she infuriated me, she was still my sister. Before she was a mess, she was my hero.

"I raised a better son who raised better girls than what the two of you have been up to lately," Grandma went on. "Well, it stops here. This summer, you clean up your act, Holli. It might be too late for Grace, but it's not too late for you."

Class now dismissed, Grandma rose from the table and headed out the side door and across the lot to the Sunset Inn front office.

I welcomed the alone time. I took care of washing my bowl and plate. I sat back at the table. The silence of the old house echoed louder than her ring tone. The silence served as its own jail sentence.

See, there was this party. I hadn't even wanted to be there, but I went because my sister asked me to. I didn't do well at parties—I tended to stick to the walls—so I followed Grace's lead. Her last request as an outgoing senior.

No party was worth what happened to get here.

Acknowledgments

♥

I love writing books set in summer. I hadn't realized how many books set during the summer I'd written already until I decided to put together a series and this theme jumped out. Thank you to the many, many people who had a hand in getting this book to where it is now. Early readers Kelly Garcia, Vanessa M. Knight, J. Leigh Bailey, Marty Mayberry, and Sarah LaPolla helped shape the story early on. As this story became part of a series, I'm thankful for the priceless advice from writers in Facebook groups, Pitch Wars, and Romance Writers of America. Thank you to Joe Kane for the details on robotics – any errors are mine. To my family and husband, thank you for supporting everything creative and for enabling my book buying habit.

About the Author

Stephanie J. Scott writes young adult and romance about characters who put their passions first. Her debut ALTERATIONS about a fashion-obsessed loner who reinvents herself was a Romance Writers of America RITA® award finalist. She enjoys dance fitness, everything cats, and has a slight obsession with Instagram. A Midwest girl at heart, she resides outside of Chicago with her tech-of-all-trades husband and fuzzy furbabies.

Photo: Leah Lewis Photography

CPSIA information can be obtained
at www.ICGtesting.com
Printed in the USA
LVHW030023161221
706193LV00004B/53

9 781954 952010